SUGAR TOWN QUEENS

Also by Malla Nunn

When the Ground Is Hard

SUGAR TOWN QUEENS

MALLA NUNN

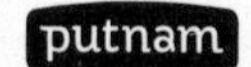

G. P. PUTNAM'S SONS

G. P. Putnam's Sons
An imprint of Penguin Random House LLC, New York

Visit us online at penguinrandomhouse.com

Library of Congress Cataloging-in-Publication Data
Names: Nunn, Malla, author.
Title: Sugar Town queens / Malla Nunn.
Description: New York: G. P. Putnam's Sons, [2021]
Summary: "A biracial girl living in post-apartheid South Africa is determined to unveil the mystery of her white mother's hidden past"—Provided by publisher.
Identifiers: LCCN 2021002390 (print) | LCCN 2021002391 (ebook)
ISBN 9780525515609 (hardcover) | ISBN 9780525515616 (ebook)
Subjects: CYAC: Racially mixed people—Fiction. | Poverty—Fiction.
Secrets—Fiction. | Family life—South Africa—Fiction. | South Africa—Fiction.
Classification: LCC PZ7.1.N86 Su 2021 (print) | LCC PZ7.1.N86 (ebook) | DDC [Fic]—dc23
LC record available at https://lccn.loc.gov/2021002390
LC ebook record available at https://lccn.loc.gov/2021002391

Manufactured in Canada

ISBN 9780525515609

1 3 5 7 9 10 8 6 4 2
FRE

Design by Nicole Rheingans
Text set in LTC Kennerley Pro

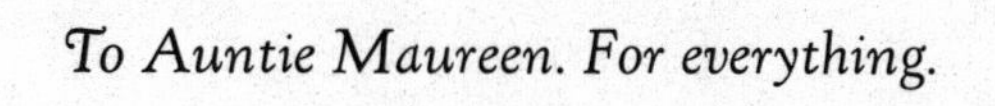
To Auntie Maureen. For everything.

1

White stars dance across my field of vision. The blindfold is tied too tight and I want to rip it off. Instead, I sit and try to rub the goose bumps off my arms. It's cold inside our one-room house, the cracks in the corrugated-iron walls wide enough to let the air in from outside. It's winter, so we have stuffed rags into the spaces we can reach. I shiver and wait patiently for the two surprises that my mother has planned.

The thing is: not all surprises are good.

"Happy fifteenth birthday, Amandla." My mother, Annalisa, who refuses to be called Mother in any of South Africa's eleven official languages, unties the blindfold and hands me a bowl of lumpy porridge decorated with multicolored sprinkles, icing sugar, and whatever canned fruit was in the cupboard. This year's fruit is pears in syrup, a step up from last year's ancient mandarins. Loaded porridge is the closest I will ever get to a birthday cake: a blessing. Annalisa is a terrible cook and a worse baker.

"Thank you." I take the bowl (surprise number one) and our fingers touch, hers pale, mine brown, both with long fingers, elegant, waiting for jewelry, or a piano. In another life, maybe. Our room is too small for a piano, and there is no money for jewels.

"Today is extra special for two reasons. It's your birthday, plus . . ." She takes a deep breath and cups my cheek with a shaky hand. "Last night, I had a vision. It was wonderful, but we have to do our part to make it come true."

The lumpy porridge sticks in my throat and stops me from cursing. Annalisa's visions have taken us into the cane fields to sing to the stars at midnight. They have told us to eat eggs, and only eggs, for four days in a row. They have led us into the heart of a storm to wait for the lightning to send us instructions. The instructions never came.

My mother is out of her mind.

The lightning was eight months ago. Every night since, I have prayed for the spirits to leave Annalisa alone and go whisper directions to someone else.

"Tell me what we have to do." I use a fake calm voice to mask the anxious feeling gathering inside my chest. I have to stay cool and make my next move carefully. "But hurry. I have to get to school."

"Hands over your eyes," she says. "Here comes the second surprise."

I cover my eyes and peek through the space between my fingers as Annalisa walks across the cracked linoleum floor in black tailored trousers, a white silk shirt, and a cropped leather jacket with silver buckles. This is her best outfit. This morning, she will disappear into the city of Durban and come home with bags of the basics: socks, underwear, soap, and a special something for my birthday.

"Open your eyes now." She pulls a piece of blue material from her wardrobe and holds it up with a flourish. "Look. Isn't it beautiful?"

"It" is a folded bedsheet with two holes cut in the fabric for the arms and another larger hole, for the head. The material is stained and held together by stitches that zigzag in different directions. She drapes the sheet dress across the foot of my cot as if it is made of raw silk and sewn together by cartoon birds with golden needles.

"If you wear this . . ." Her pale skin glows like there's a fire burning out of control inside her. "All our dreams will come true."

No. All my nightmares will come true.

"Which dreams are you talking about, exactly?" Annalisa's dreams can be anything. A brick house with ocean views. A holiday under swaying palms. Cold lobster rolls chilling in a fridge for when the temperature rises . . . if only we had a fridge instead of a cooler.

"Wear this dress," she says. "And your father will come back to us. Blue was his favorite color. You see?"

No, I do not see.

My father is not an actual person. He is a collage of blurred images thrown together by Annalisa in the half hour before we go to bed. Less now than when I was little. She would whisper that father was tall as a lala palm and black as a moonless night. He wore a sharp gray suit with a blue tie, iridescent like peacock feathers. He loved to dance, and he stole her breath away when he kissed her.

No matter how pretty a picture she paints of him, there is only one thing that I know for sure about my father.

He is doing fine without me.

"Is he here in Sugar Town?" He isn't, but I ask just in case. I have to be sure, even though I hate that there is still a tiny shred of hope left in me that he is out there somewhere.

Annalisa smiles wide, and her lips stretch tight across her teeth. "He's not here yet, but he'll come when he sees your blue dress." She grabs my hands and squeezes tight. "The wind will carry the message to him quicker than a text. Get dressed now. It's time to leave."

Today is Friday, a school day. On school days, I wear a uniform. Blue skirt or pants, white shirt, black shoes, and white socks. A black sweater or a black blazer for now in winter. Nothing fancy, but Miss Gabela, the principal, is clear about the rules: No uniform, no school. Annalisa's magic sheet will get me suspended, *and* it will frighten away the few friends I have. This is the last day of second term, but the scandal of the blue sheet will survive the holidays and live on to haunt me for the rest of the year.

No thanks. I'll pass.

"Hurry." Annalisa tugs at my nightgown. "Lift up your arms and put on your new dress. There's a good girl."

"It is not a dress." I pull away. "It is a sheet with holes in it, and I won't wear it. Ever."

"You have to wear the dress." Annalisa's smile disappears, and her expression turns dark. "It's the only way to get him back."

We stand face-to-face, breathing hard. Mother is a few inches taller than me, with fine blond hair and pale blue eyes that remind me of the sunlit ocean. She is delicate, with slender limbs and narrow hips, while I am all bumps and curves. What did the nurses think when I slipped into the world with different skin, different hair, different everything from Annalisa? They must have wondered how the two of us fit together. Sometimes, I look in the mirror and I wonder the same thing. Who am I, and where do I fit in?

"Put the dress on," Annalisa says. "Do it for me. For us."

Annalisa angry is scary. Annalisa with a bottomless darkness welling up inside her is terrifying. I see that darkness well up now. More resistance from me and she'll tumble into it. She will curl up and sleep for days. She won't talk or eat. I have been to the bottom of the well with her once. I will never go there again—if I can help it.

"Here. Give it." I take the sheet from her with jerky movements and point to the mirror hanging to the right of the sink. "Don't forget your lipstick."

"Of course." Annalisa digs through her faux-leather hobo bag that acts as a portal to another dimension. At different times, she has pulled out an orchid bulb with dangling roots, an owl feather, five mother-of-pearl buttons, a vintage Coca-Cola yo-yo, and a porcupine quill. I'm surprised my father isn't in there, too.

She takes out a tube of Moroccan Sunset, her favorite color, and leans close to the mirror to put it on. The moment her back is turned, I grab my school uniform out of the bedside drawer and push it deep into my backpack. I slip the sheet dress over my head and bend low to tie the laces of my school shoes, working up a plan to switch the dress for my uniform somewhere. Somehow.

Got it.

"Lil Bit and me are meeting early to finish up an assignment in the school computer lab." The "lab" is a room the size of a cleaning closet. One door, one window, and the faint smell of bleach coming up from the concrete floor. Come to think of it, the room might, in fact, have been an actual cleaning closet before the donated computers arrived from a Christian school in Denmark. "Got to run."

"Lil Bit and I," Annalisa automatically corrects. "And we're not finished yet. Sit, and I'll do your hair. It has to look the same as in my vision."

Shit.

"Fine." I take a seat and work through next steps. I have a plan. For the plan to work, I'll have to leave home five minutes before Annalisa, and then I'll have to run. Not my preferred activity. But run I will. Today, I will be the great sprinter Caster Semenya—strong, fast, and focused.

Annalisa wraps a curl around her finger, remembering. "You got your father's hair, that's for sure. Don't ever straighten it."

"I won't." No lie. I will keep my kinked-up curls, not because they tie me to an invisible man who haunts our lives, but because straightened hair is an imitation of white hair, and I am not white. I am brown with a snub nose sprinkled with freckles. I have hazel eyes flecked with green. I'm a genetic mutt. And I am happy to let my hair be.

"Today, your hair will be a halo," Annalisa says. "That way, your father will see the angel that we made together."

On a normal day, she plaits my hair into a single French braid that dangles between my shoulder blades, but today is not normal. Today she pulls the metal teeth of an Afro pick through my springy curls to make a bumping 'fro that casts a shadow onto the kitchen table. It is huge. An alien spacecraft could crash-land on the surface of it and sustain no damage. Beyoncé rocking a Foxxy Cleopatra wig has nothing on me. The style is loud and proud, and damn, I gotta admit that it is impressive.

"Last and best of all." Annalisa dips her hand into her bag and pulls out a tiara. An honest-to-goodness rhinestone tiara with BIRTHDAY PRINCESS spelled out in fake pink diamonds. Hideous.

"You bought this?"

"Of course not." She anchors the tiara to my head. "I found it lying on the side of the road. It's ugly, but it's perfect for today. The stones will catch the light, and the light will fly over the hills to wherever your father is."

I can barely breathe I am so angry. The 'fro I can deal with, but the sheet dress and the tiara are too much! Instead of screaming, *It's my birthday! Be normal. Just this once*, I make a list in my head. Lists soothe me. Lists are anchors to rational thought. Lists are how I survive.

This morning, I will:

1. Keep calm.
2. Run fast.
3. Get help.

"Catch you this afternoon . . ." I grab my backpack and rush to the door that leads to the lane. Annalisa blows me a goodbye kiss and tucks a strand of blond hair behind her ear. I am stunned to see her so cool and elegant. She belongs in a magazine, and I wonder, for the millionth time, how she ended up in this tiny house on a dirt strip that runs between Tugela Way and Sisulu Street. The lane doesn't have a real name. "The lane between Tugela and Sisulu" is description enough for the bill collectors to find us. When I used to ask Annalisa where she came from, she'd say, *Next door and a million miles away.*

I don't ask anymore.

2

I step outside our one-room house and into a small patch of dirt that murders every plant that's planted in it. Our front yard is a graveyard for living things. Behind me, the corrugated-iron walls of our home glow like a sunrise and rocks and old tires hold down the flat tin roof.

Annalisa calls our room "snug," as if the word alone has the power to change the fact that we have a single light bulb dangling over the kitchen table and a rusty tap with an off-and-on-again water supply. It's the twenty-first century, but we live like the people in black-and-white photographs from the 1950s.

"Ah, shit," I whisper under my breath. The lane is busy with people on their way to work—or on their way to look for work—in the city. Children skip to school, and stray dogs trot between houses, sniffing for scraps. I stand paralyzed in the yard. If I cross the lane, I will be seen in my blue sheet. If I stay frozen, I will be seen in my blue sheet. Either way, the word about me will spread like a grass fire.

You heard about that white woman's daughter? Dressed in a sheet. Big hair like an exploded watermelon. Wearing a crown. A crown! Madness runs in the family, my sisters.

The sound of keys rattling inside our shack gets me moving. I sprint out the gate and across the lane. The world around me blurs into shapes and sounds. Mrs. Mashanini's blue front door is all I see. Behind the blue door is sanctuary. I run for it although I've never been inside before.

"Mrs. M!" I pound my fist against the wood. "It's Amandla. Please open up. I need your help."

A long moment passes. Footsteps shuffle across a grass mat, and the door opens a crack. Mrs. M's blind aunt peeks through the gap, and her blindness spares her the sight of me sweaty and wild-haired.

"Yebo?" she says in Zulu. "Ubani?"

"It's Amandla, from across the lane," I answer in Zulu, and check over my shoulder. Our front door is still closed, but any second now, it will open. Annalisa has a bus to catch, and she is never late. "Auntie, *please* can I come in?"

Blind Auntie steps back and makes space for me to squeeze through. Three children and a woman sleep tangled together on a pullout bed squashed against the wall. Mrs. M's daughter and grandchildren: refugees from a bad husband and bad father who was never home anyway. Six people in one bedroom. Somehow, they all fit.

"In the back." Blind Auntie leads me through the room to a narrow kitchen with a woodburning stove and old wooden crates nailed to the walls for storage. Mrs. M, a tall Zulu woman with a tight-knit Afro, scoops seeds from a small green eggplant the size of a brussels sprout. She's busy, and my being here is awkward. In the six years that Annalisa and I have lived on the lane, we have never entered her house. Annalisa prefers to keep our neighbors at a distance.

"Sorry to disturb you, Mrs. Mashanini. It's just that . . . uh . . ."

"Your mother had another one of her notions." Mrs. M takes in the whole of me without a flicker of amusement. She is also a retired nurse who keeps an eye on the neighborhood. When Annalisa and I returned from that night in the cane fields, Mrs. M smiled at me through her window, but I looked away.

"Yes. One of her notions." A blush burns my cheeks, and the roots of my hair tingle. It shames me to remember Mrs. M watching the two of us dragging ourselves home in the rain, barefoot and soaked to the skin.

"Are you here for the day or just for the time being?" Mrs. M asks, and I get the feeling that, if I decided to stay for five hours, she'd somehow find a space for me to sit and wait.

"Just for the time being. I brought my uniform to change into. When my mother leaves, I'll head off to school."

"Auntie, go see if Miss Harden is gone," Mrs. M says, and I wonder how a blind woman will know. Yes, she knits scarves for the children at the Sugar Town Orphanage without dropping a stitch, but that's different than spying on our house across the lane.

She shuffles out of the kitchen, and I have to ask: "Mrs. Mashanini, how will she know?"

"That one can hear a pin drop in Zimbabwe," Mrs. M says. "If your mother is home, Auntie will know. If your mother is gone, Auntie will know. Put on your uniform and get ready to run. You don't want to miss the first bell."

I shrug off the blue sheet dress and pull on my school uniform. Standing half-naked in a strange room for even a short while should embarrass me. Strangely, it does not. Mrs. M sips tea and spreads the eggplant seeds on a piece of paper to dry. She worked in the emergency ward of the Inkosi Albert Luthuli Hospital for twelve years. A round-hipped brown girl in plain cotton undies is nothing compared to what she must have seen on the wards. Babies being born. The tragic aftermath of traffic accidents. Bones shattered by gunshot wounds. Death delivered by the hour.

"Unyoko akasekho," Blind Auntie says. *Your mother is gone.* She sits at the kitchen table and takes up knitting the last panel of a scarf made with leftover red, pink, and brown yarn. "But your tap is dripping. Mr. Khoza, there by the red roof? He can fix it."

Mr. Khoza. Short legs. Wide chest. Bald head. Twin daughters. He lives four doors down from us, but we don't talk. We nod hello in passing. That is all. *Why make friends*, Annalisa says, *when we'll be leaving Sugar Town soon?* That is my mother's dream. We're no closer to leaving now than the first time she said it. I can't even remember the first time she said it.

And now it is my dream, too. At night, I lie awake and imagine the wide road that will lead me away from the dirt streets and back alleys of Sugar Town. At the end of that wide road is a brick house with picture windows and separate rooms. On the kitchen table is an invitation to a cousin's birthday party, and on my mobile phone is a long list of family names and contacts. The house is a safe place for friends and the network of aunts and uncles who exist only in my imagination. Best of all, the house is built in the middle of a far-off town where the color of my skin doesn't mean anything, a town where I am at home in my roundness and my brownness.

I think that escaping from where we are is going to take longer than my mother imagines. Right now, though, being here inside Mrs. M's house, Sugar Town isn't so bad.

"Sit, Amandla. Auntie will do your hair."

I wrestle the tiara from the whirlwind of Afro curls and sit on a low stool next to Blind Auntie, who stops knitting and runs her fingertips over the contours of my skull. She parts my hair down the middle, a first. Then I feel her fingers working in rhythm. It's firm but gentle—no hair pulling, but nice and tight. My breath matches the rhythm of her fingers, until suddenly, she's done. She has plaited the sections into two chunky braids that dangle over my shoulders. Another first. When she's done, she pats my shoulder and goes back to knitting. I'd love to see what I look like, but asking for a mirror is rude, so I don't.

"Go, now," Mrs. M says. "Or you'll be late."

"Thank you. For everything." The words come out stiff and embarrassed at having to ask for refuge inside an already-crowded house. *Nothing comes for free*, Annalisa says. *Favors have to be paid back one way or the other.* How will I repay Mrs. Mashanini's kindness? My pockets are empty. Mrs. M sees my awkwardness.

"Neighbors help each other, Amandla." She pours her aunt a mug of red bush tea, adds six teaspoons of sugar, stirs, and adds another scoop to make seven. "That's Ubuntu."

Ubuntu. We learned about it in primary school: the Zulu idea that a person is a person through other people. We are all interconnected in a living, breathing ocean of compassion and humanity. If that is true, then Annalisa and I are the anti-Ubuntu: two individuals who live in the community but are not part of it. Maybe it's better that way for everyone.

Social interactions are awkward. Annalisa's voice might drift off when her memory hits a blank spot. Or visitors might be held prisoner by a ten-minute lecture on how to brew the perfect pot of tea. Or she might suddenly stare at the ground. Or at the sky. Or just walk away.

"Come by anytime, my girl. Bring your mother," Mrs. M says. "My door is always open."

I nod, speechless, and creep through the narrow front room, afraid of waking the sleeping children, all under five and too young for school. A strange feeling burns in the pit of my stomach. Not from the lumpy birthday porridge, which was all kinds of wrong, but from Mrs. M's simple *Come by anytime, my girl. Bring your mother.* Mrs. M knows Annalisa is strange—and she doesn't care. And now her daughter has crashed into her house looking for help. Despite all that, her invitation stands. *Anytime, my girl.*

Outside, the lane is quiet and the sun's rays slant over the rusted rooftops. On either side of me, Mrs. M's winter garden glows green with broad beans, thyme, and winter gem lettuce. Today will be long and hungry with just that spoonful of porridge to keep me fueled.

"Amandla!" Mrs. M is right behind me. I turn, and she puts a piece of steamed corn bread with butter in my hand. "Go!" she says. I run without even saying thank you.

The bread is still warm.

* * *

Brown, white, and mostly black teenagers pack the schoolyard outside a low classroom building painted with sunflowers on the outside and rolling ocean waves on the inside. Lil Bit, my best and only real friend, waits for me in the shade of the parsley tree where the poor but ambitious students gather.

"What happened?" Lil Bit's gaze narrows on my face, all-seeing. "Your hair looks amazing, but you're sweating a river."

Lil Bit's real name is Esther, but she hates that name, and Lil Bit suits her better anyway. She is a "little bit" of a girl: dark-skinned and slender as a dancer. Inside her delicate skull, her planet-size brain is always thinking and making connections. I don't need to pretend with her. I lay it all out:

"Annalisa had another vision. She cut up an old blue sheet and tried to get me to wear it to school. The sheet was meant to bring my father back. Blue was his favorite color, apparently."

Lil Bit is the only one I tell about Annalisa's highs and lows. We are both only children. We both have parent problems.

I have my mother and her visions. Lil Bit has her father, the Reverend Altone Bhengu, who was caught behind the church altar with a teenage girl named Sunshine. Both of them were naked. That was a year ago, but the scandal is still fresh. Together, Lil Bit and me spend hours plotting a path out of Sugar Town to the University of KwaZulu Natal in Durban, fifteen kilometers away on the map but an epic journey for two girls with no money.

"I think it's nice," Lil Bit says, and I raise an eyebrow.

"Which part is nice exactly?"

"My mother wants my father dead. First, she'd cut off his legs and make him crawl through the streets to beg for forgiveness. Then she'd dump his body in the bush for the wild dogs to eat. Your mother loves your father and wants him back," Lil Bit says. "That was the nice part of your story."

"I guess . . ." I can't imagine what it would be like to have Annalisa tell me a bedtime story about wild dogs feasting on my mythical father's corpse. I get a love story instead. Pale girl meets dark boy under a sky full of stars.

We move to the far side of the parsley tree and into the shadow of a concrete water tower with Nelson Mandela's face painted on the side. This is our place, set apart from the others and right under Nelson's beaming smile. Nelson Mandela, aka "Madiba," is our patron saint. He gives us hope that one day the South Africa he dreamed of will come to pass. His dream is slow in coming. Money and race divide us. The rich are still rich and the poor are still poor and none of us is truly colorblind. Not yet. The black kids give Lil Bit a hard time for hanging out with "that colored girl" instead of "one of her own." The white and mixed kids do the same to me. Old habits die hard, I guess.

"Happy birthday, Amandla." Lil Bit hands me a brown paper parcel tied with twine. "If you don't like it, I'll get you something different."

I have my first genuine smile of the day. "Thanks." I untie the string and carefully peel open the brown paper wrapping. Lil Bit is poor like me. A gift from her is worth more than the money that she spent to get it. My breath catches at the sight of a square sketch pad and a set of high-quality graphite drawing pencils. Nothing this fine is for sale in Sugar Town.

"You shouldn't have." I hug her, and then I hug the parcel to my chest, torn between delight and guilt. "You could have been caught."

"Please!" She snorts with amusement. "This girl never gets caught, Amandla. The lady in the store followed me around for ages, but she had no idea who she was dealing with. The Lightning Thief."

Lil Bit has a quick brain and even quicker fingers. Her talent for theft borders on the supernatural, but much as I'd like to scold her for taking stupid risks, I aim to keep the sketch pad and pencils. They are perfect, and now they are mine. Besides, Lil Bit only "shops" in the city on special occasions and never here in Sugar Town, where the store owners scrape by on the thin trade that comes through the doors. She's a thief with a conscience, which helps to ease mine.

"Thanks again." I pull her into another quick hug as the morning bell rings. "I love my present. You're the first person I'll sketch."

She shakes her head, *Not me*, and her lack of confidence is painful. I want to tell her that the Bible is wrong, that the sins of the father are not visited on the daughter. Reverend Bhengu's sins are his alone. She is Esther Junia "Lil Bit" Bhengu, a separate and sovereign being with a heart and a mind that are all her own.

"I want to try to capture your inner criminal," I tell her as we walk side by side to class.

"Sorry, my sister. I have to stay invisible. It's the only way to be free."

3

After school, Lil Bit waits outside the girls' toilets while I pull the blue sheet dress over my uniform. Meeting Annalisa straight off the city bus is a birthday tradition, and if she were to see me not wearing her magical outfit, she'd get upset and start asking questions. Resigned to being stared at, I slip on my blazer and step out into the yard. Lil Bit whistles low and laughs.

"Tuck the sheet into your skirt and button up your blazer," she says. "When your mother gets off the bus, pull the sheet out and let it hang over your uniform. If she asks, tell her that Miss Gabela made you wear the blazer. That way she'll never know that you went against her."

"Brilliant!" I follow Lil Bit's instructions, glad to get back to a semi-normal state of dress and extra glad that she's my best friend rather than my enemy. She'd get away with any crime she committed.

We walk through narrow dirt streets with tin shacks and identical government-built plasterboard homes crowding in on either side of us. To the east is a shipping container graveyard, and to the west, the endless fields of sugarcane that give the town its name. The sky is flat and vast above us and, somehow, lonely. As if we needed reminding that we live on the fringe of a great city but are not a part of it.

We cross the outer limits of town and head for an isolated bus stop on the edge of the fields. Minivans run into Durban from Abdullah Ibrahim Street, but the public bus that drops passengers off two kilometers from the center of town is cheaper. And, where Annalisa is concerned, cheaper is better.

"Here it comes." Lil Bit points to the white coach moving through the young cane stalks. We step back into the vacant land behind us as the bus pulls up. The doors swing open. Any minute now, a smiling Annalisa will appear, weighed down by shopping bags. Factory workers and sweaty dockworkers in dirty overalls pour out. No Annalisa. She never gets off the bus this late. I scan the windows for her. The bus is mostly empty now, with only a few passengers left.

Then Annalisa stumbles down the stairs with strange, jerky movements. No smile. No shopping bags. For a moment, I think she's drunk, but I know she doesn't drink.

I forget about untucking the sheet dress and rush forward to grab her arms. "What's wrong? Are you sick?"

She staggers and leans her weight against me. I stumble to the side, and Lil Bit pulls me straight to help me regain my balance. We move away from the bus and into the vacant lot next to the road.

"No," she says, straightening up. "Take me home."

The bus pulls away, and Lil Bit and me guide her onto the road that leads to Sugar Town. She walks slowly, stopping every few minutes to catch her breath. Her skin is even more pale than usual, and her eyes are puffy and red from crying.

"What happened?" I ask with a lump in my throat.

"I need to lie down. I need to sleep." She clutches her oversize bag to her stomach. "Did your father come home?"

"No," I say. "He didn't."

"We'll try again next year," she says. "Next year he'll come back to us."

"Next year for sure." I guide her into scrappy Makeba Street, and I wonder if wearing the blue dress for real would have brought Father back to us and kept Annalisa from falling apart. It's a stupid thought, but it sticks in my head, the idea that whatever happened to Mother in Durban is my fault. I made this happen.

"Easy now," Lil Bit whispers when Annalisa stumbles over the uneven ground. "Almost home, Miss Harden."

"Just a few more minutes," I tell Mother, who wears a dazed expression. "Keep hold of my hand." I'm trying not to attract too much attention along Makeba Street, but we get strange looks from a few people anyway.

Lil Bit and I steer her onto the dirt lane that runs between Sisulu Street and Tugela Way. We pass Mrs. Mashanini digging fresh chicken manure into her garden. She pulls off her gloves and rushes to the fence, concerned by Annalisa's blank expression and slow steps.

"Is your mother sick, Amandla?" she asks.

"I don't know what's wrong," I tell Mrs. Mashanini. "She got off the bus like this."

"Let me see." Mrs. M comes out her gate into the lane. She grabs Annalisa's wrist to get her pulse. "Steady," she mutters, and gently cups Annalisa's face between her palms, scanning and analyzing. "No physical injury," she says. "Just grief. And sadness."

I see it, too. A sadness as wide and deep as the ocean. How do I stop her from drowning in it?

"Time is the only cure," Mrs. M says as if she's read my mind. "And rest. Take her home. Let her sleep. Give her warm food to eat."

I can do that. Me cooking dinner at the stove while Annalisa grabs a nap between three fifteen and four is part of our normal after-school routine. "Thanks, Mrs. Mashanini." I move quickly to our house and pull Mother through the yard. She stares at the red paint flaking off the front door with a faraway look. She's here but not here. I take her bag and dig through it, searching for the key. My fingers brush against a thick stack of paper, and I pull the bag open to see what's inside.

"What in heaven's name?" Lil Bit says over my shoulder.

In the bag is a wad of cash held together by a thin rubber band. It's more money than I have ever seen at one time, though that's not saying much.

"Standing outside with this kind of cash is asking for trouble." Lil Bit checks the length of the lane with narrowed eyes. "Get in the house."

True. I find the key and open the door. Inside, I flick on the overhead light, an extravagant use of electricity when it is still day out. The tin room brightens. Annalisa blinks and comes back to the present long enough to throw herself, fully clothed, onto her narrow cot. She snuggles down with a deep sigh. Her breath slows, and inside of a minute, she is fast asleep. I creep into the bedroom area, carefully take off her shoes, and place them neatly at the foot of the bed. The soles of Annalisa's feet are damaged, the skin covered in circular scars that look like miniature moon craters. I have never been told how she got them.

* * *

Lil Bit and I stand on opposite sides of the kitchen table with Annalisa's bag between us, fat with questions and secrets. How much money is there and where does it come from? Should I look inside or not?

"Yes, you should count it," Lil Bit says with cool logic. "Your mother won't know, and I won't say a thing."

"You're right. She'll never know." I pull the cash from the cavernous leather bag and place it gently on the table, as if the money is sleeping and might run out the door if I wake it up. Next, I pull out a crushed piece of white paper, lipstick, a pen, and a broken fortune cookie with the fortune missing. My usual birthday presents: a new "best dress," a new "best pair of shoes," and seven pairs of sensible cotton underwear are missing, along with the usual shopping bags.

"How much do you think is there?" Lil Bit asks as I flick off the elastic band holding the cash together. The rand notes are soft against my fingertips. Not crisp like I was expecting. I flex my hands to stop them from shaking and count. The bills are a mix of big and small denominations, and all of them are wrinkled.

"Those notes look like a cow chewed them," Lil Bit says. "Money from the bank is different. Cleaner."

"Shh . . . I'll lose count." I build a pile of messy bills and make a final tally. "Forty-five thousand rand."

"Enough to last a few months," Lil Bit says. "If you're careful."

Living costs money. Annalisa works two days a week at Mr. Gupta's law office and stocks shelves at Mr. Chan's Dreams Come True Variety Store once in a while. I never did the math before. Her wages are not enough to keep us in a one-room shack with two beds, a gas stove, and a pit toilet in the back yard. The money on the table must help to pay for our food and shelter and my school fees.

"Where do you think she got it?" Lil Bit asks as I snap the rubber band around the wrinkled notes with a jerky movement.

"I have no idea," I say. "She goes into Durban a couple of times a year. It might be to collect the money. I can't say for sure."

Lil Bit shifts in her chair, uncomfortable. She's holding something back. Something big. Something I need to know.

"What have you heard?"

"Uh . . . it's all rubbish, Amandla. Gossip."

"Tell me," I say.

Lil Bit hesitates. She rubs her eyes. The moment drags out in awkward silence. I was right. Whatever she's holding back is big, and she needs time to build up the courage to speak.

"Okay." She traces a scratch on the surface of the table with her fingernail. "Here it is: People think your ma acts all posh but that she's the same as the women who wait for customers behind the soccer stands at nighttime. The fact that she goes into Durban to be with men for money makes it worse . . . It's like she's too good for Sugar Town."

"Oh my God!" I'm stunned by the news, and furious. If my father was white, the gossips wouldn't cast Annalisa in that light. Madiba said that all relationships are equal in the eyes of the law, but things are different down here on the ground. A white woman who sleeps with a black man is a gold digger if the man is famous, and a tramp if he's not. Love and tenderness don't come into the equation.

The insult cuts me up. Some people believe that Annalisa goes into town every couple of months to sell the only thing she has to offer: herself. Not only is she odd, she is also a prostitute. The loaded glances I've had my whole life take on a new meaning. The gossips think I might be the result of an accident with a stranger.

My face heats up, and I want to hit something. If people knew Annalisa at all, they'd know how wrong that idea is. But they don't know her. That's the problem. She is a mystery even to me, and that lets doubts creep into my mind. The money is real, and I have no idea where it came from. But I can't bring myself to believe the rumors, even as a voice in my head reminds me that I know nothing for certain about Annalisa's life before me.

"None of what they say is true." I scramble to make words. "Annalisa wouldn't let anyone touch her like that."

"Rumors, like I said." Lil Bit sighs. "It's good that your mother doesn't care about the gossip. My ma takes everything she hears about my father to heart, and some days, she doesn't leave the house."

I push the money away from me and a white piece of paper floats to the floor. Lil Bit picks it up and gives it to me, curious. I smooth the paper flat with my palm and read out loud. "'Saturday. Twelve to one p.m. 211 Kenneth Kaunda Road, Durban North. Use the private car park entrance at the rear.'"

"Any ideas what it means?" Lil Bit asks, but my mind is focused on one simple fact. Annalisa has a secret life that involves sneaking through private entryways and coming out with a stack of money.

"Do you think it's true . . . what people say?" I ask Lil Bit in a shaky voice. "Annalisa leaves home with an empty bag and comes back with a stack of notes. Explain that to me . . . I mean . . ."

"Shush." Lil Bit holds up her hand like she's stopping traffic. "Think, Amandla. If your ma can make that much money in one day, why are the two of you still living here? Why not go into town once a week and move the two of you out to a nice house with ocean views?"

"I don't know anything about her, Lil Bit, not where she's from or the kind of life that she had before me. I can guess that it was better than this, but that's not the same as knowing anything for sure."

Lil Bit turns the piece of paper and reads over the slanted letters. "This is your chance to find out. Check what's at this address and go from there."

Internet connection and electricity supply are intermittent in our township, not that it matters. Neither Lil Bit nor I own a mobile. Annalisa's old Nokia with the cracked flip screen might as well be a brick. It is always out of credit or power. Usually both.

Lil Bit checks the clock on the wall. It's 3:42. "The school computer lab is open till four," she says. "If we run, we'll get there in time to do a search."

My arms and legs grow heavy. I live with Annalisa's strange turns and blank memories every day. Now I have the chance to fill in parts of Mother's story, but I'm afraid of what I might find.

"I don't know if I want to know, Lil Bit."

"It's up to you, Amandla." She moves to the door. "At least once a day, I wish that my father's secret had stayed a secret. If it had, my mother would be happy and my father would still be living at home with us. We'd be together, but . . ."

B-U-T. Three small letters that have the power to change whatever came before them.

"But what?" I ask.

"You either live in the light of the truth or stay blind in the darkness." Lil Bit parrots her preacher father. "Those are your choices, Amandla. Whatever you decide, I'll be waiting for you outside the computer lab till it closes."

She opens the door and a flood of afternoon light silhouettes her tiny frame. Her tight brown curls make a soft halo around her head. Give her wings and she'd pass for an angel, but not the kind with a harp and a smile. No, Lil Bit is an angel of the avenging kind, armed with a fiery sword.

Goose bumps creep up my arms. Reverend Bhengu has left the township, but his talent for laying down *the word* at the right moment lives on in his daughter. Amplified. Lil Bit is a powerhouse with the lights just turning on. When the time comes for her to shine, I hope I'm there to witness it. She turns and walks outside. She gives me time to make up my mind. I stay seated. My feet are too heavy to move. Dust swirls in the laneway. Lil Bit walks through the front gate and in the direction of school.

"Wait." I jump up and rush outside.

4

We reach the computer lab stairs, sweating and out of breath but with enough time to look up the address in Durban North. I pull the crumpled paper from my pocket and silently ask Mandela on the water tower to give me the strength to deal with whatever I find out about my mother. A door slams, and Mrs. Zuma, the thickset Zulu teacher who runs the learning extension program, locks the door to the computer lab in the library with a quick turn of the key.

"Wait . . ." Lil Bit puffs. "We have time. Five minutes at least."

"Too late, girls." Mrs. Zuma drops the key into her handbag. "It will take me five minutes to open the door and start the machines, and by then, it will be time for me to close up again. Go home. It's Friday night, and I have things to do."

Arguing would be a waste of time. Mrs. Zuma is done for the term and ready to start the midyear holidays early. We have to find another way to get information. Lil Bit and me hang out with kids who have limited credit on their phones. Begging for data is the same as begging for a cigarette on the street corner. It is a sign you've hit the bottom, and Lil Bit and me won't do it.

"Have a good holiday," Mrs. Zuma says, and walks off with light steps. Two student-free weeks is a shot of summer sunshine in the dead of winter. She can't wait to get away.

"So much for that," Lil Bit says as a soccer ball sails over her head and hits my right shoulder. The ball belongs to soccer-mad Goodness Dumisa, who plays goalie for the amateur Sugar Town Shakers.

"Hey!" Goodness yells from the yard. "Kick it back to me."

I kick the ball badly, and Goodness laughs at my lack of skills. Sports is not my strong point. Sports and I are, in fact, sworn enemies that are forced to spend one torturous hour together every week at school. Lil Bit is faster and better coordinated than me, but not by much; it's another reason the two of us stay on the sidelines, both on and off the sports field. In contrast, Goodness is tall and lanky, with dyed-blond braids and killer speed.

"The holidays started an hour ago and the two of you are already back at school, begging to be let in. What do you do for fun?" Goodness kicks the ball back to me, which I don't expect. She runs with a group of girls who, like her, are at the top of the social ladder. Her father, Mr. Dumisa, owns the Drinking Hole, a popular bar a block down from the Build 'Em Up timber yard, which he also owns. The Dumisa family is Sugar Town royalty. Lil Bit and I are, well, *not*.

"Amandla and me have fun." Lil Bit kneels down and reties her shoelaces. A classic sign of nerves. "We walk and talk and read books and—" She stops short, realizing that every word she says confirms that we are dull bookworms who haunt the school library in our off-hours. She rushes to add, "Amandla needs to do an internet search. That's why we're here. Not for schoolwork."

I appreciate her trying to save us from the broke-and-boring list that the other students have written us down on in their heads. It's too late. We top the list every term. Every year. Goodness pulls the latest iPhone from her skirt pocket and swipes the screen. "The Wi-Fi signal is strong, but who knows how long that will last? Use my mobile to do a search, if you want."

Yes, I do want, but what if the address is for a topless bar or a charity that gives out secondhand clothes?! Being poor isn't a sin, but it certainly is a shame.

"Take it, Amandla. I promise not to look at the history." Goodness holds the phone out and the fake diamonds sprinkled over the silver case catch the sunlight. Goodness plays soccer with the boys and gets right up in their faces if they question her right to be a goalie, but the jeweled case reminds me that she's also a township princess.

"Thanks." I take the mobile, and a second too late to hide it from the others, I notice that my hand is shaking. After years of begging Annalisa for answers about her past, I sense that I might finally be near some part of the truth. Goodness steps away to give us privacy. It doesn't help. I feel sick to my stomach.

"Here, let me do it." Lil Bit takes the phone and types in the address, already memorized in her remarkable brain. I take a deep breath and wait for the bad news. Or the good news.

Or, knowing Annalisa, the *that doesn't tell me anything of use* news. My mother, the mystery.

"Oh . . ." Lil Bit says, her eyebrows raised. "Come see for yourself."

She cups her palm over the screen to cut the glare and a fenced-off construction sight comes into focus. I sigh. An unfinished building makes perfect sense. Where Annalisa's secrets are concerned, nothing comes easy.

"Let's check the neighbors." Lil Bit scrolls her finger across the image to search for clues to the building's identity. The Street View expands to show the entire suburb of Durban North with roads shooting off in different directions. Another swipe brings up a map of the entire KwaZulu Natal region, crisscrossed with main roads and rivers that run to the sea.

"Hellfire . . ." Lil Bit whispers in frustration, ever the preacher's perfect daughter. Goodness comes closer and holds her hand out for the phone.

"Let me see," she says. "What are you looking for?"

"A three-sixty Street View of that address in Durban North." Lil Bit inches away from Goodness, who's sweaty from soccer practice. The move surprises me. Lil Bit is polite and hates to offend anyone, which makes her behavior unusual.

"Here we go." Goodness brings up the picture of the building site and slowly rotates the image to the right. "Four floors at least. An elevator shaft. Steel scaffolding. Safety fences and portable toilets. The developers are spending serious money on the project."

"How do you—"

"My brothers build things," she says. "I know construction."

The Build 'Em Up sells cement mix, iron sheets, bricks, wood, and wheelbarrows. There's a piece of Dumisa material in almost every building in Sugar Town.

"Can you tell what it is?" I ask.

"Nope," Goodness says. "Just that it's being built right."

Lit Bit shifts her attention from the screen to me. "Go tomorrow and see for yourself, Amandla. It's the only way to find out what's there. I'd go with you, but I agreed to look after the Naboni children from nine to one and it's too late to back out now."

I groan. Mrs. Naboni and the other Christ Our Lord Is Risen! Gospel Hall ladies are vipers who are happy to gossip about Lil Bit's family on the street corners. Then they have the nerve to use Lil Bit as a free babysitting service. "Say no to them," I tell her. Or at least make them pay for it. Babysitting *is* work. Mrs. Naboni has five children, all of them devil spawn.

"None of my business," Goodness says. "But, depending on how long ago this image was taken, the building might already be finished. Take a shot at goal, brah. Get off the bench. It's the only way to win a match."

This is the most that Goodness has ever spoken to Lil Bit or me. She is tough and loud and has three older brothers who guard her like she is made out of gold and the world is out to steal her. I admit to myself that sometimes I want to be her. Or at least be close to her. I'd love a brother. Just one. I'd love a mother other women rush to for advice and a house that doesn't let the cold in.

"Why are you being nice to us?" Lil Bit demands out of nowhere. "Are you bored with your real friends?"

I hit Lil Bit on the shoulder. "Girl, shut up!"

"It's okay," Goodness says to me. Then she turns to Lil Bit. "I talk to everyone," she says, "but *you* don't. The two of you are in your own little world. Too good for the rest of us?"

"You're a Dumisa," Lil Bit says. "You have no idea what it's like to be us."

Goodness rolls her eyes, like, *Please, child, you don't understand a thing.* Annalisa says that *Into each life some rain must fall.* I bet Goodness has problems of her own that we will never know about. She bounces the soccer ball from one knee to the other for a long while. Lil Bit chews her bottom lip. I wait for Goodness to turn and walk away.

"I understand what you mean," she finally says. "But being me isn't what you think. From the outside everything is—"

A sharp whistle cuts through the conversation, and we turn to find Mr. Mgazi, the school cleaner and night watchman, standing at the gates with his wife, who helps him sweep the classrooms and rake the yard.

"Out, my sisters," Mr. Mgazi calls. "School is closed."

Goodness tucks the soccer ball under her arm, and dust smears across her school uniform. She doesn't notice or doesn't care.

"I'll be working at the Build 'Em Up or practicing at the field all through the holidays." Goodness turns toward the gates and says over her shoulder: "Come get me if you want to hit up Miss Gabela's lending library. I like books, too."

"Sure enough," I say, and Lil Bit grabs hold of my arm to stop me from moving forward. Goodness keeps walking, and we stay still. "What's gotten into you?" I whisper. "She was just being nice."

"But why?" she whispers back. "What does she want?"

"I don't know, but having a rich friend can't hurt."

"And what happens when she decides to dump us? Have you thought about that?"

Lil Bit might be right, but it doesn't feel that way. I say, "Who cares? We'll still have each other. The two of us are enough."

The words come out sweetly and with confidence, but deep down, they don't feel right, either. Goodness said that Lil Bit and me make up our own world. Friends with different voices and different points of view could help expand our "little" world into a bright, new universe.

"Walk me home." I hurry Lil Bit through the school gates. Wanting more is dangerous. Wanting more will only lead to disappointment. I have to be happy with what I have here and now.

"Will you go tomorrow?" Lil Bit asks when we turn into the lane between Tugela and Sisulu. "Just to see what's there."

"Yes, I'll go." I decide to learn what I can. And there's the matter of personal pride. How can I expect Lil Bit to stand up to the church ladies and be strong if I can't get myself to Durban North in broad daylight?

"Come tell me what you find out," Lil Bit says. "Sunday, after church."

"Why wait? I'll come straight over to your house from the bus." I open the door and peek inside at Annalisa, still sleeping. "If Mrs. Naboni asks you to stay longer, tell her no. You have places to go and people to see."

"It's not Mrs. Naboni. Tomorrow is the one-year anniversary of Father getting caught with that girl. I need to make sure that my mother doesn't do anything stupid."

I understand difficult mothers and hard choices.

"Sorry about your ma. I'll see you after church on Sunday."

Lil Bit nods and walks in the direction of Amazulu Street, where she lives in a one-bedroom house that's crowded with reminders of Reverend Bhengu: Hymnals and military history books. The small desk where he wrote his sermons. The ashtray he used to stub out his cigarettes. His one vice, they thought. They were wrong. Lil Bit's mother could sell it all, but she refuses.

She needs to burn everything, Annalisa tells me. *That's the fastest way to heal a wound. With fire.*

Lil Bit waves from the corner of Tugela Way and disappears into the pale shadows that fall across the broken shacks and the children playing football in the dirt. I rush inside and pull the new sketchbook and pencils from my backpack. The image of Lil Bit standing in our doorway earlier, backlit by slanting rays of sunlight, fierce and supernatural, is still sharp in my mind. I sit and I draw.

5

The Amanda Bollard Institute is six stories of brick and glass surrounded by a garden of aloes that blend together to make a living palette of reds, grays, and greens. It's beautiful. Nothing like it exists in Sugar Town. The word *institute* makes me wonder. An institute is for research and learning. An institute is where you go when that lump that you found growing on your chest gets bigger and only a specialist doctor can fix it. When Annalisa or I get sick, we line up outside the Sugar Town clinic and wait for hours to see a nurse, or if God is good, a volunteer doctor who wants an adventure.

There is no line outside the Bollard building, nor are there crying children with chapped lips strapped to their mother's backs. This institute is for rich people, and we are not rich. Annalisa calls our secondhand clothing "vintage," but that doesn't change the fact that we keep our long-term savings in a coin jar. Why has Mother come to this place? Unless . . .

Is Annalisa sick? Is she dying? Is her being here somehow my fault? My heart skips a beat, and suddenly it's hard to breathe.

The one thing that scares me more than having to take care of Annalisa and her problems is losing her. I will not survive on my own in Sugar Town.

Stop. Lil Bit's imaginary voice cuts through the panic rising in my chest. *Take a breath and blow it out again, the way I showed you.*

After Reverend Bhengu skipped town with his pregnant, underage girlfriend, Lil Bit had panic attacks that left her curled into a ball and gasping for air. After the first attack in the schoolyard, we moved to the far side of the parsley tree, under the shadow of Nelson's smile, where she felt safe. It was there that she taught herself how to "self-calm," a technique that she found inside *Peace Within*, a self-help book that she shoplifted from Crystals and Candles, a hippie shop in Glenwood. *I needed help*, she said. *So I helped myself.*

I take a long, deep breath. Cars drive past on the road. Then I hear a minivan door sliding open and footsteps on the pavement.

"Thanks. You got me here in record time." Annalisa's voice drifts down the block to where I stand, tucked between two buildings. She's arrived. When I left her sleeping this morning, I wasn't sure that she'd keep the date written on the paper. And, much as I'd like to run to her, I hold still and wait for her to get ahead. As far as she knows, I'm helping Lil Bit weed her mother's garden. On the first day of the holidays! It's funny what some parents will believe if it makes them feel good about their children.

I pop my head out from the nook where I'm hiding and watch Annalisa cross the road. She lives in a township, but you'd never guess it from the confident way she moves through the world. The tall buildings and upmarket shops do not faze her. She grew up surrounded by beautiful things, I think. Her elegant accent is 100 percent real, not put-on like some people in the township think.

She double-checks the address on the paper that I slipped back into her bag yesterday afternoon and stops to take a deep breath of her own. This is her first time here, too, but there's no way to tell how she feels about it. She turns into a small side street that leads to the rear of the Amanda Bollard Institute. Following her is the only way to find out what's going on.

A gap in the traffic opens up, and I cross the road with my heart hammering inside my chest and my mouth bone-dry. Annalisa has disappeared into the building, and it takes a moment for me to gather the courage to follow. My feet step one in front of the other, heavy and slow, like I'm walking through a river of honey.

A car horn brings me out of my thoughts. In the lane and inches from my right hip is a sleek black sports car with stylish cat-eye headlights. It is gorgeous. Even growling slowly next to me it sounds as if it's going a hundred miles an hour.

The driver flicks his suntanned hand to get me out of the way. I turn to the side to make room for the car, and I catch a glimpse of him: a silver-haired man with a hard, serious face behind the steering wheel. He wears sunglasses, but my instincts tell me his eyes aren't friendly, either. A shiver runs down my spine as the car accelerates past me onto the main road. If I never see that white man again, it will be too soon.

A few steps ahead of me is the entrance to an underground parking lot with a security gate and two black guards on duty. The smaller of the guards comes out to meet me with a clipboard tucked under his arm.

"Name?" he asks, and my mouth freezes. Amandla Harden is not on the list. I know that for sure. Mother isn't in the parking area or waiting by the elevator behind the guard's station. I take the risk that her name is on the list.

"I was supposed to meet my mother, Annalisa Harden, but my, uh . . ." What could hold up a respectable girl from a respectable suburb on a Saturday morning? Swimming? Horseback riding? Target practice? I tell a lie with a splash of truth. "My art class finished late and I missed my bus."

The guard double-checks the list while I wait. I'm torn between wanting to get inside the building and running home. How Lil Bit manages to stay cool while shoplifting is beyond me.

"Look. See her face?" the bigger guard, tall and broad across the shoulders, says to his companion in Zulu. "That one belongs to the queen. Let her in."

"*Eish!*" The small guard makes a surprised sound and says in Zulu, "You are right, my friend. Imagine that. A house sparrow among the white seagulls."

Okay. Now I am officially confused. Who is the queen and what do house sparrows and seagulls have to do with anything?

"Sixth floor. Room 605." The big guard walks me to the elevator and pushes the up button. Despite his intimidating size and shaved head, his manner is gentle, a rare thing in a powerfully built older man. That white driver in his fancy car could take lessons in good manners from this low-paid guard in a green uniform. I shrug the tension from my shoulders and wait. Elevators, in my limited experience, are a hit-and-miss affair. Some creak and jolt. Others move so slowly that taking the stairs is a better option. This one arrives quickly and silently. The doors glide open smoothly. Goodness was correct about one thing: this building was built right.

"Please tell the madam that Cyril sends his regards." Cyril, the big guard, holds the doors open with a bright smile, and I can't help but check over my shoulder to see if there is someone else standing behind me. The lift is empty. The smile was meant for me, a stranger.

"I'll pass your message on to the madam," I say as the doors close and the lift shoots upward. Inside, the elevator has smooth stainless-steel walls and a single glass panel with the image of a mopani tree etched onto it in silver. The tree branches spread out over a hill, inviting tired travelers to come and rest in the shade awhile. The image serves no function, but it holds my attention. It is art for art's sake. A silky electronic tone chimes, and the elevator doors open onto a hallway that smells of fresh flowers and antiseptic.

The white corridor is eerily quiet, unlike the Sugar Town Clinic, which rings with crying babies and old aunties complaining about the pain in their hips and knees. The Amanda Bollard Institute is posh compared to the clinic, but it is still a place for sick people and all their hopes and fears.

A second wave of panic swells inside me, and I beat it down. *Live in the light of the truth or stay blind in the darkness*, Lil Bit said biblically. That's the choice I have to make. If Annalisa is sick, I want to know about it. If she's dying, I want to be present for every crazy minute of the time we have left together.

An arrow painted on the wall points the way to rooms 600 to 615. I follow the arrow. The hush gives way to a nurses' station. A skinny Indian nurse looks up and then goes back to her computer screen. I follow the arrow around a corner. A little farther and I see a large door in the quietest part of the hallway. It's hard to knock on 605 without knowing what's waiting on the other side, but I raise my fist and rap my knuckles gently against the wood. The sound is loud in the empty space.

"Come in," a woman answers in a crisp voice that reminds me of Annalisa. I turn the handle and step into a bright room filled with fresh flowers. White roses bloom next to a flat-screen television. Red proteas decorate a glass table. Sunflowers glow yellow in the sunlight that breaks through the open curtains.

My eyes adjust to the bright and dark areas of the room, which is huge. On the right side and away from the window is a hospital bed, and sitting on the bed is a gray-haired old lady wearing a blue Japanese robe. Blood roars in my ears. The woman is a stranger, but the shape of her face, the wide set of her mouth, and the sharp angles of her cheekbones are achingly familiar. She is future me, hooked up to machines and decades older.

And she's white.

* * *

My mouth opens and closes, like a fish on land. The woman's mouth does the same, both of us lost for words. I close my eyes and open them wide again to make sure that I'm seeing straight. The woman is clear and in focus. She is real and she is right across the room from me.

"Come closer," she says. "Let's take a good look at each other."

I walk in a trance and stop halfway to the bed. The woman holds out her hands, but I stay where I am. Girls from my neighborhood do not run into the arms of strangers.

She drops her hands into her lap. "Do you know who I am, Amandla?"

My name, coming from her mouth, sounds delicate and rare somehow. *Amandla* is the Zulu word for *power*, but the way she says it, it's more like the name of a rare bird or a flower. No one in her world is called Amandla. I take three steps closer to the bed, pulled by an invisible thread.

"I'm your grandmother," she says when I stay quiet. "The other grandchildren call me Mayme, but you can call me anything. Granny. Amanda. Whatever you like."

Annalisa told me I was named after the kindest woman she ever knew. An angel married to a gargoyle who keeps her locked in a stone fortress by the ocean. I thought it was a made-up story, but now I'm not so sure. Amanda . . . Amandla . . . There's a connection.

I'm frozen. Delighted. Afraid. I don't believe her. Then I do. Then I *know in my bones* that this old lady is my grandmother.

A sudden new feeling wells up inside me. I am furious.

What the hell, brah? There are other grandchildren and another family that lives somewhere in rich-white-people land? My *mother told me nothing. Nothing. Nothing to prepare me for this. Annalisa's family. My family. And I never knew.*

I think of all that I've missed. Birthday parties. Family dinners. Lazy Sunday walks that lead aunts and cousins back to the same house. A long wooden table with a seat reserved just for me. The stuff of my dreams.

"You must have a million questions," Mayme says. "Ask me whatever you like, and I'll try to answer."

I do have questions. Maybe not a million, but a few. I've been kept in the dark for fifteen years, and screaming questions at an old lady in a hospital bed is not the proper way to get information. I stop and I breathe. Mayme tilts her head and patiently waits for me to say something. The silence between us grows. It's awkward, but I don't know where to start. Then I clear my throat and decide to start easy and build up to the hard questions.

"How many cousins do I—"

The bathroom door opens and glass shatters on the tiled floor.

"Amandla!" It's Annalisa's voice. "You shouldn't be here. It's not safe. You have to leave. Right now."

Her hands twitch by her side, and her body vibrates with fear. Of what, I cannot imagine. "Everything is all right." I talk her down. "See? It's just Mayme and me, and we're both fine."

Annalisa steps over the broken vase and the pink lilies scattered across the bathroom tiles. She rushes across the room and grabs my arm, hard. She tugs, red-faced and panicked. I dig in my heels. "You don't understand. You have to leave right now."

"I just got here."

"There's no time to explain. He can't know that you're here. If he comes back—" She frowns, and the blood drains from her face. "You followed me . . . Did he see you come in?"

"Who?" I ask, more frustrated than angry. I've seen Annalisa face down rude men with an icy glare. Whoever she is talking about has turned her inside out.

"My father," she says.

"I don't know your father. What does he look like?"

"Silver hair. Suntanned," Mayme says. "You might have seen him in the parking garage."

Silver-haired and suntanned. I think of the white man who beeped at me in the laneway.

"I saw him and he saw me," I say, and Annalisa's fingers dig into my arm, deep enough to leave a bruise. I peel her fingers open. "Listen to me." I keep my voice low, afraid of sending her into a panic. "He drove past me, but he didn't see me. Not really. I was just in his way. I was nobody. He won't come back because he's already forgotten about the brown girl in the driveway."

It's a strange thing to say about the man who, it turns out, is my grandfather, but it makes Annalisa laugh. I don't see the funny side. Annalisa and I are always the outsiders—why do we have to be? Wouldn't it be lovely, just once, to live in the warm heart of things? To be part of a family?

"Everyone relax. Amandla, come. Sit by me." Mayme pats a spot on the side of her bed, which is wider than my single cot. This time I make it all the way across the room, though I remain standing. "I'll order tea. Everything is better with tea and cake, don't you think?"

Well, yes, though I am more interested in the fact that tea is being ordered and delivered to a hospital room. Maybe that's how it's done in city hospitals.

"Tea would be nice." Annalisa retreats to the bathroom and bends down to gather the spray of pink lilies scattered across the tiles. "I'll clear this up."

I go to help, but Mayme takes my hand. "Stay," she says. "I'll get proper help to clean up the mess."

Proper is one of Annalisa's favorite words. Proper tea is made with tea leaves and not with tea bags. Proper beds are made with "hospital corners" that keep the sheets tucked tightly to the mattress, like they are on Mayme's bed—here in this hospital. Annalisa is religious about keeping our room clean and in order. She grew up in a house where everything was proper. I've always wondered where she learned to sweep, scrub, and make our beds so well. I imagine her as a little girl, following the maid around the rooms of a large house and making a game out of helping her to make the beds properly.

"What do you know about our family?" Mayme asks after ordering tea and cleaners via the telephone on her bedside table. As easy as that.

"Not much. When I ask Annalisa where she's from, she says, 'Close but a million miles away.' I used to think she was hiding something, but there are times when I think she doesn't remember where she came from herself."

Mayme nods, familiar with the sudden headaches that strike Annalisa when she tries to remember the past. I throw Mother a quick look, nervous about where this conversation might lead, and find her standing by the window with a bruised lily in her hand. She's caught in a moment, suspended in time. A thought strikes me. If Mayme is aware of Annalisa's fragile state of mind, then surely she must be aware that we live in a settlement that's stuck between endless cane fields and a shipping-container graveyard.

"Have you been to Sugar Town?" I ask.

"No."

"Then you don't know how we live."

"Is that why you came here today, Amandla? To ask for money?" Mayme asks, and I flush hot. The money question comes out of nowhere. It makes me angry enough to spit. An old white lady thinks a township girl is out to rob her.

Tell me something new, brah.

"Listen, Granny . . ." I lean in close, angry. "You don't know me, and I don't know you, so let me lay things out. I'm not here for *you*. I tracked Annalisa to this hospital because I thought she was sick. And why would I ask a stranger for money? I don't beg."

"Good for you." Mayme's face relaxes. "What's my name, Amandla?"

I blink, confused.

"Amanda. You just told me."

"My full name."

"I have no idea."

"Harden is my maiden name. I have a married name, too. Do you know what it is?" *Jesus, help me, what does this woman want from me? Harden is Annalisa's surname and mine also. Yes, me sharing my grandmother's maiden name is odd, but how would I know how that came about?*

"We only just met," I say, frustrated. "How would I know your proper surname?"

Mayme laughs. That drip bag attached to her arm must be filled with intense meds. Morphine or another mood lifter. Mrs. M would know exactly, but I can only guess. Two soft knocks come from the other side of the door.

"Tea, madam," a woman's voice calls out. "May we come in?"

"Of course," Mayme answers, and two older black ladies in blue uniforms wheel a tea trolley into the room. Two more women, young and dressed in green uniforms, step around them and clean away the broken glass and flowers from the bathroom. The *proper* cleaners Mayme ordered. In minutes, the mess is gone and the women have vanished as if nothing had broken at all.

"Where would you like the trolley, Mrs. Bollard?" the older of the tea ladies asks in a deferential tone. That's when it clicks. The answer to Grandma's question comes to me in a flash. Mayme Amanda is the "queen" that Cyril, the parking guard, said I belonged to.

"You're the Amanda on the front of the building. Amanda Bollard."

"Correct!" Mayme says, and the older tea lady purses her lips to hear a girl address an elder by her first name. It's not done. Normally, this is where I'd apologize to "Auntie" for offending, but I am still trying to digest the fact that my grandmother's name is slapped across the entrance of a brand-new multistory hospital. Not a wing or a floor. The entire building.

Boom. The small guard's strange bird comment suddenly makes sense. I am the sparrow, and the Bollards are the white seagulls. And, judging from his surprised expression, I'm the only brown bird in the flock.

6

I'm fifteen years old and only now have I met my grandmother face-to-face. A grandmother who could have helicoptered us out of Sugar Town to a nicer place on any day of the week but didn't. Why not? My stomach flips. I have a feeling that my black father and my brown skin are the reasons that Mother and I live separate from the Bollards.

"Amandla, you pour," Annalisa says.

I blink, and the tea ladies are gone. The trolley, stacked with cakes and scones and tiny sandwiches cut on the diagonal, is set up beside Mayme's bed with one chair on either side. Time has passed without me noticing.

I take the cover off the teapot, give the tea leaves inside a stir the way Annalisa taught me to, and place the silver strainer over the lip of a china cup decorated with lavender flowers. I pour.

"Milk, sugar, lemon, or black?" I ask Mayme as dark liquid fills the cup.

"My mother taught me how to pour tea. I taught Annalisa,

and she taught you," she says, choking up. "The world moves so fast. It's beautiful to watch you do that."

Something has changed in the room. In my grandmother.

"Black tea, Mayme?"

"Yes," she says. "Yes, please."

I place the cup and saucer into her waiting hand. Liquid sloshes over the sides, and a river of tea spreads across the white bed linen. Mayme's shoulders and arms shake, and the cup tilts. I grab it before the rest of the tea spills and notice, only then, the tears streaming down her face.

"Are you all right?" Annalisa grabs her mother's wrist and holds her fingertips at the pulse point. "Is there pain in your chest? Lie still. I'll get the doctor."

"Don't fuss, Annie," she says. "I'm fine. I just had a moment of . . ."

Sorrow, I think. A moment of sorrow. The same deep sadness that ate a hole in Annalisa yesterday. Mrs. M said the only cure for that was time and rest. Warm food helps, too. Mayme dries her tears and gathers herself together again.

The electronic monitor beside the bed blinks red, and I am ashamed of my earlier anger. The room is clean and beautifully laid out, but it is a hospital room. A place for sick people, and Mayme is sick. I split open a scone and slather it with strawberry jam and cream.

"Here. Eat. The scone is still warm."

"She can't have that." Annalisa waves me off like I have served up death itself. "Take it away."

I sit back down with the plate perched on my knees; I'm a visitor. Despite her poor memory, Annalisa fits into the quiet luxury of this plush room where high tea and doctors are ordered on demand.

"You have it, Amandla," Mayme says. "Sara, the cook here, makes the best scones. Annie, have the other half and let me catch my breath."

Annie. Mother has a nickname. It's funny. She hates shortened names. She calls Mrs. M "Mrs. Mashanini" and Lil Bit "Esther." All part of being proper. I bite into the scone and hold back a groan. Mayme did not exaggerate. The scone is the best I have ever tasted. Tonight, before I fall asleep, I will replay the light, fluffy texture of it in my head.

"Mmm . . ." The sound escapes my mouth, and Mayme smiles to hear it. The tears have dried, but a trace of the sadness still remains. *Being me isn't what you think*, Goodness Dumisa said in the schoolyard. Maybe it's the same for Amanda Bollard of the Amanda Bollard Institute, with everything perfect on the outside but messy inside. Annalisa pours tea and glances at me to examine my posture and my manners, always on the lookout for anything that will brand me as coming from a township instead of being the *proper* girl she raised. She nods her approval. I've passed the test. For this moment, I belong exactly where I am.

Tears dried, everyone calm; now I need to know why we live in Sugar Town. I need to know why Annalisa and I have been left to fend for ourselves. Why am I growing up with so little when my family has so much? I need to know who I really am.

The phone on the bedside table rings, and Mayme frowns; she's not expecting a call on the private line. Annalisa sips tea and listens in, waiting, it seems, for bad news.

"Was that him?" she asks when Mayme hangs up. "Is he coming back?"

"No, that was Julien and the boys. He's parking the car."

"Quick." Annalisa gulps her tea and waves me toward the door. "We have to leave now."

"I still have questions, *Mother!*" I'm also halfway through a scone I will remember for weeks. Walking away from tiny chocolate cupcakes with sugar flowers on top is going to break my heart.

"My brother is . . . I mean . . . we . . ." Annalisa's words scramble together. "Your uncle Julien and I . . . We haven't seen each other in fifteen years . . . Now is not the time, Amandla. Let's go."

I give the cakes a glance and commit them to memory. Tonight my dreams will be sweet and sad.

"Shh. Relax, my love." Mayme strokes Annalisa's arm. "Why don't you fill a napkin for Amandla to take home while we say goodbye?"

Mayme's voice calms Annalisa, who grabs a cloth napkin and goes to work collecting cakes and sandwiches from the trolley. One of everything would suit me fine, but I'll take whatever I can get.

"A hug before you go, Amandla?" Mayme asks, and my stubborn township self holds back. We stare at each other, and tears sting my eyes. No matter what happened before today or what happens after, there's no denying that she is my grandmother. The two of us share the same name and the same facial features. We are connected by blood and by a family history I know nothing about.

Mayme opens her arms, waiting and vulnerable. I fold gently into her embrace, afraid of hurting her. She grabs me and holds me close. I can't help it. I love the way she crushes me.

"Thank you," she whispers into my ear. "Thank you for looking after my daughter. Come see me on Monday morning. Ten o'clock? Let's try to make up for lost time."

"I'll come." Heat stings my eyes, and I choke back tears. My questions can wait. This moment, our arms around each other, holding each other tight in a warm embrace, is all I need for now.

"We have to go," Annalisa says, and when I turn around, she's already standing at the door holding a bunch of cakes wrapped in a napkin. Some will go to Mrs. M and Blind Auntie with the sweet tooth, some to Lil Bit, and the rest are for the two of us to eat after supper.

"Bye, Mayme," I call over my shoulder, and follow Annalisa into the corridor. The elevator bell rings as we turn the corner and the doors swish open. A tall white man and two teenagers with sandy-blond hair step into the hall. Uncle Julien and the boys. My cousins. I want to stop and soak in the details: their pale skin and hair, the way they move and talk. Their ironed blue jeans and oxford shirts swish in the hallway, neat and laundered. Time is up. They are between us and the elevator. If we stay where we are, they will see us.

"The stairs," Annalisa whispers, and bolts in the direction of a door marked Exit. We slip into the stairwell and take the steps down two at a time to escape. She hasn't seen Julien in fifteen years, she said.

My age exactly.

* * *

The bus bumps through the fields on our way home. Green stalks flex in the breeze, and the city grows small on the horizon behind us. I wait for Annalisa to tell me something, anything, about the Bollard family and how we came to live in Sugar Town.

And, while we're on the subject of secrets and lies, *how dare you bring me up to believe that we're alone in the world?*

Annalisa stares out the window and says nothing. Not a *sorry* or a *please, let me explain*. I cannot stand the silence for one minute longer.

"What the hell!" I blurt out. "If I hadn't followed you into town today, would you ever have taken me to meet Mayme or told me about your family? Like, ever?"

"How did you know where I was, Amandla?" she asks in a tense voice, like my being at the hospital is the most important talking point right now. And way to deflect the conversation away from the big issues, Mother. I'll play the question-and-answer game if it leads us back to why we live in Sugar Town and how we came to be there in the first place.

"I found the address for the institute in your bag," I say.

"It isn't proper to look through other people's personal possessions, Amandla." Her annoyance is almost laughable. "You should know better."

"When you came off the bus yesterday, you were sick. I opened your bag to grab the house keys, and that's when I found the note." A little white lie, but at this stage, who is the real liar here? "Why didn't you tell me about my family?"

Annalisa turns her face away. She doesn't look at me. She talks to the window instead. "My father is a dangerous man, Amandla. He threw me out of my own family and said to never come back. I meet up with Mother every few months in secret. If he ever found out that we talk, he'd find a way to punish both of us. If he'd caught you inside the hospital . . . I just . . . I don't want to think about it."

I flash back to the cool way my grandfather dismissed me in the driveway like I was nothing. Annalisa's view of the world is fractured, but describing her father as "dangerous" feels right. His face was stony. I bet his heart is, too. Only a cold, hard man would turn his child away forever. In Sugar Town getting kicked out of your own home is practically a tradition. William Caluza, our butcher, has thrown his younger brother out of his house a dozen times for being drunk or drugged out. But he *has* taken him back in every single time. How can Annalisa's father sleep at night not knowing if she is cold or hungry or hurt?

"I came back home once and he sent me away again . . . It was bad . . . He sent me to a place in the country . . ." The pause between words stretches out as the memory of what happened slips away. Finally, she gives up and turns to me. Her face is pale and her eyes are bright. "Your grandmother wants to see you, but it's too much of a risk. You're not going back. You're staying home, where it's safe."

That must be the first time anyone has declared our township a safe zone for a fifteen-year-old girl. It's funny and it's not. "You met your grandmother once and that will have to be enough," she says. "Do you understand?"

Lady, you are out of your mind if you think that's going to happen.

After today, it is impossible to shrink the world back to just Annalisa and me. My universe now contains cousins, an uncle Julien, and grandparents. Meeting Mayme has made me realize how isolated Annalisa and I are. A quick glimpse of two sandy-haired Bollard boys has made me long for impossible things: birthday parties, family squabbles, and Sunday lunches with bodies squashed around a table. For the first time I can remember, I feel lonely and alone.

"Mayme is sick," I say. "What's wrong with her?"

"Heart failure."

"Because she's old?"

"No. She was born with a heart defect."

"Is it serious?"

"Yes. She needs an operation to fix things. If she doesn't have the operation, she'll be dead in a few weeks. I know it's a shock, but promise me that you'll stay away from the hospital, Amandla." Sweat gathers on Annalisa's top lip, and her voice is low and serious. "Swear it."

"I swear," I say, and the moment the words are out of my mouth, I know they are a lie. Mayme has a few weeks left on this earth, and I intend to spend every minute of that time getting to know her and getting to know my family and my history.

7

Annalisa sleeps like the dead awaiting resurrection on Judgment Day. Yesterday's near miss with Uncle Julien and Mayme's illness have bruised her, and she will need time to mend.

Taking cupcakes to Lil Bit (Esther).
Back around noon. Amandla

I drop the note onto the table and pack two chocolate cupcakes into the napkin from the hospital. Mrs. M got the lion's share of the goodies for her three grandchildren, depressed daughter, and Blind Auntie with the sugar addiction. If Mrs. M got to eat a single cake, I'd be surprised.

Outside, the day is bright and cold. The streets are quiet. The holy are in church and the not-so-holy are settling in for marathon Sunday drinking sessions in backyards and illegal bars that will go into the night. I pass businesses with the owners' names hand-painted over the doorways or across the front walls. Solomon and His Three Wives General Store. Rayvee Fish and Chips. Sheba's Fast Fashions. People have buildings named after them in Sugar Town, too, but not six-story hospitals with underground parking lots.

The Sunday service is still in full swing when I get to the Christ Our Lord Is Risen! Gospel Hall. Five large jacaranda trees surround the churchyard, their bare limbs stark against the pale winter sky. I stand under the sprawled branches and wait for the last hymn to end. It takes a while. Paster Mbuli likes to keep the music flowing and the collection plate moving from back to front to sweep for money that might shake loose on a second pass.

The music dies, and the wooden doors swing open. Lil Bit and her mother, both dressed in blue cotton dresses that fall below the knee, are first out of the hall, the way they always are. Lil Bit sees me and comes over, but her mother hurries home. I wish she'd let the shadow of her husband's disgrace go. She didn't do anything wrong.

"I brought you something." I open the napkin before she starts in on the questions. The cupcakes are slightly squashed on the sides, but the whipped chocolate icing and the sugar flowers are intact. They are miniature works of edible art.

"A tulip and a peony." Lil Bit identifies the different blooms in a hushed voice; her slender fingers hover over the napkin. "They are too beautiful to eat."

"Well, if that's the case, I'll feed them to the birds."

"Don't you dare." Lil Bit grabs my right wrist with one hand and scoops up an iced cupcake with the other. She takes a bite and chews. She groans just like I did. Sara, the cook at the institute, is a magician. Lil Bit's Afro curls are styled into two braids that are woven tight to her scalp. It looks painful, but her smile is pure sugar-fueled joy.

"Good?" I ask.

"*Good* isn't a good enough word to describe it." She licks chocolate from her fingers. "Try *sublime* or *heavenly*. Where did you get these?!"

"The short answer is a place in Durban North," I say as Goodness Dumisa and her mother step out of the hall. People stop them to talk, to compliment their outfits, their unfailing devotion to the good Lord above. Mr. Dumisa joins them. He is tall with a skewed nose and a bull neck that make him look like a gangster. He smiles wide and laughs loud, but there's a hollow quality to his laughter that makes me think he is putting on a show. I wonder if he is something different in private. I know a little about family secrets now.

Goodness strides over to us in a tight-fitting shweshwe fabric dress that hugs her hips and clings to her thighs. Her feet, in white canvas sneakers, are at least comfortable. Knowing Mrs. Dumisa's taste for high heels, I bet Goodness had to fight to wear those kicks this morning.

"What's the news?" she asks me straight out. "Where did your mother end up?"

Seriously?

I'm grateful Goodness let me use her smartphone, but that does not give her permission to dig into my family business.

It's too soon to share information. I don't even know how to process what's happened myself yet.

"The same place you got the cakes?" Lil Bit scoops up the crumbs from the first cupcake; she's too caught up in the rush of sugar and chocolate to realize I don't want to talk in front of Goodness. But there the two of them stand, looking at me and waiting.

"The building we saw is a hospital." I give in. "The Amanda Bollard Institute . . ."

"Oh, heavens," Lil Bit says. "Is your mum sick?"

"No, Annalisa is fine. It's my grandmother Amanda who's ill."

"You met your grandmother?!" Lil Bit says.

Goodness tilts her head to the side, amazed. "Is that the first time you met your granny ever?"

An impossible situation for her to imagine. The Dumisa family lives and works together. They take care of each other and fight each other's fights. Try laying a hand on Goodness and see what happens to you.

"That's funny." Lil Bit eyes the second cupcake, her attention split between my big news and the demands of her stomach. "Your granny Amanda in a hospital with the same first name as hers."

"That's the thing," I say. "The building is named after her. She *is* Amanda Bollard."

Lil Bit's eyes go wide, and Goodness raises an eyebrow. Joan van Mark, a skinny white girl in the grade above us, loves to tell anyone who will listen that her family is rich and that, any day now, the money will hit the bank and she'll be gone in the back of a gold Mercedes-Benz. Sugar Town people have a lot of lottery fever-dreams and *money buried in the backyard* fantasies.

"For real?" Lil Bit asks in a *don't you lie to me* tone. I don't blame her. A grandmother with a building in the city would be a township first, and for an unnerving second, I doubt myself. Was Mayme real? Or am I my mother's daughter—caught between reality and what I wish reality was? I glance down at the remaining chocolate cupcake. There's my proof. The Amanda Bollard Institute is real. It exists. I was there.

"That sublime cupcake is from the Amanda Bollard Institute. What else do you want to know, ladies?"

Lil Bit laughs, relieved to find that I am earthbound and thinking straight. "So the Bollards are loaded?"

"If money gets your name on the front of a building, then the Bollards must be rich. I don't know for sure. Yesterday was the first time I ever heard that name."

"We could do a web search," Goodness says as the church grounds empty and dust from the congregation's footsteps darkens the air. "Come to the Build 'Em Up tomorrow morning. We'll use one of my brother's computers to get info."

Again, the Bollards and what they do for a living is none of Goodness's business. Free access to a working computer and printer is hard to find here, though. I can't turn down the offer. Goodness has a good plan, but I can't make it. I have a date with Mayme.

"We could use your phone like we did yesterday, if that's okay," Lil Bit says, and Goodness glances across the yard to where Mrs. Dumisa stands surrounded by other smiling women. All of them trying to get close to Sugar Town's royals.

"My mother took my phone away this morning. It's just . . ." Goodness hesitates, on the verge of sharing personal information, then goes on. "She wanted me to wear high heels and I said, 'No thanks. If I fall, I'll break an ankle and how can I play soccer with a broken ankle?' And she said it was time for me to start behaving like a proper girl. A lady. I said, 'No thanks' to that, and she said, 'No heels. No phone for two days.' That's why we have to go to the Build 'Em Up tomorrow. My brothers will let us use the computer and the printer. Whatever we want."

I'm jealous. Goodness's mother might be unreasonable about footwear, but her brothers have her back. Annalisa will fight to her last breath to keep me safe, but when she's in her dark place, it's just me, fending for myself.

"Can we do it in the afternoon?" I shove my envy to the side. "I have to be in Durban North at ten."

"No problem," Goodness says. "Between one and two?"

The yard is mostly empty now, and Mrs. Dumisa's expression has gone from sunny to stormy weather at being left waiting by an ungrateful daughter who refuses to wear high heels.

"That's great, but if you want your phone back any time soon, you'd better hurry over to your ma," I say. "We'll see you tomorrow."

Goodness turns to leave and throws a quick glance at Lil Bit over her shoulder. "You have a bit of chocolate on the corner of your mouth. Right side."

"Oh." Lil Bit ducks her head and rubs the chocolate away with her fingertip. And the way she does it, all quick and embarrassed and hot in the face, makes me think that, despite her rudeness on Friday afternoon, she likes Goodness.

"See that? She offered to help without being asked," I say, fishing for a reaction. "You still think we should stay away from her?"

Lil Bit shrugs, too casual for the gesture to come off as natural. "Can I take that home?" She fiddles with the last cupcake. "The sugar hit might cheer my ma up."

Nice deflection, Esther Bhengu, but not good enough to fool me. Why she would try to downplay the fact that Goodness is cool and having her as a friend adds a new dimension to our lives is curious. She's hiding something. I don't know what.

"The cupcake is for you." I fold the napkin over the chocolate peak and the sugar tulip on top. "Eat it or share it with your ma. You decide."

Lil Bit smiles and says, "Don't judge me if I take at least one bite on the way home. For the energy that fuels my giant intellect."

We leave the empty churchyard and go our separate ways. Lil Bit to a cramped one-bedroom brick house on Amazulu street and me to our tiny tin house on the lane. Lil Bit stops outside the gates and says, "Till tomorrow, when the secrets of the world will be revealed."

And damn, Lil Bit can't help but be a preacher's daughter. She takes words and makes them *the word*. Pity that she is tongue-tied around most people. Not me, though. And now Goodness. I never saw *that* coming.

"Till tomorrow," I say, and start walking home. Things have changed in two days. I have a new grandmother and Goodness Dumisa is suddenly a friend. And not by accident. By design, I think. She has chosen to hang out with two girls from the fringe instead of the cool kids with money. Maybe she enjoys the sense of power that helping out a couple of poor kids gives her? Or maybe there is another reason for choosing us that I've missed? Until all the secrets of the world are revealed at the Build 'Em Up, she can take up space next to Lil Bit and me as much as she wants.

8

On Monday, I creep out of the house after Annalisa leaves for Mr. Gupta's law office, where she organizes legal files and cleans up the cigarette butts and chocolate wrappers that he hides under his desk. I get to the Amanda Bollard Institute at five minutes to ten, excited but nervous at having lied to mother, who thinks I'm doing homework with Lil Bit. A part of Annalisa's rational mind must know that:

1. Me taking time out to study on the first official day of the holidays is utterly ridiculous.
2. Me staying away from Mayme is impossible and she shouldn't have asked it of me.

"Good morning, Miss Bollard." Cyril, the big guard, waves me through the parking lot with a smile for who he thinks I am. A girl from the Bollard clan. He'd have a heart attack if he saw our shack and the dirt soccer fields filled with the bad boys of Sugar Town.

The elevator arrives, and Cyril hits the button for the sixth floor. I want to say, *Loosen up, brah. No need for the show. I'm poor as an empty pocket.*

Instead, I smile and say, "Thank you, Cyril. Very kind of you."

The doors close, and my nerves kick up a notch. It took ages for me to figure out what to wear from my limited choices. I chose poorly. Annalisa might be able to pull off a pair of faded blue jeans, a white T-shirt, and a thrift shop tuxedo jacket with velvet lapels. Not me. On me, the clothes aren't vintage. They are hand-me-downs that give off a *5:00 a.m. walk of shame from a stranger's apartment to the bus stop* vibe, as if everything was thrown together in a rush. I've never been inside an apartment or done the walk of shame through city streets with tall buildings rising up to touch the low belly of the clouds, but I did read about it in a novel from Mrs. Lithuli's library. That's the beauty of books. For five hours, I lived inside the skin of a messy white girl with runny mascara and gold high-heeled shoes that pinched her toes.

The elevator glides to a holt.

"Too late to turn back," I mumble as the steel doors slide open on level six. This time, I know which way to go. When I get to room 605, there's a note stuck on the door.

Come up to the roof garden on the next level. It's a beautiful day.

"The roof garden," I say aloud, and realize that this is the first time the words *roof* and *garden* have left my mouth together. In summer, the tires that hold down our tin roof sprout wild grass and daisies. Rusty red lichen spreads over the loose rocks. A garden of some sort, but definitely not a *roof garden*. There are no car tires or rocks on this rooftop. That much I know for sure.

One level up, the doors open. In front of me, flowering grasses, golden marigolds, and silver-leafed shrubs stretch to where the edge of the roof meets the sky. Raised vegetable beds planted with spinach, squash, and beetroot with leggy purple stalks take up the right side of the space. When Mrs. M dreams of heaven, I bet this is what she sees: an abundance of flowers and vegetables worked by an army of bees collecting nectar.

I was right about the tires (not one) and wrong about the rocks. Four tall slabs of weathered sandstone stand over a blanket of winter aloes. No way did those stones fit into the regular elevator. They must have been craned up and lowered onto the roof. Astonishing.

"Amandla." Mayme's voice stirs me from my daze, and I turn to where she sits in a wheelchair parked in the shade of a potted milkwood tree. The beeping machine from her room is missing, and by her side is a boy about my age, pale-skinned and plain-faced, with sandy-blond hair the exact same shade as Annalisa's.

"Come and meet your cousin Sam," Mayme says, and I'm afraid that if I blink too hard this waking dream will dissolve. The boy, Sam, stares and stares, and sweat breaks out on my top lip. The differences between us are stark. He is white and dressed in jeans, a long-sleeved blue shirt, and a pair of black Air Jordans with bright red accents. Goodness would know the style name, and Lil Bit the price. More than Mum earns in a month. Easy.

My footsteps falter. Being here, with a God's-eye view of the city, makes me feel anxious. My clothes are all wrong. I am all wrong. Mayme accepts me, but will my new cousin do the same?

"Don't be shy," Mayme says. "Samuel is sixteen and he's the best of the Bollards. He won't bite."

Cousin Sam stands up and offers his hand confidently. I take it, and, up close, his expression is easier to read. It is not disapproval or distrust, but sheer amazement. Oh, of course. I understand. Mayme Amanda and I share the same face but in different colors.

"Remarkable, isn't it?" Mayme chuckles. "Amandla could be my daughter from a handsome black man."

Sam blushes, and I laugh out loud. Sugar Town mamas sprinkle hot sauce on their conversation to give it kick, but hearing that kind of talk coming from the mouth of an old white lady in a wheelchair is hilarious. Mayme has a naughty streak. I like it.

"Samuel Bollard," she says. "Meet Amandla Harden."

Sam's hand is smooth with a strong grip. He wouldn't last an hour in my township, but he's not soft, either.

"Walk and talk." She points to the paths that wind through the garden. "Get to know each other while I take in the air. It's good to feel the sun on my skin."

"Are you sure?" Leaving a sick woman alone in a wheelchair feels wrong. And without the beeping machine that was attached to her in the room . . . possibly dangerous.

"Stop fussing, Amandla." Mayme waves me off. "I'm old, not helpless, and I'd like a moment to sit and think."

Sam moves to the raised vegetable beds, and I follow. Walking with him is awkward and it's not. He is a familiar stranger with Mother's blond hair and blue eyes. If I belong to Granny in the looks department, he belongs to Annalisa. To my left is the wide expanse of the ocean, and to my right, tall buildings that scrape the clouds in the business district. The city of Durban spreads out below me. Cars and people move along paved streets and highways.

"I've never been this high up before," I say as a swallow swoops low over the garden and wheels toward the white sand beaches that hug the ocean. Being this far above the ground is powerful but also lonely.

"It's only six stories, plus the garden," Sam says.

Only six stories, he says. Like the sky has always been his limit.

"The tallest building in Sugar Town is three stories, and I went to the top floor of the Pavilion shopping mall once." I go with honesty even though a part of me wants desperately to lie about how low to the ground I live. "That's as high as I've been."

"Truly?" He shoots me a sideways glance, uncertain how this sparrow fits into his flock of white seagulls. *Stop trying to make sense of me, cuz.* I don't fit. My "vintage" clothes, curly hair, and brown skin give away everything. We are cousins: tied by blood, but not much else.

"Why would I lie about something so silly?" I stop and bend low over a bushy plant with bright purple, orange, and red chilies. It is the perfect distraction from the uncomfortable knot of embarrassment tightening inside my chest. People from Durban call Sugar Town a slum and a breeding ground for criminals, and they are not wrong. Sugar Town is mostly slum, and for those with an appetite for guns and stealing, crime pays the bills and keeps food on the table. Sugar Town is also where Mrs. M grows food for her family and her neighbors, and her blind aunt knits scarves for orphans. Which reminds me . . . Mrs. M's kindness has to be repaid, and I've found the perfect gift.

"Mayme," I call over my shoulder. "Can I take some of these chilies home for Mrs. Mashanini? She's a keen gardener, but I don't think she has a chili plant with different colored fruits."

"It's a fairy lights chili." Mayme names it right away. "Snip off whatever you like, Amandla. Seeds are for sharing."

I break off a small branch popping with colors and drop it into my jacket pocket. Mrs. M will dry the seeds out, and when the plants are full grown, she'll set out a basket of fresh chilies for the people on the lane to choose from.

"Where's Sugar Town?" Sam asks. Come to think of it, the name Sugar Town does not appear on any map. It is an "informal settlement" self-named by those who live inside its shifting boundaries.

"To the north. Right after the shipping-container graveyard and a few miles before the big sugar refinery."

"There's nothing out there but . . ." He stumbles to a stop, too embarrassed to call where I live a slum.

"Shacks and dirt roads and sugarcane fields." I walk on, hunting green treasure for Mrs. M. An old black man in a thin dressing gown sits on a bench with his wife, who wears neat clothes for the hospital visit. Not a rich couple. A poor one. The Amanda Bollard Institute isn't just for the wealthy after all. It lifts my heart to know there's a place here for sick people no matter how much money they have.

"You live in a township?" Sam asks straight out, brave now that we've established that there is no hidden mansion with servants and a swimming pool tucked in the cane fields. "You're a *Bollard*. What happened?"

I wish I knew for sure. I have guesses and random facts that may or may not be related to what actually happened. That is enough to start out with, though.

"Grandfather kicked my mother, Annalisa, out of home. Forever. When she tried to come back, he sent her away to the country. Someplace bad. I need to get the full story from Mayme, but the split had something to do with me. With my black father."

Sam does not contradict me. His silence tells me that he thinks the story could be true. Until Mandela came to power and said that we are all one rainbow nation with our colors mixed together, blacks and whites lived separately. They did not mix or marry or attend the same schools. Even now in Sugar Town the races mostly remain at a distance from each other.

Sam sits on the edge of a raised garden bed, and I sit next to him. He stares over the rooftops. "You should know that the best thing about our grandfather is our grand*mother*," he says in a quiet voice. "Mayme is kind, and Grandpa Neville is the opposite.

Cross him once and you're an enemy for life. Holding a grudge is his religion. When you meet him, you'll see what I mean."

In Annalisa's mind, my grandfather is more than that. He is dangerous. Even with the blacked-out spaces in her head, Annalisa's animal instincts tell her to stay away from her father. That is enough of an alarm bell for me.

"I don't think we'll ever meet. Annalisa won't let me go near him."

"Avoiding Grandpa Neville is better than trying to please him, which is what my father does. He won't walk away from the business. I hate seeing how hard he tries to get Grandpa's respect and how little Grandpa cares. It's a shame. Father has some good ideas."

The words come out in a rush, like a dam wall breaking. Sam turns and peers into the rows of marigolds and winter spinach, seeming embarrassed at speaking his mind. I want to know more, but now is not the time to press him for details on what *the business* means.

"Is your neighbor looking for anything in particular?" He moves the conversation to the safe topic of vegetables. I go with the flow.

"Mrs. M loves unusual versions of ordinary plants, like that multicolored chili."

We comb through the garden bed, searching for cauliflowers with strange-shaped heads and bell peppers in colors other than green and red. Sam reaches for a yellow pepper with rusty-red streaks and freezes, his hand stuck in midair. Raised voices reach us. "Irresponsible" and "careless," a male voice says. "My life, my decision," Mayme snaps back, and what we're hearing isn't exactly a fight; it's an argument about her being outside and unplugged from the machine.

I part the green stalks to see a tall man, tanned, with fair hair. Uncle Julien. Next to him is a handsome teenager dressed in the same simple but expensive style as Sam.

"My father and my brother, Harry," Sam says. "I'll introduce you."

"No." I pull him down beside me. "I'm not supposed to be here. My mother will lose it. You go. I'll stay."

Sam hesitates. I give him a gentle push in Mayme's direction. "Go before your dad gives her a heart attack for wanting to sit in the sun."

"All right." He stands and brushes down his jeans, which have not one crease in them. "Mayme has my number . . . It's school holidays. Let's grab an ice cream on the beach if that's okay. I'd like to see you again."

"Sounds good." Annalisa takes me for ice cream on Main Beach maybe twice every summer. We fill our water bottles from the public drinking taps, and after lying in the sun for ten minutes max, we swim out past the breakers and gaze back at the skyscrapers crowding the shoreline.

Sam goes to rescue Mayme from being lectured, and I lean into a row of vegetables to harvest the yellow pepper for Mrs. Mashanini. A long shadow in the shape of a man falls over me, and the skin on the back of my neck prickles. I tell myself not to look, but my head turns without my permission.

9

My grandfather stands at my left shoulder and stares down at me. He is tall and slim, with blue eyes and thick silvery hair, brushed back neat. His eyes aren't a normal pale blue, I realize. They are arctic blue and cold as winter. He examines my face, my hair, my skin. Where Sam seemed delighted by my resemblance to Mayme, Grandpa does not like what he sees.

"Unplugging your grandmother from her heart monitor and bringing her out into the open without a nurse or medicine," he says in a stiff English/South African accent. "You really are your mother's daughter."

Block your ears to ugly voices, Annalisa says. *Save your energy for the people you love*. Grandpa is not on the loved list. I snip the pepper from the bush and stand up slowly. I look him in the face and see Annalisa in it. Maybe even a little of me. And I see anger. And maybe even a little bit of fear.

"Morning, Grandfather." I cup the yellow pepper in the palm of my hand and hold it out for him to see. "Isn't it a beauty? Any idea what it's called?"

He glares at me, and I smile back. My fear will kick in later, but for now, I pretend that everything is fine, just fine. After Annalisa's buildup, I'm surprised to find that he is an old man with leathery skin and wrinkles on his forehead. He is the first to look away. Not me. My heart is calm. After all, what have I got to lose?

Hate me all you want, and see how much I do not give a crap.

"Amandla. Come here to me," Mayme calls in a lilting voice that I recognize from home. *Come here by me*, township mothers sing to their children in the falling dark. *Don't you wander off, now. Stick close by, girl.*

Mayme wants me safe from my own grandfather, and I am happy to oblige. I turn and walk away without an *excuse me* or a *goodbye*. Rude, for sure, but it's what he deserves after what he said about me unplugging Mayme's heart monitor.

"Amandla, this is your uncle Julien and your cousin Harry." Mayme makes the introductions, and if Sam stared for too long, Harry and Uncle Julien break his record by a full minute. They gawk at me in stunned silence. *Brown sparrow alert!* Uncle blinks and narrows his eyes, which are the same shade of Bollard blue as Mother's. He shares Annalisa's pale skin and slender build, but that's all. Dressed in slim trousers, a plain T-shirt, and a tailored linen jacket, he could be a mannequin in the window of an expensive menswear store . . . the kind with polished concrete floors and armed guards at the door. His kind of bland smoothness does not exist in Sugar Town.

"Annalisa's daughter?" Julien asks no one. "That's impossible . . . she's been missing for years."

Wait, Annalisa was missing? That can't be right. On the bus, Annalisa said that she and Mayme met up every few months in secret. That if Grandpa ever found out, he'd find a way to punish them both. Mayme and Annalisa somehow reconnected anyway. I don't know how or when or why, but I am going to find out.

"Missing isn't dead, Julien," Mayme says. "Your sister keeps to herself, that's all."

"Well . . ." Julien breaks the awkward silence that falls on the group. "This is a surprise."

The same way a parcel bomb at your door is a surprise. *Boom*. The package explodes and breaks windows and ripples through the atmosphere. That's what I am: an explosion in the heart of my mother's family.

"Mrs. Bollard . . ." A black nurse in a white uniform hurries from the lift and kneels beside Mayme's wheelchair, huffing for breath. "No leaving the room without a nurse. That is the rule, Mrs. Bollard. Now you have everyone worried."

Mayme sighs. "Look at me. I'm fine. Sitting in the sun for ten minutes with my grandchildren is the best kind of medicine."

She seems to have deliberately left Julien and Grandpa out of the good-medicine category. I smile to myself, happy to be lumped in with two other grandchildren for the first time ever.

"You've had your moment in the sun." Grandpa walks over and grips the handles of the wheelchair. He backs up and turns the chair to face the lift with no time for hugs or goodbyes. "What you need is your doctor and to get back in bed."

"Neville, wait . . ." Mayme grabs the wheels to stop them turning, but Grandpa keeps pushing toward the lift. He either does not hear her or chooses not to.

"Neville, please . . ." she says. "Stop."

He ignores her. He does not stop or slow down. He keeps walking, and that is enough for me to forget my manners. Enough is enough. Mayme was fine before he showed up.

"Wait a second." I step in front of the wheelchair, and the footrest hits my shins hard. Ow. He did that on purpose, but *Tough luck for you, brah. I'm not moving.*

"Out of the way," Grandpa says. "Now."

I ignore him. If he wants obedience, he can get a dog.

"Come here." Mayme holds out her arms, and I swoop in for a hug. This is all she wanted. A chance to say goodbye. Our faces touch, cheek to cheek, and I breathe in the sunshine and vanilla in her hair. Annalisa will be furious when she learns that I lied to her, but this moment of being loved and squeezed by Mayme is worth it.

"Nine thirty tomorrow morning," she whispers into my ear. "Bring Annalisa. It's important."

"We'll be here," I whisper back. I straighten up and find Sam and Grandpa standing side by side and staring at me, hard. Grandpa is stunned I defied him, but Sam's eyes are smiling.

"Stay and enjoy the garden, Grandpa," Sam says. "Amandla and I will take Mayme back to her room."

Excellent thinking, cuz.

Grandpa stands to the side, gracious, and I step back to give Sam room to maneuver. The nurse holds the doors open as Sam turns the wheelchair around and reverses it into the elevator. A hand clamps my shoulder when I go to follow.

"Amanda has a weak heart. If we fight in public, the strain will push her closer to a heart attack." Grandpa's voice is low and tense. "Is that what you'd like?"

Mayme alive and happy for the weeks we have left together is all I want. Grandpa knows that. Of course he does. His hand drops from my shoulder and grabs the tail of my jacket. He tugs. A threat. If I move forward, he'll yank me back and send me flying to the ground, and then there really will be a fight. Happy to oblige, but not in front of the family.

"You go ahead," I tell Sam and Mayme. "I'll collect a few more plants for Mrs. M and head back home. Annalisa will be worried when she finds me gone."

The nurse hits the down button, and I hold eye contact with Mayme, sending out love and calm. The doors close, and my heart sinks. I want to spend more time with her, but not with Grandpa here, holding me in place. The prickly-skin feeling on the back of my neck spreads down into my chest and limbs. I turn to him. *You want to fight? Then let's fight.*

"What's eating you?" I say straight out.

"Tell your mother that when Amanda goes, the handouts stop. I won't pay for her mistakes or for you—the dark-skinned kaffir girl she drags around with her. Annalisa made her bed and she can lie in it."

"Man, you must be thick to believe the crap that comes out of your mouth. You know nothing about Annalisa and me."

He rears back, offended. "Is that how they talk in the slums?"

I see him clearly now. This man is mean. He is a bully. Annalisa would rather live in a one-room shack with a bare light bulb dangling from the ceiling than ask him for help. If she has a screw loose it's because he loosened it. I hate him so bad that the feeling eats a hole inside my stomach. I want to raise a fist and punch hard. Instead, I follow Mother's example and stare at him with ice-cold calm. *How weak you are.* Then I hear Lil Bit's voice asking the right questions: *Why would a grown man attack a teenage girl? His own granddaughter?*

"Now I understand why my mother stays away," I say, and the sadness in my voice surprises me. I will never have the close, loving family that lives in my dreams. Not while this man is alive. No way will I call him Grandfather or Gramps or any other pet name with a hint of affection. Not till he's earned it. "Something is missing inside you, *Neville.* Your hate is just pointless."

"Your mother defied me, and see where she ended up?" Neville's voice is cold and clear. "No money and nothing to show for her life but you."

A part of me has always known that we live in a tin shack because of my skin, my face, my hair, but it hurts to hear it said out loud. Nothing but me: Amandla Zenzile Harden, a freckle-nosed brown girl, sketchpad scribbler, above-average student, and the architect of her mother's downfall. Or not . . .

"Whatever you're looking for, you won't find it here," Neville says. "I suggest you leave and never come back."

That is a straight-up threat. He wants me to run away with my tail tucked between my legs like the Sugar Town bitch he thinks I am. That shows how little he knows about Sugar Town bitches. We fight for what we want. And I want Mayme.

Julien stands to the side and says nothing. If I'm a Sugar Town bitch, he is a weak-assed bitch and shame on him for not standing up for Mayme and for me. I know how to play this.

"Fine," I say. "I'm going."

Annalisa taught me well. We've run through the maze of Sugar Town searching for the safe way home many times, and sometimes we take a wrong turn. Pretending to surrender while we plot our next move is standard operating procedure.

"It's for the best." Uncle Julien finds his tongue. "Annalisa has a way of upsetting things, and Mother is too sick to cope with big changes. You understand?"

What I understand is that you heard every word that came from Neville's mouth and you did nothing. Mother is the tiger that chewed off her own paw to escape. You are a worm hiding in a hole.

"I understand perfectly, Uncle Julien." I stop myself from smiling. This coward thinks he can speak for his mother, a woman who'd rather risk death in the sun than remain in a sterile room attached to a machine that counts her heartbeats. "I'll pass your regards on to Annalisa. She'll be pleased to know how kindly you think of her."

Cousin Harry blushes and stares at the ground. His father is a weakling and he knows it. Poor kid. In the next few years, he'll have to choose his own path. I hope it's one that takes him far from his grandfather and his father.

I walk to the lift and step inside. Neville's hate has left an invisible bruise inside me. I burn with anger to think about the poison Annalisa must have been forced to swallow while she lived under his roof. The doors close and I go, down, down, down . . .

10

Goodness and Lil Bit wait outside the front gate of the Build 'Em Up: an open lot surrounded by a tall brick fence topped with coils of razor wire and security lights. The thing is, I already know all I need to about Annalisa's—and my—family. Mayme and Sam welcomed me. Neville threw me out, and Uncle Julien did nothing to stop him. Harry stood to the side, unable or unwilling to take sides. I don't know how all this will end, but the way that Mayme crushed me in her arms before I left gave me a feeling of closeness and comfort. I want it again.

"Come on." Lil Bit waves me closer at the very moment I decide to turn and walk away. I don't want any more bad news, and my gut tells me there's plenty of it about the Bollards on the World Wide Web. "You're ten minutes late already!"

I want to go home and rebuild the parts inside of me that Neville broke with his contempt. His voice invades my mind, and I realize that shutting him out will be hard work. I need my friends to help me turn down the volume of his voice, and they are right beside me.

"Calm down, Sugar Town bitches. I'm here now."

They laugh.

"This way," Goodness says, and leads Lil Bit and me into a busy loading bay. Men haul timber to waiting trucks, and fork-lifts buzz across the concrete floor to collect bricks and bags of cement like ants taking apart a picnic. Most businesses in Sugar Town are barely hanging on. Customers drift in and leave with a can of condensed milk and a bag of dried lentils. The Build 'Em Up is rocking.

Goodness climbs a set of narrow metal stairs that lead to an office area above the loading dock. A loft. Or if the building was taller, an aerie.

"You first," I tell Lil Bit, and follow her up to a small waiting room with a row of plastic chairs pushed against the wall. The Build 'Em Up makes money, but none of it is spent on interior decoration.

Goodness knocks on a door with OFFICE spray-painted on the wood in navy blue. "Come on, you two," she says. "My brothers are always busy, so let's do this quick."

The office door opens and a lean black teenager in dirty khaki pants and a faded T-shirt comes out. One of Goodness's three brothers, all of whom I know by sight but have never been introduced to by name. This brother is tall and only a few years older than me. Seventeen or eighteen at the most.

"What's going on, G?" he asks, and his gaze flicks from Lil Bit to me and back to his sister as he waits for an answer.

"We need the internet," Goodness says. "And I'm starving. Do you have any food in here?"

"There's chicken and roti in the kitchen." The boy waves us into a messy work area with three desks covered in receipts and dirty coffee cups. "Use Themba's desk."

The office is a boys' clubhouse. In one corner is a mini gym with a skipping rope and a punching bag and, in the other, a sofa and a coffee table littered with papers and empty soda cans. An overweight cat sleeps on a pillow covered with its own hair.

Annalisa would shudder if she saw this place. She might be messy in her head, but not in her habitat. The regular soap goes on the right side of the sink and the special "going out" lavender soap on the left. Shoes go under our beds. Dishes get washed, dried, and put away immediately.

"Where are Themba and Stevious?" Goodness sits on the edge of the nearest desk and swings her leg back and forth, completely comfortable in this alien man cave. The mess doesn't bother her, either.

"Delivering building materials to the housing development that's going up at the turn off to the city. It's a huge job," her brother says, and takes the opposite corner of the desk. He waits to be introduced.

"Oh," Goodness says to us. "This is my brother Lewis. Lewis, these are my friends Lil Bit Bhengu and Amandla Harden."

"Lil Bit and Amandla." Our names come out slow and deliberate. Is he thinking about Lil Bit's father, the disgraced priest, and my mum, the strange white lady who goes into the sugarcane fields to sing to the stars at night?

Until this morning, I would have felt embarrassed about Annalisa's strange behavior. Now things are different. It's my grandfather Neville who should be ashamed of himself. Not Annalisa. Not me.

I cross the worn carpet and hold out my hand. "Hi, Lewis. I'm Amandla." Fake confidence gives way to the real thing. "Nice to meet you."

His handshake is tight and awkward, and standing this close, I can see that he has brown eyes and dimples in his cheeks. I don't think he knows it yet, but his square jaw, full lips, and dark brows come together exactly right. He is . . . delicious.

"Me too," Lewis answers in a rush. "I mean, it's nice to meet you as well."

Goodness rolls her eyes at his awkwardness and flings herself into an old leather chair that creaks and groans when she moves. She hits the power button and the computer monitor on the desk pings to life. Lil Bit stands close to Goodness's right shoulder, but I keep my distance; I'm too scared to confront whatever information might come up. I let Goodness be my filter.

"Where should we start?" she asks.

"With what we know for sure," Lil Bit says. "A name. A place. A date. What have you got, Amandla?"

Three facts jump to mind.

"Mother's birth name is Annalisa Bollard. Her mother's name is Amanda. Her father's name is Neville Bollard, and he is a bastard."

Goodness taps in the information, hits search, and frowns at the screen. "Neville Samuel Harry Bollard. From Durban?"

"I think that's him." Uncle Julien named his sons after Grandfather and still no love from the old man, Sam says. Poor Uncle. "What have you got?"

Goodness stares at the computer and then up at me. "Says here that the first generation of Bollards made their fortune in sugar. The next generation bought half shares in a diamond mine in Kimberley and the next generation expanded into real estate and transportation. Your grandma Amanda brought in fresh money from an investment firm and a technology company. Brah, your gramps is rich as fuck. The hell are you doing in Sugar Town?"

Like I have a choice between a shack and a glam house by the ocean!

"Wait." I step closer, eager for more news, but still afraid of what I might find. "Is my mum listed under children?"

"Annalisa Honey-Blossom Bollard. You can't make this shit up, so yeah, she's listed. Second child. Only daughter. Come. See for yourself." Goodness leans back so Lil Bit and me get a clear view of the screen. I lean in and do a quick read before breaking the information down: Old money (Bollard sugar and diamonds) meets new money (Harden technology and investments), and together they make more money.

Goodness flicks to images of the Bollards: a recent pic of Mayme and Neville at the opening of the Amanda Bollard Institute, Uncle Julien breaking ground for a new factory, and a photograph of my mother, young and suntanned and standing on a snowcapped mountain with tall spruce trees and views of a winter-white valley.

"Oh," I say. "Oh."

It physically hurts to see Annalisa so happy. She has no idea, in that photo, that her rich-girl life is about to end. That she'll end up living in a tin shack with a baby and no money. Was that a choice she was forced to make? Me or the money?

"Seriously," Goodness says. "You never thought to look this stuff up before?"

"Annalisa used her mother's maiden name, Harden. Same as my surname. She never mentioned her family, not even once. I asked. She said we were alone."

"Now that you know the truth," Goodness says, "why are you here, mixing with us poor folk?"

"Goodness . . ." Lil Bit says.

"Okay, okay. I'm just saying . . ."

I sigh.

"My grandfather Neville kicked my mum out of the house when she got pregnant with me or maybe after she had me. I don't know for sure. What I *do* know is that my brown skin is too dark for Grandpa. He's old-fashioned that way."

Lil Bit says, "Hold on. You've met him?"

"This morning, at the hospital."

"And?" She wants details.

"He is a mean old white man. And a racist."

"But you're his granddaughter!"

The words are hard to say, but I say them. "He kicked me out of the hospital, told me to never come back. And he called me a kaffir."

In America, they have the n-word. In South Africa, we have the k-word. Same difference. Both are slurs that equate blackness with laziness and lack of intelligence. Both hurt to hear. Both leave a wound.

"Lord help us." Lil Bit gasps. "To your face?"

"To my face," I say, and quickly move on. "Is there a bio link for Annalisa?"

Whenever Annalisa tries to remember things, her mind slips. Facts appear for a moment and then they're gone. My father's name. The place I was born. Her first boyfriend. Her last job. All blank. Now is the moment to gather whatever information I can.

"The last photo of your ma is from sixteen years ago, before you were born." Goodness scrolls through picture-perfect images of the Bollard family living a picture-perfect life. "After that, she disappears. Poof. Gone."

I bet Grandpa knows. He knows what happened to Mother after that last photograph was taken. He knows, but he'll never tell.

"Ask your granny." Lil Bit finds the most logical source of information. "She was there. She'll fill in the gaps for you."

"Of course." I let Neville into my head when I should have kept the memory of Mayme's open arms closer. That's on me. "Mayme wants to see Annalisa and me tomorrow. I'll ask then."

The clock on the wall strikes three, the end of Annalisa's shift at Mr. Gupta's law firm. If I rush, I'll catch her leaving the office, which is actually a blue shipping container with the words SANDEEP GUPTA, ESQUIRE. UNPAID FINES? UNFAIR JAIL TIME? BAIL HEARINGS? ASK ME. I CAN HELP! spray-painted on the side.

"Gotta go." I have to soften Annalisa up to get her to come back to the hospital with me tomorrow. It won't be easy after I confess to sneaking out to see Mayme on the sly. I don't think I'll mention the old man.

"But . . ." Lil Bit splutters. "There's *chicken* and *roti*."

"You stay," I tell her. "I gotta catch Annalisa, though. All right?"

"All right." Lil Bit throws Goodness an *is it really all right?* look to be sure. Passing up a free lunch goes against everything Lil Bit stands for. She loves food the way a flower loves the rain. Food is happiness.

"Of course, stay." Goodness clears a space on a messy side table. "I'm hungry, too. With our royal sister gone, there's more for us anyway."

"Yeah," I say. "My inheritance is coming any day now."

"I'm your best friend. I should go with you," Lil Bit whispers as she walks me to the door. She's jumpy at being left alone to eat lunch with Goodness Dumisa, though I can't imagine why. Lil Bit likes Goodness, and she adores food. The situation is a win-win for her and her stomach.

"No matter what, you'll always be my best friend." I squeeze her shoulder. "Enjoy the curry, Lil Bit."

"Drop by my place tomorrow and tell me the news?" she says.

"Count on it. And you too, Goodness. Thanks for the computer help."

I take the metal stairs down to the loading dock and tread a path through the moving forklifts and idling trucks. The air in the open yard smells of wood sap and sawdust. Not unpleasant. Halfway down the lane to Abdullah Ibrahim Street, I hear the crunch of running footsteps coming up behind me. I turn with my fists raised, ready to beat off a rude boy on a grab-and-go mission. Lewis Dumisa stops and smiles at my weak imitation of Mike Tyson on the worst day of his boxing career. I look like a fool.

"Offense is the best form of defense." I quote Lil Bit, who found the expression inside one of the military history books that her father left behind when he ran off. "Did I forget something?"

Lewis holds out a cotton shopping bag.

"Chicken curry and roti," he says. "It will save you making dinner tonight. You can bring the empty container back to the yard or to our house. Whichever."

Thanks but no thanks. I have my pride. Annalisa and I accept church charity on occasion, but we refuse personal handouts. We get by. Except the curry smells divine. My mouth waters, and my pride dissolves.

"Thanks." I take the bag and glance up at Lewis long enough to show good manners. He smiles at me, and those gorgeous dimples do strange things to my heart. I'm standing still, but I feel like I've run a hundred kilometers uphill with no water; my mouth is that dry. He holds eye contact for a moment before looking away. Dear lord! This boy is juicy. One sip from those lips would quench my thirst, and now it is definitely time for me to leave. "See you around."

"Yeah, see you soon," Lewis says. I start to walk toward home, already working on wiping the memory of Lewis from my mind. He is way out of my league. But the expression on his face when he gave me the roti is impossible to forget.

"Amandla!" he calls out, and I glance over my shoulder. "None of my business, but what your grandpa said? Don't believe a word of it."

"Thanks," I say in a voice that is strange to my own ears. "I'll try not to."

He waves and walks back to the Build 'Em Up. I walk to the avenue. Lewis is different from the township boys who snap their fingers at passing girls and call out, *Come over here, sweetness. I'll take you places you've never been.* When I looked up at him, I saw curiosity and kindness. A kindness so rare, it made my knees shake. It's just as well we live on opposite sides of Sugar Town. A tall black boy with friends and money? A small brown girl with one good friend and only change in her pocket?

No way!

Or maybe?

11

Juicy?

Top of my English class and that's the word that I come up with? Chewing gum is juicy. A ripe mango is juicy. Hot gossip is juicy. But to use it to describe an entire boy? That is . . . vulgar. Unimaginative. Coarse. Lazy, even. I don't think of myself that way.

I turn into Abdullah Ibrahim Street, preoccupied with the word *juicy*, and how it is low class but, in the end, suits Lewis perfectly, and bump shoulders with Jacob Caluza, the younger brother of William, the butcher. Bumping into Jacob is proof that the universe has a sense of humor. He is exactly what I expect from most township men who, when they see me alone on the street, see an opportunity to take advantage.

A can of grape Fanta soars out of Jacob's hand, and I catch it on the fly without thinking.

"Got it!" I grab the can and give it back to him. "Here."

"Amandla, what a nice surprise!" Jacob rips the tab open and slurps purple liquid from the rim of the can. He was handsome once, with smooth black skin and warm brown eyes. That was before he started smoking the clear white crystals we call Tik—crystal meth. Now he is thin as a skeleton. His pupils are dilated, so I know he's flying. "Still in school?"

"I have two more years before I graduate," I say. Jacob dropped out of high school a long while back. He's around twenty-five years old now and going nowhere.

"Good, good, good, but all work and no play makes Amandla a dull girl." He grins like he's the first person to think up that expression. "You should come to my friend Dion's place for a Sunday session. All nice people. I'll take care of you."

I'm sure he would—not! Those drinking sessions and smoking sessions have trapped Jacob and his friends in a drug haze. They imagine themselves riding through the streets of Sugar Town in the back seat of a tricked-out Mercedes-Benz with tinted windows. If they had the money and the time, they'd do great things. I hear that kind of pipe talk on street corners all the time.

"Thank you for asking, but I can't." Jacob is unpredictable. I once saw him turn violent when his brother refused to give him money. I will never let him get too close. "Sunday is the Lord's day, and that's when we go to church."

We *do* go to church, but only when Annalisa is moved to attend, which is once every two or three months. This coming Sunday I will turn up at the Christ Our Lord Is Risen! Gospel Hall and testify alongside Lil Bit, just in case Jacob tries to catch me in a lie.

"God ain't got no money, but I have plenty," Jacob says. "You should be out having fun instead of stuck at home with your crazy ma and her big ideas. I hear her tell my brother that you're meant for better things, and I agree with her. You need money to get out. I can help you."

I fail to see how being stuck with a twitching, itching drug addict is better than being stuck with a mother who at least has real ties to the world outside of Sugar Town. Frayed ties, yes, but ties of blood that might, one day, be useful.

"Speaking of my mother." I glance in the direction of Mr. Gupta's office. "She's waiting for me."

Jacob reaches out to grab my arm. I sidestep him with a fake smile. "Take care of yourself, all right? I have to rush."

True to my word, I rush away from Jacob and from the realization that he might be right about the amount of money it takes to break free of the township. Generations have tried and failed to make the leap.

The pile of notes inside Annalisa's bag might not be enough to pay my school fees for another two years. Neville won't do it. It scares me to think that I may never finish high school, let alone go to university. Education is my only way out.

* * *

I catch Mother leaving Mr. Gupta's shipping-container office with her handbag slung over her shoulder and a breeze from the sugar fields running through her hair. I shape my mouth into a smile, ready to lie before I get around to telling the truth.

"Surprise," I say. "I thought we'd walk home together."

Annalisa stops and stares at me with narrowed eyes. My smile dies, and the skin on the back of my neck prickles. No way can she know where I've been or who I've spoken to.

"You went to see her," she says. "After I told you not to."

"There's a roof garden on the top level of the institue." I blurt out the first thing that comes into my head. "I got some cuttings for Mrs. Mashanini."

"Tell me everything that happened." Annalisa turns into a narrow alley that takes five minutes off our journey home. "And don't bother lying. I'll know if you do."

So much for inching toward the truth. Annalisa is way ahead of me. I skip the lies and tell her about the garden, Mayme in the wheelchair, meeting Sam, Uncle Julien, and Harry. Neville and his threats. I leave out the visit to the Build 'Em Up timber yard. The pictures of her young and happy are too painful to bring up. I skip to the future.

"Mayme wants to see us tomorrow morning at nine thirty. It's important, she said."

"You made an enemy of my father." Annalisa is grim. "He'll make you pay for talking back to him. He can't forgive or forget. It's not in his nature."

"What can he do? Mayme is a grown woman who has the right to talk to whoever she wants."

"You don't understand." Annalisa grabs my arm and pulls me close. Our hips bump bone to bone. "He'll try to take you away from me again, but this time I'll be ready. This time, I will fight back."

What does she mean, *again*? I have no memory of Neville before the black sports car drove past me. Surely I'd remember brushing up against a person so mean. Unless . . .

"When did he try to take me away? Was I little?"

Annalisa stops midway down the alley. She rubs her forehead, trying to clear up the haze inside her head. Her short-term memory is fine, but going back a decade and beyond is a struggle.

"You had no name," she says. "There was a stone wall. Gardens and black cats. I don't know when it happened."

I have no idea what she's talking about. The blood drains from Annalisa's face. She goes pale. Sweat rolls down her temples, and the veins on the side of her neck pulse blue under her translucent skin. She's close to a panic attack. Her fingers dig into her skull, either trying to unearth the past or keep it buried, I can't tell which. She's scaring me now. If she pushes too hard, I'm afraid she'll fall again into darkness. I can't let that happen.

"Stop. Stop, Ma." I take her hands in mine. She stares into my face, her shoulders softening. "Mayme will help you remember tomorrow. But for now, guess what?"

I open the cotton bag and hold it under her nose, drawing her back into the alley with the scent of coconut chicken curry and cloves. My stomach rumbles, reminding me that a single slice of bread for breakfast was the last thing I ate. Annalisa laughs at my grumbling stomach. Now I know that she's with me in the present.

"Early dinner?" she says, and I lay my head against her shoulder, content to be right here, right now, with dust swirling around my ankles and low winter sunlight slanting across the mouth of the alley. I don't need the Bollards. Annalisa is my gold.

* * *

This morning, Cyril the parking guard's smile is missing. He hands me a folded piece of paper with my name written on the front in ebony-black ink. Simple and expensive. Lil Bit stole a pot of the same color from an art store in Glenwood last year. Cyril stares at the ground and avoids making eye contact. He knows the note contains bad news.

"It's from Mother," Annalisa says. "I recognize the writing. What does it say?"

I open the paper and read:

> Time has run out. The doctors say that an operation might fix my heart, but they can't guarantee it. And if something goes wrong, what kind of life would I have? I would rather have a few short weeks, alive and lucid, than six years tied to machines and in a fog. Neville thinks that I'll be more comfortable at home with my books and plants. He's right, but a part of me feels, well, uneasy. I wanted to stay another day, but he said that a quick move was better for me. Again . . . I wonder what happened between the two of you yesterday in the garden. Neville can be unkind. When you get this note, come and see me. Annalisa knows the way.
>
> Love, Mayme Amanda

At the bottom of the page is Sam's name and mobile number and, under that, a short sentence. *If you need help.*

"Of course he wants her at home," Annalisa says. "He's only happy when he's in control of everyone."

An angel married to a gargoyle who keeps her locked in a stone fortress by the ocean. That's how Annalisa described Mayme and Neville to me without naming them or explaining that her mother was the angel. Annalisa sees fantastic creatures roaming the streets in broad daylight: Mrs. Bewana, the owner of the Black Beauty Hair Salon, is a snake in human form, and Jonas, the mechanic, a mouse with a lion's heart. Sugar Town has dozens of shape-shifters whose true nature is known only to my mother. Neville as a gargoyle makes perfect sense, though.

"You remember the way?" I fold the note and drop it into my pocket. "She said to come over."

"I remember," Annalisa says. "Follow me."

Cyril watches us go, relieved that the awkward interaction is over. How strange, I think, to want to be close to the Bollards and yet fear the consequences of displeasing them at the same time.

12

Iron gates guard the two-story house and the circular driveway. In the center of the circle is an art piece: a cube of plain white marble balanced on a metal spike. I marvel at the size of the building. The house seems to look down through a dozen white-framed windows at a garden thick with plants and blooming flowers.

"Stay close," Annalisa says as we approach the gates. "Let me do the talking."

Fine by me. The white house, the paved street lined with other great houses and acres of lawn, have taken my breath away. I don't belong here, but my mother does. She played here. Walked here. Grew from a girl to a woman here, protected by fences and private security. All that security didn't keep her out of Sugar Town, though.

We get close to the gates, and three tall men in dark suits move from the garden, through the gates and onto the pavement. They come straight for us, like they've been waiting for a slender blond woman and a brown girl with a freckled nose to show up. Each man wears an electronic earpiece and has a handgun holstered on his hip. My mouth goes dry and it's hard to swallow.

"Annalisa Bollard." Mother announces herself in a polished voice. "I'm here to see my mother, Mrs. Bollard."

A beefy mixed-race security guard with pockmarked skin and light green eyes shakes his head. "Sorry, Miss Bollard. I'm afraid she's not able to see you today."

The other guards crowd around: one white and wiry, the other black and solid through the shoulders. I take in the tall trees and the garden. The wide blue skies and birdsong. It seems that today, none of this groomed beauty is ours to enjoy, even for a moment. Annalisa and I are outsiders who belong back in the township.

"I beg your pardon," Annalisa says with icy calm. "Perhaps you misunderstood. I'm here to see my mother. On her invitation."

The mixed-race guard clears his throat and says, "Sorry, Miss Bollard. I can't let you in."

"Who says so?" My voice comes back. "Mayme Amanda or Neville?"

A flash of surprise lights up the guard's green eyes. A Bollard who isn't white. He's never seen one before. Makes sense. I've been stashed out of sight for fifteen years in Sugar Town. The alley cat is out of the bag now.

"Mr. Bollard's orders," the guard says. "He was very clear."

Annalisa steps back, unsteady. Her hands and shoulders shake, and then her whole body follows in a spasm of rage and grief. She throws her head back, and the cords of her neck string tight against pale skin.

"Mother!" she screams at the top of her lungs. "Mummy! Come out. Help me. Please. Come out!"

A shiver of fear travels down my spine to hear Annalisa so raw and vulnerable. I go to pull her into my arms, to smother her with love and make her quiet. Then I hear the whoosh of blood in my own veins, whispery as the rain that falls onto our roof in the springtime. The rain is soft at first, then it gets louder. It tells me to let Annalisa scream. It tells me that I need to scream with her.

Instead of shifting away, embarrassed, I take Annalisa's hand. If we had a mobile phone, we'd call Mayme direct, but all we have are our voices. I open my mouth and scream: "Mayme! Mayme! Mayme!"

The guards panic and crowd in. They better not touch us. Annalisa and I hold our ground. Our two voices melt into one.

"Mother. Mayme. Mama!"

We call for our mother and grandmother.

"Please! Miss Bollard!" the lead guard says, frantic at the noise we're making. The neighbors will be out soon, and the gossip will go on for days. Not our problem. Let Neville deal with the fallout from banning his own daughter from her childhood home.

We ignore the guard. Annalisa's hand tightens around mine. I squeeze hers back. Something raw and primal comes out of us together. It feels awful and amazing at the same time.

"Miss Bollard!" the main guard shouts over my screams. "Stop. Neighborhood security will drive by any second now. They will pull over and pick you up. If you're lucky, they'll take you to the local police station. Or they might take you someplace else. Do you understand?"

I understand. Private security companies are a law unto themselves in South Africa. They *are* the police, except better armed, better paid, and they make their own rules. I squeeze Annalisa's hand, take a deep breath that goes all the way down to the pit of my stomach, and I lift my head one last time. "Mayme!" I scream.

Our voices die into nothingness. Silence from the house. Behind the guards, nothing moves. A white car with DIAMOND SECURITY written across the side turns into the street and drives toward us.

I put my arms around Annalisa. "Relax," I say. "Take a long, smooth breath in and a long, smooth breath out. Smell the flowers in the garden."

Lil Bit calls this slow in and out "yogic breathing," yet another trick she picked up from the stolen self-help book, *Peace Within*. It's strange that yogic breathing doesn't seem to help Lil Bit calm her emotions when Goodness is around.

"I smell roses," Annalisa says in a voice hoarse from screaming. "Lily of the valley. Lavender. Jasmine."

"You know the names, but you can't grow any of them." I laugh. "Why is that?"

"Black thumb," she says. "Except for you. You are the only perfect thing I ever made."

The guards glance at the ground, the sky, the passing traffic on the street. They ought to be ashamed to keep a daughter from her mother, and maybe they are, but they have their orders and jobs are hard to find. The private security patrol car moves closer with its windows wound down. The pockmarked guard clears his throat again. "It is time for you to go," he says.

"Fine. We're going." I tuck a strand of hair behind Mother's ear, tender. She warned me to stay away from the hospital and from Neville. I was foolish, too caught up in the fantasy of having a family to stop and think about what this would do to her.

"We can have what's left of the curry for lunch. It'll be even better today."

"Wait," she says, and reaches past the two backup guards blocking the gates with their bodies. She snaps off a single white rose from a dazzling bush covered in flowers. She drops the rose into her bag, and somehow, when we get home, the bloom will emerge with perfect petals.

The three guards close ranks to form a human chain outside the gates. This is Neville punishing us. Cutting us off from Mayme will hurt her as much as it does us, but he doesn't care. *Neville can be unkind*, the note said. Next time I see my grandmother—if there is a next time—I will explain the difference between unkind and cruel.

"Back to the bus station," Annalisa says, flat and defeated, as we turn from the big white house to begin the twenty-minute walk past the security cameras positioned along the street. The houses have dogs and razor wire, alarms, guards . . . Man, this country is screwed up. Nelson on the water tower changed the segregation laws so that all people could be free, but money, or the lack of it, keeps us in our separate boxes, fighting.

When will Neville put his weapons down?

* * *

"Annalisa. Good Lord! Annalisa. Is that you?"

A skinny white man with red cheeks and wisps of gray hair flying up from his scalp like exploding firecrackers runs out of the gates and past the guards. He wears a wrinkled black suit and a wilted clerical collar.

"Annalisa?" He hurries over with his worn heels scraping the pavement and a look of wonder on his face. "I prayed for you to come home, but sometimes the lord doesn't return my messages." He smiles. "Until now."

He reaches for Annalisa. She doesn't flinch when he hugs her. I try to remember if I've ever seen my mother being hugged by a man before. No. The security vehicle moves past us and turns into the next street. All clear.

"Where have you been?" he asks. "I was scared you were in prison. Or dead . . ."

Annalisa closes her eyes, leans against his shoulder, and says nothing. She feels safe with this man. The priest lets her go and wipes the tears from his face. He blushes, an odd sight in a man in his seventies. I see that he's old but strong. Wiry, even.

"Neville said you ran away to Joburg and that he hadn't heard from you in years."

"He lied," Annalisa says. "Obviously. Are you really surprised?"

"At seeing you, again? Yes, absolutely. At your father lying? Not at all." The priest steps back and takes in all of Annalisa and then all of me. He sighs, and I see him put the puzzle pieces of mother's disappearance and my existence together. "Ah," he says. "Your daughter?!"

"Yes. This is Amandla. Amandla, meet Father Gibson, our family priest. He married my parents at Saint Luke's Mission by the Sea, built on private land near Umhlanga Rocks. Julien and I were christened in the same church," she says. "A family tradition."

I remind myself that I am not inscribed in the family Bible. There's no chair waiting for me at Sunday lunch. I'm a missing link in the chain of my mother's family and their traditions.

"Amandla." Father Gibson holds out a bony hand, smudged with blue pen ink and streaked with dirt. He sees that I see and smiles. No offense taken. "The ink is from writing a sermon, and the dirt is from pulling up a weed in your grandmother's garden. I'm a famous slob. Ask Annalisa."

"It's true." Annalisa laughs, and for an instant, the happy girl from the photographs on the internet appears. Carefree and lovely. "It's Father Gibson's trademark."

The priest's handshake is firm and friendly. I decide right there that I like him. He made Annalisa laugh. He frowns and checks his watch, an antique timepiece with a cracked leather strap.

"I have a pre-wedding counseling session in forty-five minutes. Come, I'll walk you to the back porch, where Amanda is sitting. I still have time." He moves to the gates and checks over his shoulder to find us standing still. "Of course. Forgive me. This is a private family moment. You prefer to go in by yourselves."

"It's not that . . ." The blood drains from Annalisa's face, leaving her pale and sweating. She's ashamed to admit that we've been banned. Ashamed to be caught pleading outside the locked gates of what was once her home. She shouldn't be ashamed when it's Neville who has done the shameful thing and he isn't ashamed at all.

"We're not allowed in," I tell Father Gibson. "Neville's orders."

"Nonsense." The priest walks to the gates, sure that a mistake has been made. He says to the mixed-race guard, "This is the Bollard house and both these women are Bollards. Is there a problem, Gerald?"

"You can enter, Father, but these ladies are not allowed on the property."

"How can you be sure?" Father Gibson is calm. "Are they on a list?"

"Two females. One white with blond hair and the other mixed with a freckled nose. Both women are banned from entering the grounds and the house. Mr. Bollard's orders." Gerald breaks eye contact with the priest. At some level, he knows that turning Annalisa and me away from the house is wrong.

"Ridiculous!" Father Gibson says. "Mrs. Bollard will hear about this. Let me through right now."

A distant siren wails, the sound growing louder as an emergency vehicle moves closer to the house. A white ambulance with lights flashing turns into the street. Gerald presses his finger to his earpiece and listens to a message coming through. It's a man's voice, too faint for me to decipher.

"Move back, please, Father," Gerald says. "The ambulance needs room to turn into the drive."

The white guard waves Annalisa and me farther down the footpath while the black guard unlocks the gates. Father Gibson joins us. The ambulance slams its brakes and reverses into the driveway. The siren dies and my mind races. Has Mayme's heart given out for good?

"Stay right there, Father." Gerald points a finger at the priest before rushing toward the open gates. "Don't make me push you back."

Father Gibson steps away, arms out, surrendering to the guard's instruction. He turns to us with a frown. "When I left, Amanda was walking around, out of her wheelchair. She was the best she's looked in weeks. Happy."

Annalisa slips her arm through mine and pulls Father Gibson closer. "The human heart is a mystery. Isn't that what you taught us in scripture class?"

The priest says something I don't hear. I'm too busy listening to the noises in the front yard of the white house to pay much attention. The ambulance is parked smack in the middle of the drive, and I can't see past it. I tilt my head and listen hard. A door opens. Rolling wheels bump on the smooth drive. Mumbled voices. A male and a female. Then faint words that I have to strain to hear.

"*Fine*," Mayme's voice says. "*A precaution*," Neville answers. "*I'll pack your overnight bag*."

The ambulance doors slide shut and the lights turn on, flashing red and blue. The guards on either side of the open gates keep their eyes on the empty street. I'd rush into the yard if I could, but all I want from the white house is now inside the ambulance.

"Bye," I whisper as the flashing lights of the ambulance disappear into the distance. Neville reenters the house, and the guards close the gates to lock us out.

Neville wins again.

"Time to go, Amandla." Annalisa holds back tears. "The next bus to Sugar Town leaves soon and I don't want to miss it."

"Sugar Town!" Father Gibson chokes on the words. He is more than surprised to find out where we live. He is shocked, and it shows. "Dear God. How did you end up in a township?"

Annalisa blushes, embarrassed by the Anglican priest's dismay. Living in Sugar Town is better than being dead, but the girl who attended scripture lessons with Father Gibson and skied the white-powdered slopes of Europe is long gone.

"I'm sorry." Father Gibson realizes too late that his shock at where we live has wounded Annalisa. She keeps her face turned away, not daring to look him in the face.

"It's not like we had a choice between this house and Sugar Town," I say. "We live where we can afford to . . . the same as millions of other people in South Africa."

"Of course. Forgive me." Father Gibson takes Annalisa's hand, gentle. "I'm older but I'm still no closer to being wise. Amanda will have my head when she hears how badly I've bungled our reunion."

"Do you think we'll see her again?" Annalisa asks. "I'm scared she won't come home from the hospital."

"Try not to worry, Annalisa," Father Gibson says. "Your mother will be fine. She has the best doctors and the best care. We'll see her again." He takes a deep breath and smiles. "Come, I'll give you a lift to the station." He pulls a set of keys from his jacket pocket and unlocks an old Volvo with a dented fender and rust on the roof. The car is his perfect mechanical twin: untidy and full of personality. "Hop in. Don't mind the mess."

Annalisa takes the front passenger seat, and I find space in a back seat crowded with cardboard boxes, loose papers, and, of all things, a baby seat and a collection of stuffed animals with chewed ears and missing limbs. Lil Bit has told me that her father's girlfriend, Sunshine, is expecting. They'll need a baby seat soon . . . This baby seat, though, probably belongs to an adored grandchild who is seriously into Peppa Pig and smooshed banana.

Father Gibson throws the battered Volvo into gear and drives away with his hands gripped tight to the wheel. I think that he's still angry at the guards for turning us away and angry at himself for hurting Annalisa with his reaction to where we live. "That house is your *home*, Annalisa," he says. "Take my card from the glove box and call me. I'll help if I can." He waits till Mother has his card tucked into her bag. He doesn't know that the closest pay phone is three streets away from our house and that Mother's mobile almost never has any credit. "As for Neville, he'll have to answer to the Lord for keeping you away from your own mother."

"I have no idea what to do now," Annalisa says, and the car fills up with silence. I turn around to take a long, last glimpse of the fairy-tale house. A shadowy figure moves in an upstairs window. Neville is looking down at us driving away. It's crazy, but Cyril's nervousness when he gave me the note at the hospital suddenly makes sense. *Neville had read the note.* He knew we'd come to the house and he stopped us. As for the ambulance turning up just in time to stop Father Gibson from telling Mayme that we were waiting at the front? Too perfect to be a coincidence. I overheard the conversation in the front yard. Mayme said she was fine, and I believe her. The ambulance was Neville's way to seize control again. My face goes hot, and my throat burns. I hate my grandfather with a passion that shocks me. The feeling is too big for my body. I feel like I might explode. Or implode. I close my eyes and breathe. My shoulders relax. But the tight knot of hate that I feel for Neville?

It stays.

13

Annalisa drops the white rose into a jam jar filled with water and places it on the windowsill above the sink. The petals shimmer, and the chicken curry simmers on the stove, filling the kitchen with the smell of cardamom and cinnamon. I set knives and forks on the table and imagine a lazy lunchtime in the big white house. A long marble counter gleams in the soft light that falls through a tall window with views of a lawn with trees at the back. Mayme and I work at the counter, our hands covered in flour and sticky dough. The oven is hot. The rolls, laid out by us in perfect rows on a tray nearby, are ready to bake. Then Mayme washes my hands with hers, pushing the dough from my fingers under warm water. "We're a mess!" she says, and we laugh together. Happy.

"I should have taken you to meet her earlier." Annalisa's flat voice breaks the fantasy. "She begged me to bring you to her, but I was afraid that my father would find out. Now . . . it might be too late to bring the two of you together."

"We will see her again. I promise." I believe what I say.

The ambulance was bullshit. A stunt. I know it but I do not say it, just in case I made a mistake and it wasn't Neville standing at the window. He was too far away for me to see his expression. He might have been sad instead of gloating, but I doubt it. Or is that my hate talking? I don't know. Not knowing is the part that worries me.

"Did Neville kick you out because my father was black?" Nelson Mandela on the water tower would be disappointed to see how stubbornly the colors of the rainbow refuse to get along.

"I . . ." Annalisa's memory struggles again. It always falters on the things that have to do with me. She sits at the table and waits for the food to be served. This is our usual routine. Me in the kitchen, cooking. Her, seated at the table, waiting for phantom servants to appear with meals. Before Mrs. M snuck across the lane to teach me how to make the basics, everything we ate came from a can. "I'm sorry," Annalisa says at last. "I don't remember the details. Things are jumbled up in my mind."

"Neville is a mean bastard. He kicked you out. That's all you need to know," I say, and normally I would never, ever, on pain of a twisted ear, use the word *bastard* to describe an older person, much less a relative. Well, I didn't know I had relatives until a few days ago, so I should be forgiven. Annalisa hates swearing, but after this morning, I've earned the right to call Neville whatever I want.

Annalisa chews a warm piece of roti, but her mind is somewhere else. I put the plates of curry down, and we start to eat. The flavor is deeper than yesterday, the chicken falling off the bone. It's delicious, just like the boy who gave it to me. I push

Lewis out of my mind. I felt something in the way he looked at me, but I'm not kidding myself. He can do better than the brown sparrow who lives in a back lane. He can do better than me.

"Seeing the house again . . ." Annalisa says after a while. "I had a flash of my father in a big room with a desk. I must have been about nineteen. It was night. I could hear the crickets chirping outside. He said, 'You can have one or the other. Not both. You choose.' He was angry. I don't remember what I had to choose between, but I think I chose wrong . . ."

"You are his only daughter," I point out. "He should have stuck with you no matter what choices you made. And Mayme should have come out when you called."

"None of it matters, Amandla. My father always wins."

We eat in silence, and the curry is finished too soon. I mop up the sauce and plan tomorrow's dinner. Rice and beans or spinach and lentils. Two of the cheap basics that Mrs. M introduced me to. Annalisa stares at her empty plate and sighs.

"Check the cupboards, Amandla. See what we have."

The answer to *What's in the cupboard?* is always the same: enough to get by on for a week or two. We never starve, but we don't have much. I get up and check our supplies. Three cans of lentils. Onions. Rice. Cornmeal. Packets of dried mashed potato. A row of canned soups and a full bag of flour. And, on the top shelf, an unopened box of Romany Creams biscuits waiting for a special occasion.

"Run to the Supa-Value and get two cans of kidney beans and two cans of beef in gravy." Annalisa takes the stack of money from her bag. The pile of notes is slimmer than it was three days ago, thanks to two unscheduled trips to Durban North and one minivan ride to the family home in Umhlanga Rocks.

"Mayme give you the money?" That's what Neville said, but Lewis Dumisa is right. I can't believe anything he tells me.

"Yes, and this is the end of it," Annalisa says. "The moment Mayme dies, my father will cut us off. We have to spend as little as possible while I look for more work. Buy dented cans with expired labels if you can find them."

Dented cans with expired labels. That's new. I love a bargain, but . . .

Oh, I get it. Annalisa's job puts food on our table and shoes on our feet, but Mayme's money keeps us afloat. My school fees are paid on time and in full at the beginning of the year. We live in a one-room house with running water, electricity, and a toilet out back. Mrs. M has five people squashed into a tiny space. I have taken what we have for granted. Yes, we are poor, but things could be much worse. With no money but Annalisa's wages coming in, we might not be able to pay the rent. People who can't pay their rent end up on a stretch of mud behind the shipping-container graveyard. It's called Hopetown, but those who live there have little hope of ever getting back into Sugar Town once they've been forced out. And what about school?

"Be fifteen minutes." I take the notes from Annalisa and grab a cotton shopping bag from the hook by the door. I step out into weak sunshine. Iron rooftops glow red and silver. A crow swoops low to feed on insects buzzing over a pool of stagnant water in front of Mrs. M's garden gate. I have dreamed of leaving the lane so often that the dream has worn a groove in my mind. Now I'm faced with the possibility of being evicted from it, and I am just scared.

* * *

I pay for the dented cans, all beyond their expiry date, and head for Amazulu Street, where Lil Bit lives with her mother in a one-bedroom house with mice in the ceiling. They used to live on Bompass Street in a brick house shaded by a giant Natal mahogany tree. That was before the congregation caught Reverend Bhengu and his girlfriend in an unholy embrace. They kicked the family out of the priest's house that afternoon.

I knock, and Lil Bit opens the door, eager to hear the news. She reads my dazed expression and leads me into a living room where two stuffed sofas, three bookshelves, a writing desk, and two side tables fight for space. Small as she is, even Lil Bit might have trouble finding a way through the maze. Mother is right: Mrs. Bhengu needs to burn the stuff or sell it and start fresh.

"Sit down." Lil Bit plops onto a ratty velvet sofa. "Tell me what happened."

I sit next to her. I tell her what happened.

When I finish, I notice that Lil Bit's mouth is curved in a soft smile. "It isn't funny," I say. "Not even a little. I was so angry. And so was Mother."

Looking back, a part of me wonders if Annalisa and I made a mistake. Did we say the wrong thing, do the wrong thing to make Neville turn so mean? He is doing everything he can to keep us away from Mayme. It makes me wonder: Is there more to the situation than I can see?

"I don't mean to laugh." Lil Bit picks at a hole in the moth-eaten sofa. "You had a terrible day, but it makes me feel better to know that my family isn't the only one with problems. That other people are also unbalanced."

"Unbalanced is a nice way to describe Annalisa's family and Neville in particular. He hates me, and I hate him right back."

"I hate my father, too." She nibbles her bottom lip, and the next words come out in a rush. "But I miss him as well. Is that strange?"

"Not strange," I say. "Complicated."

"How is it complicated?" Lil Bit asks.

"Neville's house is something out of a magazine. It has more windows than I can count and a white marble sculpture in the front garden. It is perfect. When the guards turned us away, I wanted to set fire to it, but a part of me was desperate to go inside. I hate him, but I also . . ."

"What?"

"I also want him to love me. Is that sad?"

"Not sad," Lil Bit says. "Complicated."

* * *

Lil Bit walks me home past the tiny shops selling single cigarettes, soft drinks in plastic bags, and lottery tickets with their yellow and blue logos. We also pass street stalls selling mangoes and mobile phone credit for tiny amounts. It's two in the afternoon and groups of children run wild on the street, drunk with school holiday freedom.

I look ahead and stumble over my shoes. Jacob Caluza stands across the road with two friends in their early twenties; they're slouching twins with devil horns tattooed on their foreheads and spiderwebs tattooed on their necks. Prison tattoos. The crude images of knives and guns inked on the tops of their hands hint at the crimes they have committed. Jacob's friends are the sort of men that girls like us cross the street to avoid.

"Hey, Amandla." Jacob waves me over. "Come here."

I keep my eyes on the footpath and pretend not to hear him. I don't want to make him mad, but I sure as anything don't want to be near him or his prison pals. Lil Bit edges closer so that our arms touch.

"You *know* him?" she whispers.

"Not really. He wanted me to have a drink with him and I said no." Shuffled footsteps sound on the pavement behind us. Jacob and his friends are following. The hairs on the back of my neck prickle with warning.

"Ignore them," I tell Lil Bit in a fierce whisper. "Keep walking."

I want to run, but if I do, Jacob and his friends will chase me.

"Amandla! Amandla!" Jacob calls out in a singsong voice. "Why the rush?"

I have to answer now. No choice. "My friend and I have homework to do. I can't stop."

Jacob jogs past us and stands in the middle of the pavement with a crooked smile. He is high again. Across the way, a group of old ladies stop and stare. They won't interfere, though. I don't blame them. Going up against men with prison tattoos will only bring them trouble, and like everyone else in Sugar Town, they have problems of their own.

"Sorry," I tell Jacob. "Not today."

"Don't be like that," he says. "Come meet my friends. We can go, grab a drink. Your little girlfriend can come with. We have plenty to go around."

The tattooed twins move in on Lil Bit with wide grins and animal eyes. She holds her ground but flinches when the twin on the right leans close to her ear and whispers, "So tiny. I could break you in two without even trying. You might even like it."

I grab Lil Bit's hand and pull her to my side. Jacob is a pest, but the twins are something much more menacing. We need to get away before the situation turns dangerous.

"Thanks but no thanks for the invitation." I am polite but firm. "We have catch-up homework to do, like I said."

I sidestep Jacob and his friends and pull Lil Bit with me. Jacob clamps a bony hand onto my shoulder and tries to pull me back in his direction. I tear out of his grasp and turn on him. The drugs have made him bigger in his mind than he is in real life, and he needs to know I will not be manhandled in the street. Neither will Lil Bit. Enough is enough.

"Listen, Jacob," I say with the calm my mother uses in situations like this. "You asked me to go with you and I said no. No, thank you. Now please, leave me alone. I have work to do."

Jacob's smile vanishes. My cool manner was a mistake. I should have stayed soft and sweet, a clueless little girl in awe of his tattooed friends and flattered by his attention. He sucks his teeth, annoyed.

"You really think you gonna make it out of Sugar Town, Miss High and Mighty," he says. "You are as crazy as your mother if you think you're gonna do better than me, girl."

I snap. I look straight at him.

"Seriously, Jacob? You think you're the best I can do?!"

He goes quiet.

"I've been polite. Now leave me alone!" I say it loud enough for Mr. Solomon, the owner of Solomon and His Three Wives General Store, to poke his head out of the doorway. One look at the twins and he ducks right back inside. Jacob and his friends slowly back off.

"If she speaks to you like that again, you have to show her who's boss!" the twin with the words *Pain Is Love* tattooed across his cheek says. "A woman has to respect her man."

As if.

Lil Bit tugs at my skirt. "Come on. We're running late."

I don't have to be told twice. I walk away. I do not look back. My body vibrates with rage at being touched without my permission. First Neville and now Jacob. My patience with lousy men has evaporated. I should be scared. Instead, all I want is a chance to take them both down with one clean hit.

"Are they following us?" I ask Lil Bit. "Take a quick look for me."

Lil Bit peeks over her shoulder. "No, they're just standing and watching."

We turn the corner, and I let out a long breath I didn't know I was holding. My hands shake. Lil Bit grabs them and squeezes tight.

"That was tense, but you were *amazing*," she says. "You told him to back down, and he did."

How long will that last?

"I don't understand what's gotten into Jacob. He didn't notice me before, and now suddenly . . ."

"Father says that once he saw that girl, Sunshine, he couldn't get her out of his mind. She filled up his eyes. Maybe it's like that."

"I hope not. I have to find a way to stop this nonsense for good."

"Ask Goodness to help you out," Lil Bit says. "Her brothers can talk to Jacob and warn him off, nice-like."

"I can't ask for a favor from her brothers," I say. "They don't owe me anything, and Annalisa already has too much on her mind with Mayme in the hospital and money running out. I have to find a way to handle Jacob myself."

"Good luck," Lil Bit snaps back. "You saw his friends, Amandla . . . twin criminals out of jail but never out of trouble."

"I don't know what I'll do." That is the truth. "I have no room in my head for Jacob and his friends, Lil Bit. They are next week's problem. Seeing Mayme again is the number one thing. She has the keys to Annalisa's past. I just have to figure out a way into the white house."

Lil Bit reaches over and plucks Mayme's note from my jacket pocket. She unfolds it and points to Sam's mobile number and the cryptic message. *If you need help.*

"Call him. Ask for help like your granny said."

14

At 10:55 the next morning, I throw Lil Bit a brave smile and pull the clean curry container from my backpack. Lewis said to bring it back to the Build 'Em Up—or the Dumisa house—so here we are. Lil Bit stands next to me, flush-faced and nervous. I get it. We never come to this part of Sugar Town and being here feels strange. The houses are big, not as big as the house Annalisa grew up in, but big enough, and built of brick.

"Knock." Lil Bit tugs at her T-shirt. "All we can do is ask. If she says no, we'll make another plan. Simple."

Today, Goodness gets her mobile back, and I need a phone with unlimited data and endless credit to plan my next move against Neville. I knock, and we wait. The door opens, and a short black woman with smooth cheeks and a wide mouth frowns at us on the porch. For a second, I think she might turn us away.

"Yes?" she says.

"Lewis asked me to return this." I hold out the empty container. "And I was wondering if Goodness was home."

"Come in," the woman says, and walks through a living room with two sofas covered in plastic and two easy chairs with crocheted doilies draped over the armrests. A three-tier diamante chandelier with fake candles hangs from the ceiling. Annalisa calls this "granny fashion," though I can't imagine Mayme's furniture covered in anything but soft leather.

"Goodness!" the woman calls at the kitchen door. "Two girls to see you."

Goodness sits at a long wooden table with a late breakfast of bacon and eggs in front of her. Dressed in a black Adidas tracksuit trimmed in white and with her bleached braids pulled into a high ponytail, she's ready for a game of soccer or a marathon shopping spree at the mall. Lil Bit's stomach rumbles, and my mouth waters. In our house, bacon is a Sunday-morning treat, and today is only Wednesday.

"Hey, my sisters." Goodness smiles and waves us into the kitchen, which smells of coffee and bacon grease. Mrs. Dumisa must have wanted a pretty little miss for a daughter, but Goodness, with her elbows propped on either side of a heaped plate of food, is fabulous in a totally different way. "Have you eaten?"

If a slice of bread and a weak cup of tea counts, then yes, Lil Bit and I have both eaten breakfast.

"We were so busy discussing Amandla's grandfather that it slipped our minds." Lil Bit lies as easily as she steals. "Wait till you hear what he did."

"Sit. Tell me." Goodness turns to the black woman who opened the front door and says, "Two more helpings of bacon and eggs for my friends, please, Mina. Thanks."

We sit, and I tell Goodness everything that happened. Except for the part about Annalisa and me screaming. I leave that bit out. If our friendship lasts beyond the school holidays, maybe I'll tell her what it's like to have a mother who has lost part of her mind and that, for a moment, I let part of mine go, too. That it felt good. That maybe I might be a little crazy, too.

When I finish, Goodness gets a serious look on her face.

"What are you going to do?" she asks. "Men like that? Give them an inch and they'll take the whole village. No way can you let your gramps win. You have to fight back."

My thoughts exactly, and now's the time to ask for that favor.

"My cousin Sam might know a way into the house. I need to call him and find out."

Goodness slides her iPhone across the table without hesitation. No need to ask or beg.

"Thanks, Goodness."

"No problem, Amandla. Power to the people!"

She gives Lil Bit a crisp piece of bacon to hold her over while Mina cooks a second round of breakfast.

"Use the speakerphone," Goodness says. "Saves you repeating the conversation afterward."

Fair.

I dial Sam's number, which I have memorized. The note from Granny Amanda is tucked safe inside the pages of my sketchbook. It might be the only letter I ever receive from her. That makes it precious and worth keeping.

The phone is picked up on the other end.

"Hello?" It's Sam.

"Hey, it's Amandla. Your cousin."

"My one and only," he says. "Ready for that ice cream on the beach?"

"I am, but it'll have to wait. You're on speaker with my friends Lil Bit and Goodness. I have something I need to talk to you about."

He has no idea what's happened, so I tell him about being turned away on Neville's orders. How it's not right, what he did. That Annalisa told me Grandpa always wins and isn't it time for him to suck on failure? "Okay. That came out wrong. What I mean to say is, if Mayme is home from the hospital, I plan on getting into the white house, one way or another. Will you help?"

"Mayme came home last night, and yes, I'll help," Sam says. "There's a separate entrance for the servants that opens with a security code. One problem, though. The maid and the gardener and the cook have worked for the family for decades. Me coming in through the servants' entrance is no problem, but they'll call the guards on a stranger."

A stranger. He means *me*.

"Can we sneak in somehow?" I wonder out loud, knowing that Sam is our only way into the white house. I'm too shy to ask him to get physically involved in our plans. We are family, but we don't know each other. Not really. Lil Bit leans over the table and says into the phone, "Where is the servants' entrance?"

"Down a small lane to the right of the front gates," Sam says. "The entrance door is made of steel. Unbreakable."

"Can the guards see the door from the front gates?" Lil Bit asks.

"There's usually only one guard," Sam says. "Manfred. And he's asleep on the job most of the time."

"Describe Manfred to me," I ask Sam out of curiosity. "Old or young?"

"Old. Fat and bald. Been there since my dad was a kid. Wears a coat that's two sizes too big for him."

"Neville has three guards on patrol now," I say. "All young and fully awake. All professionals with earpieces and guns."

"All there to keep you from getting into the white house," Goodness points out. "Your gramps didn't trust the old guard to turn your ma away from the family home."

That makes sense. The way Sam tells it, Manfred and the Bollards have decades of shared history. Annalisa grew from a child to an adult under his watch. No way would he have made us stand on the sidewalk like beggars.

"Manfred won't be back till after Mayme has passed. That's my guess," I say. Neville is cautious. He is cunning. He plays to win. What can a colored girl from the township do to a white man who has all the power?

"One guard or three, it doesn't matter." Lil Bit chews a mouthful of bacon. It seems like the smoky flavor is opening up neural pathways in her clever brain. Her eyes close for a moment and then fly open.

"I know a way in," she says.

* * *

We sit around the phone and listen to Lil Bit's plan. When she finishes, I ask her, "Are you sure?" She rolls her eyes, full of drama.

"Yes, I'm sure. And don't try and ditch me, either. If the plan goes wrong, you'll need backup."

"This could work," Sam says on the other end.

Goodness holds up her hand before I get another word out. "Don't ask me to sit and warm the bench, Amandla. That's not going to happen. It's all of us working the plan or it's none of us. That's how a team works."

Friends and now a team. An impossible situation to predict four days ago, but here we all are, planning a break-in together.

"Nine a.m. tomorrow. We'll leave from the minivan stand on Abdullah Ibrahim Street at eight." Goodness puts her stamp on the deal and waits for me to object. I nod, all resistance gone, and she smiles.

"Sam?"

"Yeah?"

"I've never had a cousin before, but I think you're a good one," I say.

"You are, too, Amandla. I wish it didn't have to be like this. But Mayme's worth it."

"See you soon."

"No problem. The Bollard brigade is ready for action, brah."

He hangs up, and we do, too.

"Now that that's decided, what should we do till lunch? I have soccer practice at two, but there's plenty of time to check what's new at Mrs. Lithuli's library," Goodness says.

Mrs. Lithuli hunts the suburban libraries of Durban for old and damaged books to stock the wooden shelves on the back porch of her house. None of the books are for loan, but you are welcome to sit and read on the porch or in the garden. Annalisa and I visit Mrs. Lithuli's haven of peace and quiet at least once a month. I'm not going this time.

"You two go ahead." I grab my backpack and swing it onto my shoulder. "Annalisa was asleep when I left the house this morning. I need to head back and make sure she's okay. The standoff with Neville shook her up."

Not a lie. Last night, after lights-out, Annalisa slipped into my cot and held me in her arms. She sang a sweet song that echoed inside the rusted walls of our shack and brought tears to my eyes. The song was in Zulu, a language she barely speaks. Did my father teach it to her? Back in the time before me? Annalisa fell asleep before I got the chance to ask, and I lay wake with an empty space inside my heart where the stories and memories of him should be. You'd think I'd be used to having a mystery for a father, but that mystery aches. I want a name and a face to put to the black man who fell for the white girl and made me.

The Dumisas' front door opens, and I hear the sound of footsteps moving through the living room to the kitchen. Mina grabs a cooler bag from the countertop and carries it to the far end of the table, ready to be picked up. Lunch for the brothers working at the Build 'Em Up, I'm guessing. I am secretly, stupidly, hoping that it is Lewis in the hall.

Then, as if I've summoned him from my fantasies, Lewis walks into the kitchen in blue jeans, a green T-shirt, and his trademark black sneakers. He sees me and does the absolute worst thing. He smiles. A slow curve of his lips brings out the dimples in his cheeks and the heat to my face. When Lil Bit blushes, her skin darkens and glows. It's cute. When I blush, my too-light skin turns red and my hazel-flecked-with-green eyes shine like I've got a fever. It's the opposite of cute.

"Thanks for breakfast." My chair scrapes against the floor tiles with a loud screech. "I've got to get home like I said."

"I'll walk you." Lewis swoops down and picks up my backpack with loose-limbed grace. There ought to be a law against that combination of kissable lips and deep brown eyes. It's distracting. If I were driving a car, I'd have an accident. "Goodness can take lunch to the Build 'Em Up."

Goodness sucks her teeth at the suggestion, but Lewis is older and a boy, and if she refuses, her mother will hear about it.

"Fine," she says. "Lil Bit and me will go."

Lil Bit blushes, kinda the same way that I blushed on seeing Lewis, and her expression is difficult to read. Embarrassment. Joy. Shyness. A mix of all three? I can't tell. It's puzzling and interesting to see a new and different side of her than I'm used to.

"Ready?" Lewis says.

"Don't worry about me," I say. "I know all the shortcuts. I'll be home in no time."

"Good." He steps aside to let me out of the kitchen first. "You can show me."

"Fine." I walk past him and into the living room, scared that my delight and confusion are written across my ridiculously freckled face.

* * *

I stand outside our "snug" dwelling, embarrassed by the rusted walls and the roof held down by stones and old tires. Neville's grand white house dwarfs the Dumisas' redbrick home, and their redbrick house dwarfs our shack in size and comfort. We live on the bottom rung of a long ladder that drops even farther down to Hopetown's mud floors and dust-bowl gardens.

"This is it," I tell Lewis, my voice tight. "This is where Annalisa and I live."

"I know," he says, and that knowledge throws me off balance.

"How?" I ask.

"No secrets in Sugar Town, Amandla."

"True," I say, even though I'm sure that a river of secrets runs below the surface of the township. He nods, and I stay rooted to the ground, too embarrassed to invite him inside and too well-mannered to ask him to leave. It's awkward, and it is past time for me to check on Annalisa.

"You should head back," I say. "Your brothers will be wondering where you got to."

"I'll wait while you go in." Lewis steps back to let me pass, and it is hard to ignore his . . . presence. This skin-tingling sensation, I tell myself in a stern voice, is exactly what led to Mother's pregnancy and free fall into poverty. A gorgeous black man. Smooth skin and kissable lips. I know how the story ends. Right here, in a dirt lane that runs between Tugela and Sisulu. Annalisa wants more for me. I want more for me.

"Thanks for walking me back. Get home safe."

Lewis turns in the direction of Tugela Way and then turns back to face me, determined to speak his mind. "Whatever business you're cooking up with Goodness and Lil Bit is your affair," he says. "But think twice before getting involved in one of my sister's wild schemes to spice up the holidays."

"What business?" I try for a cool tone, but the words come out high-pitched and thin. I am a terrible liar. So terrible that Lewis smiles to see the heat rise from my throat and into my cheeks. My face is hot.

"Listen." Lewis keeps a friendly tone. "My father is a hard man. He thinks that women should be soft and sweet and obedient. Goodness is none of those things. Any chance she gets to cause trouble, she takes it. You don't want to get caught between her and my father. Believe me."

"Understood," I say. He thinks that Goodness is the one leading me astray, not the other way around. Testing the limits set down by her father might well be the reason Goodness is so keen to get involved in our plan to bust into the white house.

"If you have to go through with a scheme that she's cooked up, be safe and careful," Lewis says. "And, if you need help, ask me."

And there it is again. The heart-stopping kindness that warms every cell of my body. The distance between us is suddenly too great. I want to step closer and lay my cheek against his chest.

I want to know how it feels to be held tight in the circle of his arms. Just for one minute. Or an hour. Maybe longer. A lot longer. Good God above. I like Lewis. I really, really like him. My hopeful heart jumps at the idea of the two of us together, laughing and kissing. Definitely kissing.

Girl, stop this foolishness and pull yourself together before you drool on his shoes!

"I'll think about what you said," I tell him. A promise I intend to keep. "You should go before your brothers come looking for you."

"See you soon." He heads for Tugela Way with an easy stride. I stand in the yard and take a long moment to appreciate how good Lewis looks both coming and going. Across the way, Mrs. M digs a trench into the soil, ready for spring planting. She waves at me, and I blush. She's caught me staring after Lewis Dumisa the same way that a drunk stares at a bottle of booze locked inside a liquor store. So close yet so far . . .

I wave back at Mrs. M and make my way to our front door. A movement at the corner of my eye catches my attention. I turn to look across our dead garden toward Sisulu Street. A plastic bag caught on a barbed wire fence waves in the wind, and the Khoza twins cry in their shared cot four doors down. Everything is normal.

Then the shadows under the wild mango trees beside the public toilet block flicker and move. A stray dog with two black paws trots out with a dead bird in its jaws. That must be what I saw in the dimness, a dog hunting dinner. It's strange, though. I'd swear that the flickering shadow that first caught my attention was standing upright. It might have been a person waiting for an empty toilet or an old granny taking a rest in the shade. Either way, it's silly to imagine that a sinister presence is hiding behind the mango trees.

Really, who has the time to spy on me from the end of our street?

Jacob Caluza?

Jacob is unemployed. He's free to roam Sugar Town from morning light to midnight. And after I publicly turned him down yesterday, he might think it's time to teach me a lesson in respect. My heart beats loud in my ears. I step closer to the front door. If Jacob comes running, I'll have plenty of time to rush inside and bolt the lock.

The dark space under the trees stays solid. I stare for a minute longer. Still nothing. I seriously doubt that Jacob Caluza could stay still for that long. My shoulders relax. Finding his next hit of tik is what drives Jacob. Not me.

"Amandla?" Annalisa opens the front door and peers out through puffy eyes. "What's the matter?"

"Nothing." I shrug off the creepy feeling and go to meet her. She's awake and ready for baked beans on toast and a cup of tea. A good sign. I kiss her cheek and go inside to fill the kettle. My mind works through what happened in the yard. I might have seen more than was actually there. Or the tall shape in the shade might have been a thief casing the lane for valuables to loot. A waste of time. There is little precious to steal from the shacks, plus the combination of Mrs. M's eagle eye and Blind Auntie's crazy-good hearing are more effective than an electric fence. We are as safe as it's possible to be in a township.

Annalisa pours fresh water into the jam jar on the windowsill and strokes the velvet petals with her index finger. The white rose that she snatched from Mayme's garden will soon fade, but she is determined to extend its life for a while longer.

"Who was that boy you were talking to?" she asks.

"A prince," I say.

"They all look like princes at the start," she says. "Be careful, princess, but not too careful. Love is the sweetest thing. I'd give anything to dance with your father one more time."

That longing for Father is an excellent reason to stay away from Lewis.

Annalisa is right. Love *is* sweet. But it's also dangerous.

15

A red sports car with a silver jaguar leaping from the hood roars out of the gates and turns left toward the main road that leads to the Durban business district. Neville is on his way to work four minutes earlier than Sam predicted and in a different car than the one he drove the other day. Wow! He has two sports cars. Imagine that. Gerald, the mixed-race guard who turned Annalisa and me away from the house, presses a button on the security panel inside the entrance, and the gates slide shut. He stays and keeps a watch on the street while the other guards disappear into the property. They are the real worry; their exact location is impossible to predict.

"He's late," Lil Bit says from where we stand in a park a block down from the big house. "Are you sure he'll show?"

"Neville left early." The timer ticks down on Goodness's mobile. "Sam will be here," I say. "Wait and see."

Two minutes pass in awkward silence. Doubt creeps into my mind. Sam has no skin in the game. He has nothing to gain from being involved with my plan. Why risk his golden life for me, a cousin he barely knows?

"Is that him?" Goodness juts her chin at a white boy in rumpled clothes and rumpled hair walking the footpath in white sneakers with a black swoop on the side. "Off-white Blazers." Goodness clocks the sneaker brand straight off. "That's some serious cash hitting the concrete."

"That's Sam. Right where he said he'd be and right on time." I'm proud to say it.

It might be that he's looking to spice up the holidays, like Goodness, but he's here and she's here, and I am glad. Their presence means that Lil Bit and me are not alone. With Sam, we are an army of four, and together we will make the first cut in Neville's armor—if the plan plays out the way it's supposed to.

"There he goes." Lil Bit chews her thumbnail, nervous. "See if he makes it in."

Sam saunters up to the gates with a casual white-boy swagger. No need to rush. No need to iron my clothes or brush my hair, either. I belong here. Get between me and what I want and watch me speed-dial the family lawyers.

Gerald nods and opens the front gate. We are too far away to hear a word that's said, but I imagine Sam giving his name and the guard responding with a polite *Please come through, Mr. Bollard.*

"Five-minute countdown." Goodness resets the stopwatch on her mobile. "We'll go first to give you cover, Amandla. If it's all good, we'll slip into the side lane. If not, Lil Bit and me will cruise past the guard, get his attention, and join you in fifteen minutes. Remember to leave the servants' entrance open a crack."

That is the plan. Clean. Straightforward.

The alarm chirps, and I follow close behind Goodness, who is taller and wider at the shoulders than I am, so you'd have to look hard to identify me. Lil Bit is too little for that job. Stuck behind Goodness, I can't see if Gerald has come out the gates or if he's patrolling the entrance.

"We're clear," Lil Bit whispers. "The guard is playing a game on his phone or texting his girlfriend."

We veer into the narrow lane that runs along the side of the house and leads to the servants' entrance. Sam holds the steel door open and waves us inside. I slip through into the forbidden land of green grass, flowering azaleas, and the winking blue swimming pool at the rear of the house. My heart beats like crazy. Annalisa should be here, I think. This is her home, not mine.

"This way." Sam ducks low and runs through the gardens to a glass door that leads inside the house. "The guards are eating breakfast in the kitchen, so we'll be fine for at least forty minutes. After that . . ." He shrugs off what might happen in less than an hour. *Que será, será, guys.*

"We're here now," I say, and follow him into a sunny space with three long wooden tables covered in terra-cotta pots, bags of soil, and green clippings. A planting room. If Mayme and Mrs. M ever got together, they'd have a great time.

"Quickly." Sam waves at Lil Bit and Goodness, who stand in the doorway with their jaws hanging open at the sight of a room set aside for plants. "Get inside. Mayme's room is down the hallway."

He leads us into a wide corridor with paintings and black-and-white photographs of beach landscapes hanging on the walls. I love the beach, even if we only go twice a year. Lil Bit and Goodness hang two steps back to give us privacy, their eyes flickering over the width and the length of the corridor. Vases filled with fresh flowers. Photographs. Paintings. It's quiet. In Sugar Town, the sounds of life pour in through the walls. Night coughs and boys fighting. Parents calling their children home at twilight. A car engine backfiring and girls laughing in the distance.

"Mayme's proper bedroom is on the second floor, but with her heart condition, Grandpa decided that using the stairs was too risky. This is a guest room." Sam knocks on a door halfway down the corridor. "Mayme," he says in a loud voice. "It's me. Sam. I have a visitor to see you. Can we come in?"

"Of course," Mayme answers. "Come through."

Sam opens the door, and now that we're here, inside the castle, the awkward feeling of being out of place seizes me. I don't belong here. What was I thinking?

"Go, Amandla." Lil Bit understands my fears. She has them, too. "Your granny invited you. She has the answers to all your questions about Annalisa, and she wants to talk."

She's right. I'm here for myself and I'm here for my broken mother, who can't remember the things we both need to know. Mayme can help. She can unlock the past. I take a deep breath and follow Sam into a room that is double the size of our shack, and much, much nicer.

* * *

"Amandla." Mayme stands by a tall window, wrapped in a dressing gown with white cranes flying across a blue sky. She holds out her hands to invite me closer. "I had a table set up on the back porch for you and Annalisa yesterday morning, but you didn't come."

The sunshine slanting through the glass picks up the fine lines and creases at the corners of Mayme's eyes and mouth. She is paler, older than in the institute, her shoulders sloped under an invisible weight.

"There was a problem with the gates." The lie comes out in a high voice. "The security keypad broke and the gates locked and we . . . uh . . . we couldn't get in. That's why I came back today."

"With Sam." Mayme is skeptical. "And no Mummy?"

"She had work today. She'll come next time." Now that we know that the plan works, we can use it again, till we're caught. "Should we sit down?"

Sam says, "I'll show your friends around the house while you two talk."

"Wait." It is suddenly important for Lil Bit and Goodness to meet Mayme face-to-face and to know that she is real and not a fantasy cooked up by a lonely teenager. In the years to come, the three of us will have a shared memory to talk about. "Let me introduce them first."

Sam opens the door. Lil Bit and Goodness step into the room side by side: tall and small, shy and bold. Township girls with wide eyes.

"Mayme, meet my friends Lil Bit and Goodness. We go to school together," I say. "You can guess which is which."

"I certainly can. Nice to meet you," she says.

"You too, Mrs. Bollard," Lil Bit says.

"Nice to meet you, Mrs. Bollard," says Goodness.

She smiles. "You can call me Mayme. Sam, show the girls the games room or take them onto the porch where it's sunny and warm. You choose."

"How about a game of Ping-Pong?" Sam asks on the way out. "Or a game of pool?"

"Pool." Goodness likes the sound of that. "Show me how to play and we'll have a match. If that's what it's called."

There's a grubby pool hall in Sugar Town where trashy girls in tight clothes go to mix with bold boys in loose T-shirts and baggy jeans. Lil Bit and I are not allowed inside. Not because we are too young; there is no such thing as "too young" in the township, but because Lil Bit's mother and Annalisa have said that the pool hall is where girls get into trouble. Whether they want to or not.

Lil Bit waves goodbye, and Sam closes the door. I am alone with Mayme in a bedroom with a long linen couch for sitting and a tall window that lets in the sunlight.

"I'm glad you came alone this time," she says. "It gives us time for something important." She goes to a writing desk and pulls a yellow envelope from a stack of papers. "When Annalisa disappeared, I hired a private investigator to find out what happened to her. The answers are inside this envelope."

I see that the envelope is sealed and brown at the edges.

"How old is that?" I ask.

"I'm ashamed to say it's almost as old as you," she says. "I didn't open it because I was afraid to face the truth." Mayme is painfully honest. "The damage to Annalisa is my fault. Whatever she went through in the months that she was missing was my doing."

"That's not right." Neville is the one behind Annalisa's disappearance. I am sure the contents of the envelope will prove it. "Let's read the report together, and that way you'll know exactly what happened."

"No." She paces back and forth with the report held tight in her hands, agitated. "I was a coward sixteen years ago, and I'm a coward now. Promise me that you'll read the report after I'm dead. Not before."

"But why?" The request stuns me. "Everything you need to know is right there in your hands. Open the envelope and find out who's really to blame for whatever happened to Annalisa."

"I already know the truth." She turns to face me. "When your mother fell in love with your father, Neville threw her out of the house. I didn't stop him. I sent money to pay for her apartment, but that was the easy way out, helping her from the shadows, too afraid of what other people would say to stand up for my own daughter. Now I realize how many years I wasted, how much damage I've done. All that time I could have spent with you and Annalisa. I failed you both. I failed myself. That's the truth."

"You pay for our rent and other stuff . . . don't you?"

"Small amounts scraped together behind your grandfather's back." Her words cut across mine, sharp and bristling with self-loathing. "I could have done more . . . should have done more. When you didn't turn up yesterday, I thought that something bad had happened. To imagine that I might never see you or Annalisa again put everything in perspective." She stops to catch her breath, and it hurts to see her hurting. "I have a weak heart because I *am* weak."

"Mayme, we should read it now. Together. And then get over it," I say.

"Please, Amandla . . ."

I want to tear the envelope open. Instead, I reach out and let her put it into my hand. "All right. I promise to only read this after you're gone and not one minute earlier."

"Good. You can hate me when I'm dead, but not before."

I put the envelope into my backpack. Mayme didn't challenge Neville, and she has to live with that shame. Oh, I know what it's like to live with the shame of being poor and stranded between black and white, but I don't know what it's like to abandon your own daughter. Annalisa will never experience that feeling, either. She'd die for me. If she lets it, shame could pull Mayme down into the same black hole that swallows Annalisa.

"We can't change the past, but we have *now*. I'm here with you, Mayme. Right now. Let's not waste the time we have left."

She looks at me in a way I've always wanted to be looked at, with loving kindness and warmth.

"Clever girl," she says, and touches my face. She leans down and kisses my forehead. "Let's you and me make the most of now."

"Oh . . . I wanted to tell you that Mrs. M loved the fairy lights chili and the yellow pepper from the hospital garden. She's saved some seeds to plant in the spring, too. With a few more plants she'll have an excellent chance of winning the Best Garden in Sugar Town Award."

Mayme smiles. "I have some speckled tree orchids that your Mrs. M might be interested in."

There is no Best Garden in Sugar Town Award, but the thought of it has perked Mayme up and taken away the regrets that weighed on her.

"Let's go look." I stand and move to the door, suddenly glad to get out of the room that holds the same volume of sadness and regret as any shack in Sugar Town. Wherever you live, it seems that life finds you.

The door opens before I get there and Father Gibson sticks his head into the room with his flyaway hair and wide grin. I step to the side, surprised, and he doesn't see me pressed to the wall.

"Look who's come to visit," he says, and my mother walks into the guest bedroom, wearing her second-best outfit: a tailored blue dress with a white hem. She is simple and elegant, a style she inherited from her mother but, unfortunately, did not pass down to me.

"Annalisa. You got time off work." Mayme is delighted. "How lovely to have the two of you here at home. At last."

Mother glances at the family priest, confused, and then, as if by magic radar, sees me stuck to the wall. I step forward, caught in a lie for the second time in days.

"Oh . . ." Annalisa blinks and says, "I, uh . . . I forgot to tell you that Mr. Gupta gave me a half day off. Father Gibson picked me up from the station so the three of us could spend a few hours together. To make up for yesterday."

That is a big fat lie. She found a way into the house and didn't think to bring me along. I'm offended, hurt even, but now is not the time to call each other out. Both of us want to spare Mayme the truth of what happened yesterday.

"Because of the broken security panel and the locked gates." I jump in with the fake reasons I gave Mayme for our missed visit. Mother raises an eyebrow. *Really? That's what you came up with?* I shrug off the sharp look. If telling lies is a family talent, then I have missed out.

"You've come just in time," Mayme says. "Amandla and I are going to the garden room to pick out cuttings for Mrs. M. With a few more exotics, Amandla says that she might win the Best Garden in Sugar Town Award."

Mother nods and smiles in my direction, impressed. *Excellent lie*, the smile says. *Keep up the good work.*

It's the first time I can remember being congratulated for lying, but we are far from home. Things are different in the big white house, I guess.

"I'll leave you three to it," Father Gibson says. "If you need me, I'll be on the back porch, smoking a cigarette. With your permission, Amanda?"

"Smoke all you want, Tony. My lungs are fine. It's my heart that's the problem." She squeezes his shoulder on the way out, affectionate. "And thank you for bringing my girl home."

The two are good friends. I wonder if Mayme ever imagines how her life might have been if she'd married a poor Anglican priest instead of a wealthy businessman? When it came time to choose between loving her daughter and granddaughter or keeping her social position, she chose the latter. The township bitch that lives inside me thinks that she deserves an empty room and regrets. If I hadn't followed Annalisa to the institute that morning, would she have lifted a finger to find me? No. She has, in fact, done nothing to build a bridge between us. Nothing!

Rational me pushes township-bitch me aside. Mayme has her faults, same as anyone else. I'm not ready to walk away from the only connection I have to Annalisa's past and my own. And maybe, just maybe, to Father as well.

16

At the potting table, I learn that Annalisa cut her leg open while surfing when she was fourteen and hiked the Annapurna track in Nepal with a friend at nineteen. Uncle Julien, on the other hand, was cautious and sensible. Mayme uses the words *sensitive soul* to describe him three different times, and decoding what she really means is easy. Mother was strong-willed and Julien wasn't.

"Neville had big plans for Annalisa." She pushes a vivid pink geranium with a white center across the wooden table to me. "He was certain that she'd take over the company one day. He liked that she had her own mind . . ."

"Until he didn't," Annalisa says. "We had a fight. After that, I can't remember what happened. There was a dirt road with mountains . . . but I don't know how I got there. Or how I got those blisters on my feet."

I shoot Mayme a sideways glance, waiting for her to fill in the blanks. Surely she has something to add? The time, the date, the reason for the fight? Anything at all. She stays quiet and keeps her hands busy shoveling soil into a row of seedling pots. The only sound is her hands working and the shuffle of the clay pot on the table.

"The fight started at dinner," she says at last. "You wanted to invite your boyfriend to a charity event at the Botanic Gardens. Neville said, 'If you mean that Zulu bartender that you're running around with, the answer is no.'"

My father was Zulu. He worked in a bar. Small pieces of information that I've never heard before. I grab the new facts, greedy for more.

"He told Julien and me to stay in the dining room while he talked to you in his office. In private. I should have gone with you. I should have stuck by your side, but I didn't. I left you to deal with your father alone."

Three sharp taps rattle the planting-room window. Father Gibson waves me into the garden where he stands with a flushed face.

"We have to leave," he says. "Say goodbye to your grandmother and meet me at the side gate right away. Bring Annalisa with you."

"But my friends—"

"I've got them. They're already at the gate. Hurry."

"Okay. Out in a minute." I slip back into the planting room. I don't know what excuse to give for leaving so soon. Annalisa reads my strained expression and begins packing the potted seedlings into a small wooden tray.

"We have to go, Mama," Annalisa says to Mayme. She forces a smile. "Mr. Gupta gave me the morning off and it will take an hour to get back to Sugar Town."

Mayme sighs. "You're angry at me for leaving you to fight with Neville instead of standing up to him. Rightfully so."

Annalisa says, "I'm not happy about it, but I'm not angry, either. Father always gets his way. We know that." She hands me Mrs. M's box of seedlings. "I want to know about the place in the mountains and what I was doing there. We'll talk about that next time?"

"I don't have answers to all of your questions," Mayme says. "The seven months between when you disappeared and when you turned up in the countryside with Amandla in your arms are a mystery. I promise to tell you everything that I know about your life before the day that you went missing."

All the answers to Annalisa's questions are inside the report that Mayme refuses to read. A report that will be opened only after she is safely in the grave and free of the shame that weighs on her. Annalisa will be disappointed, but right now we have to leave.

"Till next time." I kiss Mayme on the cheek and hurry through the garden with the seedling box bumping against my hip. I leave Annalisa to say her goodbyes in private. If there's trouble waiting for us in the garden, I will hopefully have time to defuse it before Annalisa comes out.

Ahead of me, the side gate is open. Lil Bit, Sam, and Goodness stand to the side while Father Gibson talks to Gerald, the green-eyed guard with the pockmarked skin. Shit! We're sprung.

"This is a private matter," the priest says. "There's no reason to involve the authorities."

Authorities?

Lil Bit meets me halfway to the gate.

"The police," she whispers.

"What?"

"In the side lane."

"But . . ." I glimpse a patch of blue behind Gerald's shoulder. "Why?"

"Don't know. The priest came to the games room and told us to come out. Now he's trying to get the guard to send the police away."

My ears strain to pick up the conversation between Father Gibson and Gerald, who stands with his hands on his hips in what Lil Bit calls the "power pose." Another gem she picked up from the self-help book that she liberated from the shelves of a hip Glenwood store.

"Sorry, Father. It's out of my hands. You, you, you, and you"—Gerald points to Goodness, Lil Bit, me, and then to Annalisa, who has finally made it through the garden to the gate—"are being arrested. The police are here to take you into custody. Go quietly and things will go easier for everyone."

"You serious, brah?" My mouth jumps into action. "Things will go easier for all of us if you stand aside and let us pass. After that, you'll never see us again."

A lie, but whatever . . .

Gerald doesn't reply. He steps to the right to let two constables into the garden, one black, one white. They are tall, serious, and in body armor. The black officer says, "You are all charged with criminal trespass. Follow me to the van. We'll need your addresses and then we're taking you to the Umhlanga Rocks station."

"I'm here to visit my *grandmother*!" I say. "Amanda Bollard is my grandmother. She invited us."

The black constable says, "Come quietly. We're not going to have the conversation here."

Annalisa leans close to Father Gibson and whispers words I cannot hear. He nods and walks back toward the house . . . to take care of Mayme, I guess, and to shield her from the shock of seeing the police arresting her family in her garden. Goodness and Lil Bit follow the cops, and then I follow.

"You're not under arrest, Mr. Bollard," Gerald says to someone behind me. "You can stay."

"I don't think so," Sam says. He moves to my side. He's coming with us. "I let them in, so technically, I'm the guilty party. We'll see what the police say."

"Your grandfather doesn't want you in jail." Gerald is tense. "Just the others."

"Let Grandpa know where I am. If he doesn't want me in jail or with a criminal record, he can send his lawyer to deal with it or he come down to the station himself."

Sam, you rock star. Vive la révolution, cuz.

"Let's go." The white constable pushes my shoulder. "Quick and quiet."

I hold on to Mrs. M's seedling tray and zip my mouth shut.

* * *

We squeeze into the paddy wagon, Sam on one side of Annalisa and me on the other. Lil Bit and Goodness sit across from us, quiet and self-contained. A cruise in a cop wagon is nothing compared to the rough treatment that the police dish out in Sugar Town. No one says anything for a moment. The engine starts.

"Annalisa, meet Goodness Dumisa, my friend from Sugar Town," I say. "And meet Sam. Your nephew."

She nods hello to Goodness and turns to Sam. She studies his face for almost as long as he studied mine on the roof garden. "Well," she says, "we may be a screwed-up family, but we are a good-looking one."

He laughs. "I take after you, Auntie."

"Good-looking, like I said." She smiles and leans back against the caged windows, relaxed. "Okay, listen up, my fellow criminals . . ."

We lean in.

"Be polite. Be chilled. Don't volunteer any information."

Nods all around.

I realize this isn't Annalisa's first time in a police vehicle.

* * *

Inside the police station, we sit in a row of plastic chairs pushed against the wall. The constables who arrested us said to wait here until they are ready to process us. The police station is less scary than I thought it would be, but still, we could be here for a while. And, if the charges stick, Lil Bit and I will end up in a youth center for juvenile offenders. Goodness and Sam have a good chance of walking free. The Dumisa family connections and the Bollard family lawyers will keep the heat off them.

A dozen police walk by us and stare at the multicolored catch of the day. We are the rainbow nation that Nelson Mandela dreamed of: white, brown, and black together. Only, in jail. Not how he planned it.

I think about all the people in South Africa who have come to places like this and never come out. Nelson was in jail for twenty-seven years. The number sinks in, and the pain of it hits me in the heart for the first time. He was locked behind bars for almost twice my lifetime, and when he was released, he walked out with nothing but love in his heart. *Respect. One week in a prison cell would break me.*

"I'm sorry." I lean toward Goodness and Lil Bit, who gnaws at her thumbnail. "It's my fault we're here."

"Rubbish," Goodness says. "The guards saw us playing pool through the window, and your grandfather let the cops take us. We're here because of them, not because of you."

"But . . ."

Goodness holds her hand up. *Shut it, sister. Not one more word.*

"You went to visit your granny, Amandla. That's the beginning and the end of the story." She digs her phone from her jacket pocket. "The real story is right here. The guard. The cops. The priest asking the guard to let us go and the guard telling him that Mr. Bollard wanted us arrested. I sent a copy to myself and to Lewis. For insurance."

Annalisa and Sam gather around to form a circle that hides the phone from the police, who should have confiscated it during the arrest. Guess it didn't occur to them that a black girl from Sugar Town had the latest iPhone stashed in her pocket. Goodness taps the screen. A video of our arrest plays, the guard standing aside for the police. The police crowding Annalisa and me in the garden and the big moment when I say, "I'm here to visit my *grandmother*!"

"Sweet," Sam says.

"*Hayibo!*" Lil Bit says. "Let the girl visit her granny, my God . . ."

Even Annalisa laughs. It's a black comedy.

"Quiet," the white constable who arrested us says from his desk. "Or I'll put you in the cells."

"Sorry, constable." Annalisa is sweet and calm. "We realize that visiting family with the wrong color relative is a serious offense. Forgive us?"

He sends her a death stare.

She smiles. It's radiant.

In a flash, I see the young Annalisa: playful, confident, and unimpressed by authority. She stares back at the constable, the two of them locked in a silent battle for power. Annalisa's smile fades, and her face takes on an expression of complete assurance. The policeman looks away.

I bet that was the exact expression she had on her face when she argued with Neville in his office. A look that says, *When all this is done, I'll be the one left standing.*

Annalisa unbroken.

"Uh-oh." Sam points to the station entrance. "Trouble incoming."

We turn as one toward the front doors. A red-faced Uncle Julien talks to the female constable at the reception desk. He's making a lot of noise, and then the officer holds up her hands at him in a *stop* motion.

"Sir!" she says loudly. "I will not allow you to see your son until you calm down."

He goes silent. She lets him pass, and he makes a beeline for my mother.

"How dare you drag my son into one of your insane schemes?" he says in a furious whisper. "It's not enough that our mother will be dead in weeks because of you and your township-trash daughter. You had to involve Sam."

Annalisa stands. "Nice to see you again, Julien. What's it been . . . fifteen years?" she says, and slaps him hard across the face. *Bam.* He jerks back in shock with his hand to his cheek. The cops tense and wait for the violence to escalate. When no more comes, they go back to what they were doing. Maybe they see this kind of stuff all the time?

"My daughter's name is *Amandla*, and nobody, *nobody*, gets to call her trash. Same old Julien. You just repeat whatever Dad says."

A muscle twitches in Uncle Julien's jaw, and something inside him snaps. I see him go from stunned silence to burning anger in a split second. He grabs Annalisa by the shoulders and shakes her hard.

"And you still do whatever you like. No matter what it costs the people around you." His fingers dig into her flesh. "When are you going to think about anyone but yourself?"

"And when will you learn to think *for* yourself?!" Annalisa punches him in the chest, and he lets go of her. He grabs her wrists and pins her arms to her side. She yells and kicks him in the shin. Both are panting now. The female constable jumps to her feet, ready to throw them both into the cells. Lil Bit and Goodness stand and place themselves between the policewoman and us. In Sugar Town, family fights are a private matter.

"Enough!" I wrap my arms around Annalisa's waist and pull her backward. She resists.

"Coward." She spits the word at Julien.

"Spoiled bitch," he spits right back.

This is old stuff from their childhood, I think. Annalisa, the favorite child, and Julien, the overlooked prince. Sam wedges himself between the pair and lays a hand on his father's arm, calm.

"Dad, Dad. Listen to me," he says. "Nobody dragged me into anything. Amandla asked me to open the side gate so she could see Mayme, and I said yes."

"That girl is banned from the property for a good reason." Uncle Julien's cheek glows red from the slap and wrestling with Annalisa. "She has no idea how to behave around a sick old woman . . . unplugging her machines, taking her up to the garden without a nurse or medicine."

"Dad, that was me," Sam says. "Mayme asked me to take her to the garden, and I did. She said she needed to get out of her room and into the sun."

"Why would you do such a thing?" Uncle Julien asks. "It's dangerous."

"Because Mayme is sick, not dead," I say. "She'd rather have a few short weeks alive and aware than six years tied to a machine and in a fog. Her words. Not mine."

"My mother is a private person." Uncle Julien is superior and all knowing. "She doesn't share her emotions with strangers."

Nice. I've been promoted from a piece of township trash to a *lying* piece of township trash. Mayme's emotional radar is broken. Uncle Julien is not a sensitive soul. He is jealous and insecure. We can tussle over *my* place in the family tree for weeks, but nothing will change the fact that Annalisa was expected to take over the family business—not him. Even with my mother out of the competition for fifteen years, he has failed to prove his worth to his own father.

"You were warned to stay away from the house and you didn't listen," Uncle Julien continues, eager to put Annalisa and me back in our place. "It's time the two of you learned there are legal consequences to your actions."

"You're going to press charges?" My mouth says the words, but my brain cannot believe that anyone, even Uncle Julien, would sink that low. Like, *why*?

"Yes," Uncle says. "You have to take responsibility for—"

"Oh, please. Shut it, brah." I cut him off. Hurt or not, he is an ass. "Even you don't believe the crap you're saying."

I step forward, ready to explode. Annalisa holds me back. It's like we're a tag team.

"I'll handle this," she says with a dreamy smile, and please, God, do not let this be the start of a bizarre vision that demands we sing or dance or stay absolutely silent. Lil Bit and Goodness close the gap to stand on either side of me. Together we make a solid block of township girl power ready to throw down if that's what it comes to.

Annalisa says, "I live in a tin shack on the edge of the sugarcane fields. No money. No swimming pool. No nothing. You have everything. *Everything*, but I still wouldn't be you for all the gold in South Africa. Hanging around waiting for our father to die."

Uncle Julien tries to say something, but the truth of Annalisa's words silences him. He stares at the ground, breathing hard.

I learn something. *Truth is a powerful weapon.*

Then, as if called to life by a black magic spell, Neville appears. He walks past the front desk and into the office space and stops to shake hands with the police captain. Then he comes toward us. Annalisa takes a shaky breath to see him so close and in the flesh after so many years. Goose bumps prickle my arms. I'm scared for her. To be honest, though, Neville frightens the hell out of me, too.

"What are you doing here, Father?" Uncle Julien asks. "We agreed that I'd handle this."

Neville ignores Julien and walks up to Mother. He says nothing. His face is impossible to read.

"Oh, Father . . ." Annalisa studies the fine lines at the corners of his eyes and the thatch of white hair that was once black. "You've grown old."

He stands absolutely still, his heartbeat pulsing softly under the skin of his neck. Is he guilty, sad, disappointed? Or does he feel nothing at all?

"You had everything," he says. "And you threw it all away."

"That's not what happened." Annalisa is tender, almost kind. "It was you who threw me away. Your only daughter. Poor Daddy. So sad."

Neville's face stays blank, but the telltale heartbeat at the side of his neck kicks hard and fast. He is not bulletproof or dead to his emotions. He just knows how to hide them really well.

"You have no idea what you're talking about. Your memory is so full of holes, it's a wonder you remember your own name."

Annalisa sways on her feet, hit hard by Neville's words. I loop my arm around her waist, expecting her to melt down in the face of his meanness. Instead, she tilts her head to the side and studies him like a curious bird inspecting a bug.

"Did Mother tell you that I had trouble remembering?" she asks. "She wouldn't have. After she found me in the country, I told her to keep our meetings a secret. She doesn't trust you, and neither do I. How do you know about my memory?"

Excellent question. *What's the answer, old man?*

Neville stares at Annalisa for a beat before he turns and walks away. He stops to talk to the captain again and then moves past the front desk and out into the sunshine.

The police captain comes over to us.

"Mr. Bollard has dropped the charges," he says. "You're all free to go."

17

Being held by the police changes the way you see the world. The streets of Sugar Town, still as dirty and mean as when we left them, now glow in the bright light of freedom. *Amen*. Mrs. M holds Mayme's seedling box to her chest like it's a winning lottery ticket and invites us in for tea. Annalisa, who believes that neighbors are useful only in an emergency, surprisingly says yes. We sit on Mrs. M's shallow porch and drink red bush tea as Blind Auntie's knitting needles click through another scarf for the orphans, this one in a mix of bright orange and green.

"How many scarfs do you knit a year, Auntie?" I ask to cover Annalisa's strained silence. She might be rethinking her decision to break the rules that keep us apart from the others, but I'm not leaving. Our being here feels good.

"I knit three scarfs a week . . . If I have the wool, I also knit sweaters and hats." She pushes the plate of sugar biscuits across the table to Annalisa. "Eat, Miss Harden. A small woman needs meat on her bones to get through the winter."

Mrs. M nods in agreement, and Annalisa throws me a look that says, *And how does she know that I'm a small woman?*

I shrug. "Auntie knows things . . . like how our kitchen tap is dripping and that Mr. Khoza with the twins can fix it. She can hear a pin drop in Zimbabwe, isn't that right, Mrs. Mashanini?"

"True." Mrs. M chuckles. "She's blind, but she sees much."

Annalisa nibbles a sugar biscuit. "'There are none so blind as those who will not see,'" she says, and my jaw drops open to hear her quoting proverbs. "I was eighteen before I realized what the world really looked like. Before that, I only saw the pretty things that money could buy."

Mrs. M sips tea and thinks on what Annalisa has said. I wonder if she ever had the luxury of viewing the world as *pretty*? She's worked for over a decade in the emergency department of a busy hospital, so I seriously doubt it.

"And now that you live here in Sugar Town, Miss Harden, you can see all the ugly things that happen when there's no money," Mrs. M says. "Me? I'll take the pretty things and the money!"

Annalisa laughs, and the moment passes in quiet understanding. Blind Auntie pours a second round of tea, and Mrs. M passes the sugar biscuits around. We live side by side in Sugar Town. We breathe the same dusty air and walk the same dusty streets, but till now, we hardly knew each other. From now on, though, we are connected. We have each other.

Later, Annalisa and I walk the streets, holding hands. We're free to turn right, left, or go straight ahead, whatever we want.

After our brief time in police custody, it feels good to walk in any direction we choose. If Neville had pressed charges, we'd be in a much darker space right now, with court dates and lawyers and the threat, for me and my friends, of doing time in a youth center hanging over us. Which reminds me . . .

"Why did Neville have us arrested and then set free?"

"He did it to show us that he has the power to lock the door or keep it open," Annalisa says. "Classic Neville."

Sounds right, but there's more to his walkout. He's hiding something. I don't know what, exactly. The less we talk about Neville, the better, so I keep quiet. We pass Pastor Mbuli weeding the patch of balding lawn in front of the Christ Our Lord Is Risen! Gospel Hall in preparation for the Friday-morning prayer meeting. He waves, and I nod.

"Will I see you on Sunday, ladies?" Pastor Mbuli throws a flowering thistle onto a pile of winter weeds and brushes dirt from his hands. "Man and woman shall not live by bread alone but on every word that comes from the mouth of God."

"Sure thing, Father," I say. This Sunday, I will warm the back pew of the gospel hall to pray for Mayme's good health and because that is the excuse that I used to turn down Jacob Caluza's initial invitation. He might have forgotten all about me and moved on to chasing some new girl, but the feeling inside my stomach says he will check up on my whereabouts.

Annalisa leads us in the direction of the Ox Tongue and Fresh Offal Sold Here butcher stand on the corner of Cedric Way. She's moved up our weekly Sunday meal of four roast chicken legs to this evening, to celebrate our release from police custody. We reach the open-air meat market, the air thick with the smell of blood and innards, and join a long line of customers waiting for cheap cuts. William, the butcher, throws us a strange look while he chops a sheep's head in half. I worry for his fingers. One slip of the cleaver and his butchering days are over.

We reach the front of the line. Annalisa examines the meat on offer and makes unhappy noises about the quality, the way she might in a store with four walls and a spotless tiled floor.

"Four chicken legs," she orders in a brusque voice. "Only the best, William."

"Of course, Miss Harden," he says with a warm laugh that shakes his belly. William wraps the legs in brown paper and clears his throat. "Jacob tells me that the two of you are getting married and that he needs money to pay a bride price to your mother. Is this true, Amandla?"

I am stunned by Jacob's lie and embarrassed by the hopeful expression on William's face. He wants it to be true. He thinks that love and marriage will save Jacob. He believes that, young as I am, I will cure his brother.

"I'm sorry," I mumble. "That's all in his head. He asked me to a Sunday drinking session and I said no. There is no bride price."

Under Zulu custom, the bridegroom pays the bride's family an agreed sum for the honor of marrying their daughter. The price is paid in cows, cash, furniture, or new shoes for the bride's family, whatever they agree on. There's not one true word in the engagement story. Jacob must have lied to get money out of his brother. A common story. Ask around. Everyone knows somebody who's been fooled into handing over cash to an addict who's looking to get high.

"I'm a fool." William shakes his head, disappointed. "Jacob lied about everything, and I never saw the two of you together. But still. I hoped he was finally on the right path. A man needs a wife and children to make his life complete. Forgive me, Amandla. I should have known . . . a nice girl like you . . ."

"Did you give him the bride price?"

"I gave him a five-hundred-rand deposit and promised to pay the rest after I'd talked to you and Miss Harden." His shoulders slump. "He sounded lovestruck, and I was desperate to believe him."

William's sadness is deep and real, but I can't leave him with false hope. He has to know that he is right. Jacob and I will never happen.

"Sorry. I'm not the right woman for Jacob." I pay him in worn notes and take the chicken legs. Annalisa glares at me. I know that look. Questions are coming. I pull her away from the stand before she starts the interrogation.

Never fight in public is one of her rules. I let go of her arm and walk away from the listening ears of the people waiting in line. She catches up and leans close to me.

"Are you running around with that useless man, Amandla? Tell me the truth."

Suddenly, the two of us fighting on the street is no problem.

"How long have you known me?" I say back. We look normal as we walk down Cedric Way, but we are actually yelling in whispers out of the sides of our mouths. "You really think I'd hook up with a drug addict?"

"Well, did you encourage him?" she asks, and it's hard to keep my voice low and under control.

"If by *encouraging*, you mean bumping into him on the corner and walking down the street while he and his friends followed Lil Bit and me, then yes, I'm guilty. The only way to stop encouraging these guys is to stop breathing. Stop walking to school. Stop talking to my friends." I shake my head, disappointed by her question. "I'm not responsible for Jacob or any other man in Sugar Town."

Annalisa strokes my arm, and we both cool down. "I'm sorry," she says. "You're right. It's just . . . what makes Jacob think that he's good enough for you?"

We've lived in Sugar Town my entire life, but mother is still blind to reality.

"We are poor," I tell her straight out. "Jacob has seen us haggling with his brother over food. You may be white, but you still live here with no money and with me. Jacob's figured it out: I could do worse than him."

"Over my dead body," she says. "The next time I see him, I'll tell him exactly what he can do with that marriage proposal."

"Please, don't." I stop her right there. "Jacob made up a story to scam money from his brother. That's all it was. Talking to him will only make things worse. Ignore him. He'll soon find another girl to bother."

That's the hope, though I pity whoever catches his eye next. I push thoughts of Jacob aside. In my mind, Neville is a bigger threat. Jacob is deluded. Neville is sharp and vindictive. One word from him landed us inside a police station, and one word from him set us free. His sudden change of heart bothers me. His walkout puzzles me. He was happy to insult Annalisa till she asked him how he knew about her memory loss. How did he know?

The private investigator's report stashed inside my backpack might have the answer to that question and a dozen more. Mayme made me promise to keep the envelope sealed till after she dies, but if Neville has his way, Annalisa and me will never speak to her again.

Where's the harm in reading the file and keeping what I find out a secret? Nobody will ever know.

Except me.

* * *

My mind keeps me up while Annalisa snores. After our run-in with Uncle Julien and Neville at the police station, I fully expected her to have a nightmare. Instead, I am the one lying awake. I'm tortured by the report in my bag. Knowledge is power, Lil Bit says, and the quickest way for me to gain power over my grandfather is to tear open the envelope, but then I would be breaking the promise I gave to Mayme.

I slide out of bed and tiptoe into the kitchen. Moonlight slants in through the window above the sink and illuminates the floor. I unzip my backpack, pull out the report and my sketch pad, and lay them both on the table. Lil Bit also says that *a little knowledge is a dangerous thing*. There is a chance that the information inside the envelope will mess up the world as I know it.

But . . .

If the report gives up secrets that will help me understand who I am, who Annalisa is, how maybe we can make our lives better, then that's a risk I'm willing to take. I push my thumbnail under the sealed flap and push slowly upward. Finally, the truth will come out.

"Amandla?" Annalisa's voice stops everything. "What's the matter?"

"Nothing." I cover the report with the sketch pad, flip it open to a fresh page, and grab a pencil. "Just going over what happened this morning."

My pencil automatically glides across the paper, filling the blank space with fine lines and soft curves. I have no control over the image that takes form out of nowhere. Mother strikes a match, lights a candle, and holds it high to see better in the darkened room.

"Is that me?" she asks.

Is it?

I peek down at what I've drawn. Or rather, what my hand and my mind have drawn without my permission. It's Annalisa, the same age as she is now, but different. Her hair is tied up in a messy bun, a style she never wears. Her expression is cool and defiant. She is Annalisa Honey-Blossom Bollard. Rebel. Smart and outspoken.

"I remember . . ." she says. "I remember being that girl."

"I saw her inside you today, waking up from a long sleep."

"If I remembered more of the past, I could work my way back to her, but my mind switches off and on and I can't tell what's a dream and what's a memory." She brushes her fingertips along the edge of the page, making contact with that long-forgotten girl. "It's good to see her, to know some part of her is still there. What else is inside your book? Show me."

I flick to the sketch of Lil Bit, the avenging angel with wings made up of a hundred singing birds. I half expect Mother to laugh at my grand vision of Lil Bit Bhengu, who is so small and unassuming in regular circumstances that she can make herself invisible at will.

Instead, she says, "You got the heart and soul of her exactly right, Amandla. 'Though she be but little, she is fierce.'"

"Shakespeare?"

"From *A Midsummer Night's Dream*. We studied it in high school."

It takes a second for the importance of the moment to sink in. Annalisa remembered two facts from the past at the same time and in order. No mind static. No hesitation. Talking face-to-face with Grandpa and Uncle Julien has briefly opened up a door to the past. Maybe each new fact is a plank. Gather enough planks together and she can build a bridge to the past that will be strong enough to hold our weight as we journey back to get answers.

Annalisa flips to the next page of the sketchbook and her attention drifts away, the miracle of Shakespeare and high school fading faster than watercolors in the rain. One plank saved. For now.

The portrait of Grandpa Neville, sketched after our meeting at the hospital, is brutal and ugly. Harsh black lines and sharp angles make up his face. His pupils are tunnels that kill the light. It's embarrassing to see my loathing for him drawn so clearly.

"Now, this one's wrong," Annalisa says. "There's more to him, Amandla. Your grandfather can be kind, when it suits him. He made me laugh when I was a little. It's sad to think you'll never see that part of him."

Not my fault. He threw the first stone, and I returned the favor. Our relationship is biblical. An eye for an eye and a tooth for a tooth. Annalisa flips the page. The last sketch is of Mayme, freckle-nosed and smiling from her hospital bed. It's a pretty likeness of a sweet old lady, but it's false. Behind the smile and the warmth is an ocean of regret at failing to protect Annalisa. Even now, with death at her door, she prefers ignorance to facing the truth inside the report. She has a weak heart because she is weak. Even so, I can't hate her for it because that smile in the institute was all for me.

"You take after her," Annalisa says. "Same mouth and curve of the eyebrows. The same lovely cheekbones and smooth skin. Just a different color. That's all."

That difference means everything to Neville, it seems. He hates that I'm not the pretty little white granddaughter he should have had. Deep down, I want to believe there are other, less obvious, more complicated reasons for the terrible way he treated me on the rooftop garden. But there aren't. My hair is too frizzy and my body is too curvy for him to accept. My clothes are too ordinary. Finding fault in myself is easy, an old habit that comes with being not one race or the other.

The truth about Neville is simple, though. And it hurts.

He is a bigot.

He called me a kaffir.

The kaffir daughter that Annalisa drags around with her like a shameful ball and chain. Was Neville born with an aversion to black skin or did it creep into his mind over time? The poisonous roots of his racism are probably buried deep in South Africa's brutal history. Neville probably grew up in a house where black people were the servants and whites were the masters and the line between them never crossed. Till Annalisa fell in love with a Zulu man. What a shock that must have been.

I wish I could have seen his face the moment he found out.

"Do I take after my father?" I ask Annalisa, hoping the door to the past is still open enough to let another memory through into the present. A name would be good. *Boris. Phineas. Homer. Funani. Shaka Zulu.* I'll take any of them. Annalisa only ever calls him "your father." He is a series of faded images: A sharp dresser. A dancer. A wonderful kisser.

When I try to imagine him, he is never alone. He is always with Annalisa, the two of them standing on a terrace at night with the moon shining on the ocean behind them. She laughs, giddy in love, and he sweeps her into his arms, the two of them melting into each other. I want to love someone that way, too. Despite the fact that it hurt my mother forever.

"You have his hair." Annalisa winds a curl around her finger. "And sometimes, when you're cooking at the stove, I get a flash of a man scrambling eggs with his sleeves rolled up."

"Was he a cook, too?"

"No. He liked to cook. Same as you."

I cook because cold baked beans and soggy peas from a can are not real food. When Mrs. M figured out that our meals mostly came from the tinned-food shelves at the Supa-Value, she taught me to make the basics. Boiled eggs. Stir-fried onion with fresh chili and spinach. Soup made from whatever was in the kitchen. Black beans and rice. Cheap food, but warm and filling.

As for Annalisa's memory of a man scrambling eggs at the stove with rolled-up sleeves? I don't trust it. It might be my father or one of the dozens of servants who cooked and cleaned and indulged her for most of her young life. Me included. Still, I'll take what I can get.

My father:

1. He was a Zulu bartender.
2. He had curly hair.
3. He made a scrambled egg to remember.

Three more planks to build a bridge to the past. Annalisa yawns and stretches out, exhausted from the fight with Julien and from the shock of coming face-to-face with Neville for the first time in years. Approximately fifteen years is my guess.

"Come to bed," she says. "We'll see my mother again. I promise."

In Sugar Town, promises are cheap, but the hope they create is priceless. They also help us to sleep and to dream of the good things waiting for us around the corner. Mayme is out of our reach for the moment. Our hearts know the obstacles. This week or maybe the next, Mayme will figure out that she is an individual free and separate from her husband. That all she has to do is walk out of the gates and come find us.

18

"What happens now?" Lil Bit kicks a soccer ball across the dirt field where Goodness plays goalie for the up-and-coming Sugar Town Shakers. A cold wind nips my nose, and dust swirls around my ankles. A few days ago, it was impossible to imagine the three of us trading shots during the holidays.

"What happens now is *nothing.*" I accidentally kick the ball far to the right of Goodness, who runs it down with easy grace. "Next time around, Neville might press charges and we'll end up in real trouble. It's not worth the risk."

"He won't press charges." Goodness is confident. "Your gramps is hiding something. That's why he walked away when your mum asked him about her memory. He couldn't answer. Or didn't want to."

Reading the report is the only way to find the facts, but Mother waking up at the exact moment that I started to open the envelope? That was an omen.

"I'm not sure that Neville has a conscience, but it doesn't matter in any case," I say. "Fighting him is too risky. There's no way to tell how he'll react, and we have all the problems we can handle right here in Sugar Town."

"So he wins?" Lil Bit huffs.

"The battle. Not the war."

Sam's mobile number, we found out this morning, is disconnected. Uncle Julien must have him locked down for the holidays. Three teenage girls up against a mean old man with something to hide? That's a fight we'll never win. Tough go, but there it is.

"Here's what we do." Goodness bounces the soccer ball from one knee to the other, thinking. "First, we forget the rules our mothers taught us. Forget good manners and smiles and high-heel shoes. We ain't no ladies watching from the sideline. We take action."

"All right." Lil Bit is spellbound by the picture that Goodness paints of us. "What comes second?"

"We go to your grandpa Bollard's office in the city and we fuck him up."

"And exactly how do we fuck him up?" I ask. "With an iron pipe or a big stick?"

"Both. But only if we have to." Goodness is dead serious.

"I'm not going to the youth center, my sister," I tell her. "The girls inside those places are rough. I won't last a day."

Goodness will be fine. Her father will buy her freedom while Lil Bit and me will be left to serve out our sentence for assault with a deadly weapon. Hurting Neville is fine in theory, but in reality, me and Lil Bit will be the ones who suffer.

"Wait." Lil Bit's eyes shine bright. "We won't need to use force. Your gramps called you a kaffir, remember?"

Yes, I will remember that insult for years and even decades to come.

"Think about it," she says to Goodness and me. "Who uses that kind of filthy language in Nelson Mandela's South Africa? I'll tell you. A prejudiced man. A bigot who was brought up with racist attitudes and hasn't changed his thinking. In his head, black and mixed people are still inferior. That's our way in, right there."

Goodness reaches over and taps the center of Lil Bit's forehead with the tip of her finger. "Slow that big brain of yours down and tell us what you mean. Use small words. What's the plan?"

This time, Lil Bit does not step back from Goodness or jerk away from her touch. Instead, she lets out a shaky breath and smiles, pleased by the attention and the mention of her big brain, which a less confident girl than Goodness Dumisa might find intimidating.

"If Amandla's skin color bothers her gramps, then we can use that against him. All we have to do is turn up. Three dark girls from the township waiting outside his office? People will talk. The receptionist. The office assistant. The security guards. Word about us will spread. And what does the boss man get up to after hours with those girls, they'll wonder."

"Eww. I don't want people to think that we . . ." The words dry up. I can't even put my thoughts into words. Neville in an intimate situation is just too disturbing to imagine. "Besides, if Neville really is a bigot, nobody will believe that he'd . . . you know."

Lil Bit rolls her eyes. "Are you serious? This country was founded by hypocrites who said one thing and then did whatever pleased them after dark! Besides, your grandpa's employees will eat up the idea that he's been naughty. We may not get into the main office, but our being there will shake things up."

The logic behind Lil Bit's plan sinks in. The odds of three black teenagers making it past the ring of Bollard employees that guard Neville's lair is close to nil. Now I see that we don't have to breach the corporate floor at all. Instead of begging for entry, we can put on a show for everyone to gawk at. It might actually be fun.

"Sharp thinking," I tell Lil Bit. "We'll be township girls with bad attitudes."

"Yeah. I've always wanted hoop earrings, a crop top, and tight, tight leggings. I'd do it, too, except the church ladies will see me and then tell my mum. I can't go out in public dressed like that," Goodness says.

"Maybe Lewis could drive us, and you could wear whatever you want! He did offer to help." The moment the words are out, I regret them. Lewis and I have spoken to each other three times and suddenly it's okay for me to ask him to do me a favor? Thinking that he owes me anything but politeness is an Annalisa-level delusion. I rush to take back the words, but Goodness gets in before me.

"About that . . ." She rolls the soccer ball against a rickety grandstand that creaks and sways in the wind. It's a death trap that offers the possibility of "death by fire," "death by stadium collapse," and "death by crushing crowd" as part of the experience. Three good reasons why Annalisa and I never attend the deafening Saturday matches.

"There is this one thing . . ." Goodness sweeps down, grabs the soccer ball, and passes it to me with an underhand flick. It lands straight in my hands, a gift from a sports star to a toddler. Goodness Dumisa is uncomfortable.

"My, uh . . ." She stops and starts again. "My brother Lewis is interested in you, but don't get your hopes up. My parents have a list of Zulu girls lined up for him, and you're not Zulu, so you're not on it . . ."

I duck my head to hide the anger that shoots through me. Having a Zulu father makes me part Zulu, but not the "pure Zulu" that Lewis's parents want for him. Funny. I am not white enough for my own grandfather, and I'm too light to get on Mr. and Mrs. Dumisa's list of acceptable girls. *Too black. Too white. Never quite right.*

Being excluded hurts more than it should, but damn! It doesn't matter that Lewis is out of my league. I like him. I want to kiss those plush lips and run my fingertips across those insanely cute dimples that appear when he smiles. Who am I kidding? *Like* is too small a word to describe my feelings. I want that boy in my life, but does he like or want me enough to go against his parents' wishes?

For all I know, Lewis has already decided to walk away from the pulse of warm feeling that beats between us. Tears sting my eyes. I deliberately throw the ball long over Lil Bit's shoulder and then chase it down. I need a private moment to pull myself together.

"Amandla . . ."

Lil Bit calls out my name. She wants to help, but I need a hot minute to feel the pain of losing my white grandmother *and* the boy *who now I know actually likes me back*!

I crouch to retrieve the ball from under a stack of blue plastic chairs. Black sneakers covered in sawdust step into my field of vision. Lewis. *Speak of the devil*, the church ladies say, *and he will appear*. A second pair of shoes, off-white with worn heels, step into the space next to Lewis's sneakers, beside which they appear comically small. The white shoes belong to Annalisa.

* * *

Annalisa and Lewis stand side by side: white and black, small and tall. Seeing them together stuns me. They've never met or talked. Annalisa is famously odd, and the Dumisa family is famously rich inside the township; they are practically strangers. Annalisa's creased blue jeans and messy bun get my attention. Nothing short of an emergency would push her out of the house and into the streets looking less than "proper."

"What is it?" I ask. "What's happened?"

Lewis says, "I went to your house and your ma showed me the note that you left on the table. I guessed where the three of you might be."

That does not answer my question. I try again.

"Oh, uh . . . What's up?"

"Can you talk?" he says. "It's important."

Heavens! The Dumisa family are serious about warning me off. First Goodness and now Lewis in person. I don't need to hear it twice.

"Don't bother. I understand. You're Zulu and I'm mixed. Goodness told me about the list. We'll never match up, and that's fine with me."

Lewis frowns, and I realize, too late, that I have jumped to conclusions. Lewis is here to talk about something else entirely.

Idiot.

"Tell her," Annalisa says as Lil Bit and Goodness sidle closer.

"Jacob Caluza and two of his friends dropped by the Build 'Em Up for a talk. He says you and him are together. His brother is collecting the bride price and I have no business walking you home or talking to you."

How does Jacob know that Lewis walked me home the day before yesterday? Oh. The shadows moving under the mango trees outside the toilet block. It wasn't my imagination. Jacob was watching me from the end of the lane. I almost shiver.

"You know none of that is true. It's all in Jacob's head."

"That's what I thought," Lewis says. "My brothers and me will find him and tell him, politely, that you're not interested and he should leave you alone."

"What if he keeps on?"

"I'll tell him that I will walk you home whenever I want and I'll talk to you whenever I want." Then he adds, "But only if that's what you want."

Goodness groans, but I am melting. Lewis's unique combination of clumsy and kind, with the added bonus of juiciness, is rare.

Do I want? Yes, I do.

"All right. We can talk and walk whenever you'd like."

Lewis smiles. I return his smile, and the moment stretches out with no need for words. We are two flies stuck in honey and drowning in sweetness. I don't care about the list of Zulu girls, or our different circumstances, or being disowned by my mother's family. My whole vision is taken up with Lewis Dumisa. Annalisa clears her throat, and I glance her way. She glares at me. I receive her message: *Schoolwork before boys, miss. That's the rule.* After graduation, I am free to ride in cars with boys and park out there behind the bleachers. But that is two years away. I narrow my eyes and send her a return message: *I can do my homework and have a boyfriend at the same time. It's not rocket science!*

Annalisa gives a small nod, agreeing to a balance between attending school and spending time with Lewis. Good, that settles it. I swing my attention to the boy in question, and honestly, I could stare at him all day. The warm feeling that connects us holds strong. I feel it pulsing inside my chest, right in time with my heartbeat. Lovely!

Goodness coughs, and Lil Bit giggles. The noise breaks the spell and reminds me that there are other people in the world besides Mr. Juicy Lips And Gorgeous Dimples. How long did Lewis and I gawk at each other in silence? Twenty seconds or two minutes? There's no way to tell. Time just disappeared.

"You'll talk to Jacob?" Annalisa says to Lewis. "I hate to think of him walking the streets, saying whatever he wants about Amandla."

"Sure thing, Miss Harden. Me and my brothers will find him and have a face-to-face. If he doesn't listen, my father has a few friends in the police. I hope it doesn't go that far."

"Thank you for doing that," I say. "And please thank your brothers also."

"Soon as I get back to the Build 'Em Up." Lewis sticks out his hand. I take it and we shake with a clumsy up-and-down motion. Amateurs. Goodness pulls a face and grins.

"Smooth," she says. "Go back to work before you kill your chances, brah. It's the safest place for you."

Lewis backs away and straight into Annalisa, who loops her arm through his with a cool smile and bright eyes. I know that face. Poor Lewis. He's landed in hot water. She's about to commence an assault on his intentions.

"Stay with your friends, Amandla." Annalisa uses her steely *do not test me* voice. "Lewis will drop me off on his way back to work."

"Of course, Miss Harden." Lewis surrenders with the grace that Goodness displays on the soccer field. Fighting Annalisa is a waste of energy, and somehow, he knows it.

"Wait . . ."

My mother ignores me and strolls off with Lewis, her prisoner, in a firm grip. She does not slow down or turn around. On the way here, Jacob was her focus. Now that focus has switched to Lewis. Annalisa will grill him on everything from his favorite colors to his future plans. And somewhere along the line, she will tell him that Sugar Town isn't forever. That I am meant for bigger and better things. University. A job in the city and a house on the beach. All that she lost. Our leaving is a far-fetched dream that we have lived on for years. Except now, I think, what's the rush?

19

Annalisa shakes me awake at dawn on Saturday morning. Faint blue light falls through the kitchen window, and the Khozas' rooster crows four doors down. I groan and snuggle under the blankets. During the holidays, I get to sleep in till nine. I have nowhere to go and nothing in particular to do. "Get up," Annalisa says. "We have to tidy the house. Visitors are coming."

We never get visitors, and our house is always tidy. Floors scrubbed twice a week. Dishes washed and put away. Cobwebs swept out into the lane whenever they appear. The bedsheets and blankets tucked tight to the mattress corners. What is there to do?

"What visitors?" I ask when Annalisa taps my shoulder like a pecking hen. "When are they coming?"

"I don't know who they are," she says. "Just that they're on their way."

Arguing is a waste of breath. Once Annalisa's mind is made up, that's it. Resisting her will is futile. I go with the flow. I get out of bed, grab a broom, and attack the clean spaces under our beds. A light fluff of dust comes back. "Don't forget to do the ceiling." Annalisa dips a brush into a bucket of soapy water and starts scrubbing the floor of the kitchen area. It's a wonder the linoleum hasn't worn through to the ground from the friction of the bristles. "The house has to be perfect."

One hour later, my shoulders ache and my knees throb from scrubbing, sweeping, and dusting to make the house ready for our phantom visitors. The sudden cleaning binge should worry me, but Annalisa is relaxed and happy. She hums through the work. When we finish, she hugs me and smiles.

"Perfect," she says. "Now you can go play with your friends."

I pull on jeans, a T-shirt, and a "pre-loved" camo jacket and skate out the door before Annalisa decides to clean the dirt in the front yard.

* * *

"Your turn." Goodness throws a girls' magazine into my lap from the comfort of her double bed, where Lil Bit sits beside her like a cat in the sunshine. It's late afternoon, and we lie around in a post-lunch coma. Walking, talking, taking lame shots at goal (none of which get past Goodness), and a visit to the Build 'Em Up to find the address of the Bollard Company headquarters and to plan our assault on Neville's reputation made the day go fast.

I flip the magazine open to the advice column, always good for a laugh. I read out loud in a high, girlie voice: "'Dear Sisi, My grandmother says that cucumbers are the devil's food and makes me wear gloves whenever I wash or cut them. I don't understand why she thinks that cucumbers are sinful or why she says that I'm too young to be left alone in a room with them. Can you explain what's going on?'"

We collapse on the bed laughing. Sinful cucumbers. It's too crazy to be true!

Two sharp knocks rattle Goodness's bedroom door. She springs to her feet and pulls it open. Lewis, dressed in an old T-shirt and khaki work pants, stands in the hallway. My heart lifts inside my chest. This boy walked Annalisa home yesterday and told her all that she needed to know. Blue is his favorite color. His middle name is Thando, which means *beloved* in Zulu. He loves to work with his hands. When he's finished training at the Build 'Em Up, he will become a carpenter. *Yes, he can scramble eggs.* I got home to Annalisa in a sunny mood. Gorgeous-dimples Lewis Dumisa made my mother smile.

He makes me smile, too.

"Well?" Goodness demands when Lewis cranes his neck to spy into the room. "What do you want?"

"Miss Harden is looking for Amandla," he says. "I asked her in, but she's waiting on the porch."

"Annalisa is here?" My voice is thin and high. "Now?"

"Yebo."

Annalisa does not drop in on anyone for any reason. Ever. I slip into the hallway and say over my shoulder, "You know where to find me."

Lewis leads me past the living room, where his mother sits in a plastic-covered recliner chair at the head of a circle of important town ladies, all of them dressed to shine. Mrs. Dumisa smiles and waves goodbye to me, and the sparkling purple polish on her nails catches the light from the diamante chandelier. She wears a matching purple dress and white high-heeled shoes with purple stars sewn onto the leather.

I was nervous to meet her, but she turned out to be nice-ish. Goodness introduced us. She gave Lil Bit and me a nod of approval before turning her attention back to the ladies. I doubt she remembers our names.

"This way." Lewis presses his hand to the small of my back, where it fits perfectly. The intimate gesture gets his mother's attention, and I find that I don't care one way or the other what she thinks of me, of us. Yesterday, on the sports field, Lewis and I told each other we would be together whenever it pleased us. Our being together this minute pleases me fine.

Lewis opens the front door and pulls me gently onto the shallow porch that runs the length of the house: a perfect winter sun trap. Annalisa waits at the foot of the stairs with her hair twisted into a neat bun and pinned at the nape of her neck. She wears blue jeans and a long-sleeved shirt with a collar. Simple. Stylish.

"Are we going somewhere?" I ask, afraid at first, and then relieved to see her smile. Thank the Lord. Annalisa is fine.

"Come quick," she says. "Mrs. M picked too many broad beans from her garden, and she's invited us for dinner. The children eat early, so we have to get back soon."

Dinner at Mrs. M's and Annalisa said yes. That's a first. Taking tea with Mrs. M and Blind Auntie broke the ice and made neighbors of us all. I head for the stairs, vaguely aware of Goodness and Lil Bit standing in the doorway. The living room curtains twitch open. Mrs. Dumisa and the ladies appear at the window, eager to see what's going on.

"Do I have to change?" I ask, and take the stairs down. Mrs. M picked the exact right amount of vegetables to feed her family *and* Annalisa and me. She is an Ubuntu machine, building connections inside the community with love and green beans. Lewis reaches around me to push the garden gate open.

"Here," he says. "I'll walk you home."

"You know that walking me home for a second time this week will get people talking." I want him to be 100 percent sure of what he's getting into.

He shrugs. "My mother and her friends can say whatever they like. I'm old enough to make up my own mind and I'm of a mind to walk you and your mother home."

Lil Bit and Goodness follow us through the gate and into London Avenue. They hang back to give us space. "It's true that my mother has a list of potential girlfriends, but I say that we make up our own lists and choose who goes on them. What do you think?"

It's a wonderful idea, but I don't answer his question right away. Instead, I ask one of my own.

"And how many names are on your list, Mr. Dumisa?" Lewis likes me, but he also has his pick of silky-skinned girls with small waists and curved backsides.

"One name only," he says.

"Oh . . ." A tingling feeling fills my chest. "Do I know her?"

"You might," he says. "She lives in Sugar Town, but she has one foot on the road to somewhere else. Some people say that she's a snob, but that's because her mother has taught her good manners. She doesn't swear or fight in the street. She gets good grades and stays home instead of going out all the time. She's different, and that's why I like her."

"I think I know who you mean," I say. "I hear that her mother is strict, though."

Annalisa picks up the word *mother* and tucks me close to her side. We turn the corner into Harlem Street, and Lewis looks ahead, scanning for potential dangers. The street is quiet. Long rows of minivan taxis wait to take passengers to Durban and Richards Bay and destinations as far away as Jozi. Johannesburg, that is.

I check over my shoulder to make sure that Goodness and Lil Bit haven't fallen too far behind. They are too busy talking to notice anyone but each other. Lil Bit laughs at something Goodness says, and it clicks. The world has opened up for Lil Bit and me over the last few days. We were a country of two. Now our tight circle has expanded to include new family and friends: Mayme, Sam, Goodness, and Lewis . . . I take a second as I walk side by side with Mr. Juicy to feel gratitude. There's that warm tingling inside my chest again.

"And you?" Lewis asks. "How many names are on your list?"

"One name for now." I keep my vision trained on the road ahead. Lewis turns his head toward me. I can feel him studying my face, but I don't look back at him. I'm afraid of another extended *looking at each other for way too long* episode.

We turn down my shortcut, an alley that takes us onto Winnie Mandela Way. I never go down this way at night, but now, in the afternoon and with Lewis by my side, I feel no fear at all. It makes me realize that I feel safe with him. It also reminds me that the township is a hard place for a girl, any girl, to ever feel safe. How sweet it would be to lay all my problems down, even for the length of this walk, to know that I have Lewis to help me cope with mother's ups and downs and maybe even to build the life I want for myself. But what happens when Lewis isn't here?

Then again, he *is* here. Right now. And it feels wonderful. I see that my shoelace is undone and stop to tie it. Annalisa walks ahead, and my fingers fumble with the knot. She is five steps ahead of me and almost at a broken-down section of wall. The wind blows honeysuckle perfume into the lane.

I hear feet on gravel behind the wall, and the hairs on my arms stand up.

20

"Annalisa! Stop!" I jump up and run full speed to close the gap between us. She's right in front of the broken wall now, her head turned to catch what I've said.

That's when Jacob Caluza steps out from behind the wall with a knife in his hand.

"Mummy . . ." I grab her around the waist and try to pull her away. My right hand goes out to shield us from the blade. Jacob slashes my palm. I cry out in pain and stumble sideways. Jacob raises his knife, aims it at my chest. Annalisa puts herself between Jacob and me as the knife falls. She screams "No!" as she blocks the blade that's meant for my heart. Then she makes a sound that I've never heard before: a groan and a soft sigh of breath that whispers in the lane. Jacob pulls the knife from above her left breast, and she falls to the ground. Blood sprays from the wound. It makes a river in the dirt.

"Mum!" I sob. "Mummy . . ."

Jacob steps over her to get to me. "You think that boy will marry you?" He slashes the knife at my stomach and misses. "You think you can do better than me, girl?"

He charges with the knife aimed right at me. Lewis jumps forward and slams a fist into the side of Jacob's head, but he shakes it off, drawing energy from the drugs racing through his system.

Lewis lands a second punch that sends Jacob reeling. Jacob straightens up, dazed, and comes at me again. He trips and falls against me with the knife wedged between us. I slam his chest back to push him off me. Lil Bit appears out of nowhere. She tries to grab Jacob's knife hand and gets a smack across the face for her trouble.

She lands hard on the ground, and I lose track of her. I grab Jacob's wrist and twist with all my strength. He's stronger than me, too strong for me to hold him off for more than a moment. I turn away from the gleam in his eyes and see Lil Bit holding Annalisa in her arms.

Jacob struggles to free his hand, teeth clenched, waving his knife in the air. An object flies toward us, and I hear the crunch of bone. Jacob rocks to the side and falls against me. He's been hit in the head with something heavy. Warm blood soaks my shirt, and a blunt object presses into my chest. Pain radiates out to my arms, my neck, my shoulders.

Lewis pulls the barely conscious Jacob back by the throat and throws him to the ground. Goodness stands over him with a brick raised high above her head, ready to smash Jacob's skull again if he moves an inch.

Blood gurgles from Jacob's mouth. His limbs twitch and go slack. The knife handle sticks out of his bony chest. His shirt is bunched up, so I can see where the blade is buried near his heart. I collapse against the wall, dazed and shaking. My mind is frozen. I open my mouth to speak and no words come out. Then I hear Lil Bit calling Annalisa's name and saying, "Stay with us. Hang on."

"Is she breathing?" I gasp out the words. "Is she alive, Lil Bit?"

Lil Bit puts her ear to Mother's mouth. "Still breathing," she says.

Goodness takes off her T-shirt and presses the balled-up material to the bleeding wound on Annalisa's breast. "We have to get her to a hospital. She needs a doctor."

The Sugar Town Clinic closes at 4:00 p.m., and the nearest hospital is forty minutes away by car on roads filled with potholes. I try to think what to do next.

"Mrs. Mashanini." My brain is working again. "She's a nurse. She can help."

"Show us the way." Lewis lifts Annalisa into his arms and cradles her to his chest. "I'll follow."

My mind goes blank. I don't know where to go or which direction to turn. Lil Bit grabs my hand and pulls me toward Sisulu Street. She has made the journey to our shack a hundred times, and now she leads the way. I stumble along beside her, soaked in blood and in shock.

"Follow me." Lil Bit cuts across Sisulu Street and scoots into our lane. Children play hopscotch and soccer in the dust.

They stop and stare. Others run to their homes to spread the news. The white woman is whiter than white, her red blood dripping in the dirt.

I give Goodness my key. "Go. Open the door for Lewis."

She bolts ahead and unlocks our door. I break right and catch Mrs. Mashanini hurrying to her gate to see what's going on.

"Help," I croak. "Annalisa is hurt. She is bleeding bad."

"Hurt how?" Mrs. M demands, and takes in my blood-soaked shirt.

"Jacob Caluza stabbed her."

"Go. Keep pressure on the wound. I'll get my things and come right now."

"Hurry," I beg. "Please."

"I will do what I can. Now go to her. Tell her to stay with you. Tell her to hold on to the sound of your voice."

* * *

I flick on the electric light. Mrs. Mashanini enters, and with Lil Bit's and Goodness's help, she rips away the clothing around Annalisa's wound. Then Lil Bit and Goodness light candles and place them on the dresser beside Annalisa's cot to give Mrs. Mashanini extra light in the "bedroom" area. Lewis is either gone or just waiting outside to give us space to work. I hold Annalisa's hand and ignore the pain radiating from the cut in my palm.

My body is a hard, cold stone. I am terrified of life without Annalisa. Despite the fact that her visions and strange behavior drive me insane, her love is what makes me, *me*.

I bargain with God. I make promises to the angels. Give her back to me and I will:

1. Be a kind and good neighbor.
2. Help others without being asked.
3. Embrace the way of Ubuntu.

After half an hour or less or more, I can't tell, Mrs. Mashanini mops the sweat from Annalisa's face and sits back with a sigh. She has done all she can with what little she had in her nursing kit. When the bandages ran out, we pulled the blue sheet dress into strips to bandage up the jagged wound on Annalisa's chest.

I confess, I was happy to see it go.

Mrs. M turns and looks me directly in the eye.

"Your mother has lost a lot of blood. I cleaned the wound, stitched, and bandaged it, but she's still in danger. If the knife damaged her heart . . . We need a doctor to see to her, Amandla. Not tomorrow. Not after waiting five hours in the emergency ward, but now. Tonight. Do you know anyone that can help?"

When we are sick, Annalisa and I take potluck at the Sugar Town Clinic along with everyone else. I do not know any doctors. But wait. I do know a *priest*. Father Gibson. He might have a connection to someone with medical skills who'd be willing to come out to a township before the sun goes down. Worth a call.

I grab Annalisa's leather bag and rummage inside for the card that Father Gibson gave her. I pull out a ball of string, a starling feather, and an old Durban postcard addressed to a Mr. William Williams. The card is neatly tucked in a side pocket with Father Gibson's name, address, and phone number in black ink on the plain white paper.

"Can I use your phone?" I ask Goodness, who wears a turquoise-colored T-shirt with a frayed neckline that we found in Annalisa's drawer. The T-shirt that she used to staunch the wound will have to be burned. That amount of blood can't be washed out.

"Of course." Goodness hands me her diamond-bling mobile. It is the brightest object in our dull shack.

I dial the number, and the phone on the other end rings. And rings. *Pick up*, I beg Father Gibson. *Please!* A moment later, the receiver lifts.

"Father Gibson? It's Amandla Harden. Annalisa's daughter." I cut him off before the routine exchange of pleasantries. Instead, I barrage him with all the information that's important. "Annalisa is hurt. Stabbed. She needs a doctor. The infirmary is closed, and even if we get her to a hospital, it might take a while to get treatment. You promised to help her any way that you could."

"Give me your address," Father Gibson says, and I tell him that we live in the lane between Tugela and Sisulu. *Ask anyone in Sugar Town. They'll know.* "Tell your mother to hold on. I'm coming with help."

"Thank you, Father." I end the call and the muscles in my jaw and neck relax. Help is on the way. "Will she be all right for another hour or two, Mrs. M?"

Mrs. M says, "I'll pray on it," and I go to give Goodness back her mobile. The phone's diamond cover is stained with blood from my hands. Rubbing the surface against the leg of my jeans makes things worse. Red and pink streaks across most of the diamonds, and the cover will have to be replaced to stop the blood from flaking off after it dries.

"Sorry." I hand the phone back. "It's ruined."

"Blood diamonds," Goodness says, deadpan. "Very African."

What she says is funny, and I laugh, high-pitched and witchy. I laugh and I cannot stop. I laugh till I am bent over double and gasping for breath.

"Hysteria," Mrs. M says. "Soon the bubble will burst."

Lewis enters the shack. His T-shirt is soaked red from holding Mother close to his chest, but it's his face that gets my attention. His jaw is tight, and his skin has lost its color. He rinses his hands at the sink for a long time and cleans the blood from under his fingernails. Then he lights the gas stove and puts water on to boil.

"What happened? Where did you go?" I ask, all tense and worried.

"To wait with Jacob's body till the police arrived," he says.

Oh, that's right. We left Jacob lying in the laneway with a knife sticking out of his chest. I'm ashamed to realize that I haven't given his death a second thought . . . not when the knife that he plunged into Annalisa's chest might have cut her heart. Still, it's awful to imagine Lewis standing alone in the falling dark with Jacob's body going cold on the ground.

"I'm sorry. Thank you for doing that," I tell Lewis as he throws loose tea leaves into a teapot and pours boiling water over them. The smell of the brewing tea hits my nostrils, and something unwinds inside me. *What a day. What a terrible day.*

I rest my palms on my knees. Suddenly, it's hard to find oxygen and hard to see through the tears that blur my vision and run down my face. Racking sobs replace my earlier laughter, and Lil Bit throws an arm around my shoulder. I stand and lean against her, and Goodness leans against me. They hold me tighter, and I don't want them to ever let me go.

"Pour the tea," Mrs. Mashanini tells Lewis over my sobs. "Tears and tea are good medicine."

Mrs. Mashanini guides us to the kitchen table with a brusque, "Come, girls. Let Miss Harden rest."

I dissolve into the chair, drained of laughter and tears. Lewis sets a cup of red bush tea on the table.

"Let me see that hand, Amandla," Mrs. M says. I uncurl my fingers to expose my slashed palm. She examines the cut and cleans it with soap and warm water. Then she applies disinfectant. It stings but it feels good. The sensation wakes me up. I think of the moments before we turned into the alley and how good it felt to walk with Lewis and the others. Then I remember that it was my idea to take the shortcut. My heart sinks.

"I shouldn't have taken us down that alley."

"What?" Lewis kneels near me as Mrs. M applies the last of the bandages. He is exhausted from the fight with Jacob and from carrying Annalisa from the alley to our house, but he is maybe more beautiful than ever. Brave. Kind. Strong, inside and out. "None of this is your fault, Amandla. Don't even think that."

I blink back fresh tears.

"If Jacob had stayed home this afternoon," Lil Bit says, "nothing would have happened. If Jacob had dropped his knife and walked away, same thing. He's responsible for everything bad that went down today. Not you. Not me. Not your mum or Goodness or Lewis. You aren't to blame."

"That's right," Goodness says.

Lil Bit continues, "And I'm not to blame for what my father did and you're not to blame for your mother's mixed-up memories. We are ourselves. We don't control other people."

"Amen." Mrs. M finishes bandaging my hand. "No stitches necessary," she says, and downs her mug of tea in one hit. The last hour or so has sucked the energy from her but has also, strangely, made her glow with inner light. Healing people is her calling.

Lewis stands and rests his hand on my shoulder, a soft touch. "I'll be back soon. You rest."

"Where are you going now?" Fear sharpens my voice, and I grab hold of his hand, impulsive. He squeezes my fingers.

"I have to go and tell William Caluza what happened to his brother. The police told me where to pick up the body. I have to tell him that, too."

Goodness throws Lewis a hard look that reminds me of her father, Mr. Dumisa, the businessman/gangster. "Take Themba, Stevious, and Daddy with you. That way William will understand that this is the end of it."

Oh, of course. William might take it into his head to retaliate for Jacob's death by coming after whoever killed him. Even though it was Jacob who fell on his own knife. Blood feuds can simmer and boil over behind Sugar Town's closed doors.

"Be careful," I tell Lewis, who nods and walks out of the room in his blood-soaked shirt and jeans. He is going to tell William that his baby brother is dead and that is where the violence ends. There will be no payback, no more bloodshed.

Annalisa's chest rises and falls. Her skin is pale, and I pray that Father Gibson gets here soon.

She was right. There are visitors in the house and more are on the way.

How did she know?

21

The clock strikes 7:00 p.m., and the light outside the window has faded to black. Annalisa lies still and pale in her cot, her chest barely moving under the blue bandages. I go to the door and check the lane for signs of Father Gibson. No one yet. The wait is agonizing. Mrs. M shoos Goodness and Lil Bit home to wash and find clean clothes while we listen for approaching footsteps. Another hour passes. Still nothing.

I sit on the edge of Mother's cot and hold her hand. I tell her, "Hang on. Father Gibson is on his way. He's bringing a doctor."

If she hears me, she gives no sign. In desperation, I lie and say that I have found all the pieces of her story. When she wakes, I will tell her every detail, down to the name of the dirt road that leads to the mountains she remembers seeing on the horizon.

Voices filter in from the outside, and I run to open the door. Father Gibson and a short black woman holding a doctor's bag stand in the empty yard with uncomfortable expressions. Whatever they imagined they'd find in Sugar Town, our shack is worse.

"Come in, Father." I cross the yard and hook my arm through his. Our neighbors gather in the lane to hear the news. They expect it to be either *The white woman has gone to the ancestors*, or *Praise be. It was not her time.*

Father Gibson clears his throat and pretends that the dusty air and the rusted buildings don't bother him. Maybe they don't. Maybe he just sees his fellow human beings bound together by poverty. The doctor struggles. She's dressed in a raw-silk pantsuit and a long woolen coat that ties at the waist. Gorgeous, expensive clothes. Her immaculate hair hangs down her back in a single woven braid. She is dazzling but nervous. Bet this is her first visit to a township.

"This way," Mrs. Mashanini calls from inside, where she waits to assist. "Quickly, please."

Father Gibson moves aside, and the doctor walks through the kitchen to the cot where Annalisa lies. She kneels on the grass mat and takes Annalisa's pulse. After a few moments, she lays Mum's arm back down on the bed. With her thumb, she pulls down the skin under Annalisa's right eye, and with the other hand, she shines a penlight into it. The pupil contracts. A good sign?

"More light," she tells Mrs. M, who grabs a candle from the dresser top and holds it high to cast a bright circle in the dimness. When the doctor pulls down the blanket, I see that the bandages are red and wet. Did the blade get to Annalisa's heart? How much more blood can she lose and still survive?

The doctor opens her bag, pulls out a blood pressure machine, and wraps the cuff around Annalisa's arm. She pumps it up, lets it deflate, then checks the reading.

"Blood pressure is stable," she says, and listens to Annalisa's heart with a stethoscope. We all go quiet, anxious to ensure that the doctor hears everything she needs to. "Lungs are clear, heartbeat is strong. Let's look under the bandage. Gloves and scissors from my bag, please, sister," she says to Mrs. M.

Mrs. M follows the doctor's directions with quick and efficient movements. She is right back in her element. The doctor puts on her gloves with a pop and opens her hand for the scissors. Mrs. M leans forward as the doctor cuts through the makeshift bandages with four quick snips to reveal the wound above Annalisa's right breast.

The cut is long and raw but sewn up evenly by Mrs. M. The violence of it forces me to turn away, sick to my stomach and afraid. If I want to sleep at all tonight, I have to ask . . .

"Is her heart okay, Doctor?"

"Her heartbeat is weak but regular. It's a good sign." The doctor looks up at Mrs. M. They have work to do. "Sterile water, sister. We'll clean the wound and rebandage. You did an excellent job closing the wound, by the way. If you hadn't, the bleeding would have put the patient in a much worse position. You saved us a lot of work."

Mrs. M says, "Miss Harden is tough, Doctor. She's small, but she's a fighter."

Father Gibson places his hand on my shoulder and gently turns me toward the door. "Let's leave Dr. Dlamini and . . ."

"Mrs. Mashanini," Mrs. M says. "Nurse. Retired."

"Dr. Dlamini and sister Mashanini need room to work. Is there a park we can walk to? Someplace quiet."

"I wouldn't go to a park now that it's dark, but we can walk down Tugela Way." I'm not one of the girls who hangs out with the drinkers near the wall painted with a rainbow in Mafalo Park at night. I have one foot in the township and the other planted in an imaginary future where I live on a sprawling university campus with gardens and stone buildings. If that future doesn't work out, maybe I'll change where I spend my evenings.

When we get outside, the crowd moves closer. They look to us for news. Their expectant faces make me want to scream at them to go home. I don't, though. They haven't done anything wrong. I am just too full of everything that's happened to me and Annalisa over the last few days.

Father Gibson senses the tension inside me. He clears his throat and tells the crowd, "With the doctor's help and by God's good grace, Miss Harden will live to see the morning."

It's enough to send our neighbors back to their homes to share the news with their families. Death has a seat at every table in Sugar Town, and with each loved one gone comes a lesson. *Don't walk down that lane after dark, my daughter. Never play under the dead marula tree on Alfred Street. If a man in a blue car offers you a lift, don't get in.* Every new danger creates a new rule to keep us safe from harm.

"She stepped in front of Jacob's knife," I tell Father Gibson as we take a right onto Sisulu Street with its locked and barred shops. "It should be me on that bed, not her."

"Your mother acted out of instinct. Burying your own child is the worst kind of pain." Father Gibson sidesteps a pool of stagnant water swarming with mosquitoes. "When my youngest daughter died, I cursed God for taking her instead of me. If it was you on that cot, it might have killed Annalisa anyway."

Annalisa called me her "perfect thing" a few days ago. The only perfect thing she ever made. Me, the brown baby that wrecked her life and led her down these dirt streets. Will I ever feel the same level of deep, blind love for another human being?

"She ended up in Sugar Town because of me, I think." We swing right onto Plain Street, which connects with Tugela Way. "Do you know what happened before she went missing? How did she get here?"

Father Gibson walks and thinks. He tries to find the right words. "Does your grandmother know that you live in a township?"

"Yes," I say. "She saw Annalisa every couple of months and gave us money to survive."

Father Gibson stops to consider the information, and I pull him forward. At night, you have to keep moving through the streets. You don't stop and let thieves close to your pockets or yourself.

"As far as I know, Annalisa disappeared when she was eighteen years old. A runaway, Neville said. She took up with a bad crowd in Jozi."

We hit Tugela Way and take another right, circling the block. "That's what Neville told everyone, and I didn't question it. I should have, but he pays for the upkeep of Saint Luke's Mission by the Sea, and he helps with my grandchildren's school fees . . . I let the sleeping dogs lie. I shouldn't have."

Father Gibson is honest, and I appreciate it. "And Mayme never said."

"No." He gestures to the barbed-wire fences and dirt yards. "She knew where you lived. How you lived. But she didn't trust me with the information, and she was right not to. I have been a weak old man, pretending that everything was all right when it was all wrong. I'm sorry, Amandla."

Father Gibson's regret is written on his face, but his words are just that: words. Like the old aunties say, *Talk is cheap and whiskey costs money.*

"I have questions that need answers."

"Ask," he says.

"Will you tell my mayme what happened to Annalisa?"

"Yes, I will. She needs to know. Neville won't hear a thing from me. That I can promise."

We turn onto the dirt lane, lit by lanterns and candles and electric bulbs burning in the shacks with windows. Father Gibson heaves a long sigh to see the rusted holes in every wall of every tin building.

"To imagine someone from your family living here . . ."

He's right, but I prickle at his tone. This is my home.

"We have shelter," I say. "We have enough."

"Enough to survive is not enough to build your best lives, Amandla. Your family should be ashamed of themselves. The gospel of Timothy says: 'If anyone has no care for his family and those in his house, he is false to the faith, and is worse than one who has no faith.'"

More words. I agree with them, but other worries creep into my mind. The police investigation into Jacob's death for one, and the possibility, however unlikely, that William Caluza will try to avenge his younger brother. Jacob was an addict, but William had hope that one day he would find a good life with a good woman. Now that hope is gone.

We find ourselves back at my house. I push open the door and lead Father Gibson inside. Dr. Dlamini and Mrs. M are cleaning up dirty bandages and wiping down the bedside table. I concentrate on Mrs. M's face and try to read her expression. Is she worried or hopeful? She looks away, and Dr. Dlamini says, "The wound is cleaned and closed, but it's still touch and go. The next few hours are crucial. Nurse Mashanini will monitor her through the night."

"But she'll be okay? She'll live?"

"Her chances are good if the bleeding stops and if an infection doesn't set in . . ." Dr. Dlamini says. "If not, we'll have to move her to the intensive care ward at the Bollard Institute."

If the bleeding stops. If an infection doesn't set in . . . The word *if* means there's a chance that Annalisa could die. That can't be right. I lean into Mrs. M, desperate for reassurance.

"Calm your mind, Amandla. Your mother is young and strong, and when she wakes up, she will have a scar to remind her of her good luck." Mrs. M told me the same thing when she bandaged the cut on my hand earlier. Scars are lucky charms, signs to the ancestors that you have already suffered and now God must go and test someone else. Mrs. M believes our old suffering wards off new suffering, despite our township being full of people who have been hurt over and over again. Some of them die. True fact.

I push down my fear and go straight to Annalisa. She's still unconscious. The rise and fall of her chest is barely discernible, but she seems peaceful. She almost died for me today. Part of me wants to scream at her for doing it. What was she thinking? Instead, I grab a wet cloth and wipe her face with even strokes, the same way she did for me whenever I had a fever. Annalisa is not perfect, but in this moment, she is my one perfect thing.

If she wakes, I will tell her.

22

Father Gibson stands between Dr. Dlamini and Mrs. M at the kitchen table. We hold hands, and he bows his head to pray. Annalisa believes in angels who take a personal interest in everything she does, whether it's shopping or sleeping or working a crossword puzzle. I'm lukewarm on the idea of a hands-on God, but how can a quick word with the boss upstairs hurt? It might help Annalisa pull through the night and into the light of a bright new morning.

"Heavenly Father, thank you for sparing Annalisa today. And for bringing Mrs. Mashanini and Dr. Dlamini to help. Surround Annalisa with your unfailing love and care at this time of injury and pain. Help her to heal."

Short and sweet and to the point.

"Amen," we all say. And we mean it. We open our eyes and raise our heads.

"Amandla," Mrs. M says, "put the kettle on, my girl. It's time for tea."

I fill the kettle, light the gas, and admit that I'm scared but not yet terrified. A nurse, a doctor, and a priest came to Annalisa's aid. It doesn't matter whether or not there is a higher power looking out for us. Today proves that people down here are looking out for each other.

"Thank you." I include everyone present. "For helping my mother."

Dr. Dlamini stretches her arms above her head and turns from side to side to loosen her tight muscles. She is toned and stylish and smells of cardamom and other warm spices that I can't identify. Dr. Dlamini is the black version of Annalisa before *the fall*. "Amandla, it is my pleasure to help Amanda Bollard's daughter. *And* her granddaughter," she says. "Your grandmother has been very kind to me and so generous in her support of the wound care department at the Bollard Institute. This is the least I could do."

I understand. The Bollard family's money buys more than food and shelter. It buys doctors who will come when you need them.

"Please, sit." I remember my manners. "I'll pour the tea."

It's not the English breakfast or black Darjeeling tea that I imagine the doctor and the priest are used to drinking, but rooibos, a red bush tea that grows in the craggy Cederberg mountains. We ran out of the good stuff a week ago, and with the money pile thinning out, the second-best stuff is all we can afford. I reach up and grab the unopened Romany Creams biscuits. If ever there was a time to crack them open, it is now.

I pour water into the teapot. Dr. Dlamini takes a Romany Creams and passes the packet to Mrs. M, who takes two of them and bites into the first one with a long sigh. It's only 9:20, but it's already been a long night.

The door creaks open and Goodness and Lil Bit walk in, followed by Lewis, who dumps a burlap sack in the corner. They are clean and dressed in fresh clothes, and if you didn't know that Jacob was lying dead somewhere, you'd never guess that the four of us helped kill a man today. Or rather, we stopped him from killing us today.

"Father Gibson and Dr. Dlamini, meet my friends Lil Bit, Goodness, and Lewis. When Jacob attacked us in the alley, they helped to fight him off. Without them, both Annalisa and me might be dead."

Dr. Dlamini nods, and Father Gibson shakes each hand held out to him. "Thank you," he says. "It's good to know Amandla has friends she can rely on."

"No problem, Father," Lewis says quietly, and touches my arm. Everything that happened today propelled us past the friendship-with-flirting stage. It feels like the four of us are blood brothers and sisters now.

"How's your ma?" Lil Bit asks, and I turn to Dr. Dlamini and Mrs. M, who cleaned and stitched the wound. I let them give the prognosis. If I speak, I will cry.

Dr. Dlamini says, "If she gets through the night without a major bleed, she should recover. I've left painkillers, antibiotics, and instructions in Mrs. Mashanini's capable hands."

"Not to worry." Mrs. M is confident. "I will take good care of Miss Harden."

The doctor packs her medical bag and snaps the lock closed with a loud click. I shuffle from foot to foot, nervous at saying what has to be said.

"You came all this way, and I'm sorry, but I have no money to pay you, Dr. Dlamini . . ."

"Consider the biscuit payment. I'm taking another one before I go." She grabs a second biscuit on the way out and eats it in two bites. "If you need anything, call Father Gibson and we'll arrange it. Take good care of your mother. Take good care of yourself. I hope to see you again, Amandla. In a nonmedical situation, though."

I soak in the details of the doctor's angular face and high cheekbones, her brown eyes that slant down at the corners. Even now, dressed in a bloodstained pantsuit and with her long braid of hair unraveled into a frizz of curls, she is a queen. She is everything I want to be in the future: educated, confident, and skilled.

"Thank you again." I open the door to let her and Father Gibson go home. I'm humbled by their generosity and strangely embarrassed to be on the receiving end of it. Annalisa says that we live in Sugar Town, but that we don't belong here, and tonight proved that she is at least partly right. We are connected to the world outside of the township, and a single phone call brought a doctor to our door—something that our neighbors will never experience.

"We'll walk you to your car," Lewis says, and an exhausted Mrs. M waves us out with a yawn before collapsing onto my cot. Lil Bit and Goodness come out into the garden, and it's comforting to have the four of us safe and together. "Where are you parked?"

Father Gibson squints the length of the lane in one direction and then the other. It is night now, with a half-moon rising. "In front of a pink house with a blue door. The number has slipped my mind."

"Maggie Mabula's house," Lil Bit says. Impulsive Maggie Mabula, who once ran into the street in a pink bra and panties to save her one-eared dog from being hit by a dump truck. Maggie, who distributes letters and packages to the right address when the postman is too busy or too scared to approach a house with a dog in the yard.

"Down here, Father." Lil Bit and Goodness lead the way, and Lewis and I fall behind. Not on purpose. It just happens. It's strange to walk through the Sugar Town streets in the dark. Normally, we lock the door at seven sharp and do not go outside till after dawn. In my own way, I have been guided and protected and kept from harm by Annalisa's constant presence.

"Who are they?" Lewis asks as we walk side by side.

"I told you. Father Gibson and Dr. Dlamini."

"No," he says. "I mean, who are they to you?"

Lewis is right to ask. Doctors do not make house calls to shacks in Sugar Town. Doctors are gods who keep short hours at the clinic and disappear back into the city, defeated by the number of patients still waiting for treatment.

"Father Gibson is the family priest, and Dr. Dlamini knows my grandmother."

"Not many people in Sugar Town have those kind of connections, Amandla." Lewis gives me a long sideways glance. "So your ma was right. You don't belong here, and one day soon, you'll be gone."

If Annalisa lives, there's a chance that our dream of moving out will come true. If she doesn't make it through the night, well, who knows where I'll end up?

"There's a difference between dreams and reality," I tell Lewis. "Let's just say that I'm not going anywhere soon."

Maggie Mabula's house is a few feet ahead; Father Gibson stops at a white car with tinted windows and white hubcaps that have, by some miracle, escaped the notice of our local car thieves.

We reach the new-model sedan, gleaming and perfect. Dr. Dlamini pulls a ring of keys from her coat pocket and presses a button to open the doors. She takes the driver's seat. It's thrilling to see a black woman behind the wheel of a powerful automobile. *Lady . . . I want to be you in ten years' time.* Father Gibson pulls me into a bear hug. "I'll let Amanda know what's happened, and I'll be back tomorrow. Call me if you need anything."

"I will."

The engine of the immaculate car growls. It pulls into the badly lit street, turns toward Durban, and disappears. After a moment, we walk back home together in the softly lit darkness. Goodness bumps her shoulder against mine.

"Oh, by the way, we're all staying overnight at your house," she says. "My mother grumbled about it and Lil Bit's mum grumbled about it, but I told them both straight, 'No arguments. It's happening.'"

"But why?" I ask.

"You'll see," Goodness says, and my face burns to think of Lewis lying close to me in the dark.

23

Lil Bit pours petrol into the metal garbage bin that Lewis rolled from the corner of Tugela Way and into our front yard. I dump Annalisa's bloody bandages inside, light a match, and drop it in. The match falls, and flames lick the bandages before they catch fire and burn. Flames rise.

"I love fire," Lil Bit says. "Let it build."

Goodness drags the burlap sack that Lewis brought with them to the edge of the crackling barrel. Smoke billows, and I rub the sting from my eyes. I will have to shampoo twice to get the wood-fire stink out of my hair.

"Now what?" Lil Bit asks Goodness. "Do we go in order or all at once?"

"There is no order." Goodness opens the sack, and the metallic smell of blood is strong. "All right, everyone. I called my Auntie Mags. She said to burn everything with blood on it. She's a sangoma, a healer, so she knows the right way to do things. The fire will get rid of the bad luck. After this, we have to wash in a river or in the ocean, to make sure that every bit of blood is washed away."

Traditional religion and Christianity go hand in hand in the township, but this will be the first time that I've taken part in a Zulu ceremony. I find it comforting to be shown a way through the terror that still beats inside my heart. The moments in the alley are etched in my mind: the stone wall, Jacob with his knife, Annalisa bleeding on the ground, Lil Bit and Lewis attacking Jacob, and Goodness using the brick to send Jacob reeling into me with the knife pressed into his chest. I want it all gone. Wiped away. If burning our clothes and washing in a river or the ocean helps, I will follow every word of Auntie Mags's advice.

"I'll go first." Lewis reaches into the sack and pulls out his shirt and jeans, dark with Annalisa's blood. His hand shakes as he drops the filthy rags into the flames. The fire splutters, then ignites the material.

"Now me." Lil Bit pulls out her clothes and drops them into the bin. I grab the sack and snag my T-shirt, jacket, and jeans, all soaked in Jacob's blood. I sacrifice them to the flames and notice, too late, that I have accidentally dumped the T-shirt that Goodness used to put pressure on Annalisa's open wound.

"Oh . . . I didn't mean to burn your stuff."

"No big deal," Goodness says. "The ancestors will understand."

The T-shirt saved my mother from bleeding out in the lane, and it is my honor to feed it to the cleansing fire.

"I'll do the rest." Goodness throws the entire sack into the bin. Bloodied bandages and sheets. Annalisa's T-shirt and jeans. They all burn to ash. I hold my hands out to the fire and feel the heat lick my fingers. My body warms up, but, deep inside, a part of me stays cold.

Jacob is dead. He fell on his own knife while we fought to save ourselves and Annalisa. We acted in self-defense. So why does his dying feel so bad? Why do I feel so guilty for attracting his attention in the first place? I must have done something to draw his eyes to me. Did I laugh too loud at one of Lil Bit's jokes? Are my clothes too tight? Is my smile too bright? I have to find what I did wrong so that I never do it again.

"Is Jacob's body still in the lane?" I ask.

"No," Lewis says. "The police picked Jacob up from the lane and took him to the morgue. My father dropped by the police station and told them that we talked to William and we've sorted the matter out between ourselves. They recorded Jacob's death as 'accidental,' and that was the end of it."

But it's not the end. Not for a long, long time. Not ever. Even Jacob Caluza was loved by someone.

The dark shape of a person enters the lane from Sisulu Street, and the four of us tense. Goodness grabs a stone from the ground, and Lewis's hands flex into fists. We are still nervous from today and expecting some form of payback.

I squint into the low light and see that it is William Caluza, carrying a small bundle wrapped in wax paper and tied with string. Goodness holds the rock up, ready to throw. *Stay right there if you know what's good for you.* He stops and opens his arms in a gesture that indicates he's not here for more violence.

I wave him closer, relieved. He comes over to the fence and holds the package out to me. "Chicken legs for your mother," he says. "The best for Miss Harden."

"Thanks." I take the gift, and the fire throws light onto William's tight jaw and swollen eyes. He wipes his nose with the back of his hand. He is sad and afraid. Lewis and his brothers have told him to forgive and forget, and that is what he is here to do.

"I'm sorry for what happened to you and your mother, but at least now I can sleep at night. No more worrying about Jacob. Is he sick? Is he well? When will he go to jail again?" William says. "All that is over."

He walks away, a lonely silhouette. Tears stream down my face. William has lost a brother, and I feel his pain.

* * *

Goodness's Auntie Mags says that we have to stick together till dawn; if we are alone, the demons will pick us off one by one. Demons love the taste of human fear, and with Annalisa still in danger, I have plenty of fear stored up. Auntie Mags said that if we stick together, we will be too strong for the demons to attack. Together is how we can send them back to the darkness they came from.

We roost like chickens in the small amount of space available inside the house. Mrs. M sleeps in my cot, too tired to make it across the way and into a house crowded with children.

Lil Bit, Goodness, and I squash together on the kitchen floor, and Lewis takes the space under the table. We are packed together, and it feels safe. I've never had a brother or sister, so being this close to this many people is new and different for me. I could get used to it.

"You wanted action on the holidays and you got it," I tell Goodness. "Bet you wish that you'd stayed away from Lil Bit and me now."

"No." She stretches out like a cat. "I was with you in the alley. My being there made a difference, and it had nothing to do with anyone in my family but me."

"But your parents give you everything," Lil Bit says. "You're one of the lucky ones."

Goodness turns to face us. "That's the problem. I have everything, except none of it is mine. When people smile at me, they are smiling at my parents. The same with my brothers. But me, Goodness, myself? I don't fit. All that township social stuff doesn't have anything to do with me."

"Oh . . ."

In the dark, I think about what people might say about Goodness if she wasn't a part of the Dumisa family. *Have you seen her on the soccer field? Boots and shorts and mud on her face. She might as well be a boy. I wouldn't trust her around my daughter!*

"I'm sorry that your ma got hurt," Goodness says. "But I'm glad I was in that alley. You understand?"

I stare up the kitchen wall and see the faint wink of a star that shows through a tiny crack high above the window. "I get it. Jacob didn't care who your parents were. You threw that brick. You saved my life."

"Lil Bit and Lewis helped," she says. "We all played a part."

"Us being together was a lucky thing." Lil Bit yawns and snuggles under the thin blankets. The three-bar electric heater, the use of which Annalisa normally rations like gold coins, glows in the corner. It is enough to cut the chill in the air but not enough to warm the entire room. Tonight, we'll stay close together to share our body heat. Lewis is nearest the heater and already asleep. I hear the steady inhale and exhale of his breath, and I know for sure that Auntie Mags is right. Our being together has power.

"It's funny," I say. "Annalisa is hurt. Mrs. M snores like a drunk with a blocked nose, and the floor is hard on my hip bones, but I feel lucky to be where I am."

"Not lucky," Lil Bit says. "Blessed."

Blessed? Here, in a one-room shack on a dirt lane with a broken dresser and starlight falling through cracks in the wall?

Yes. Lil Bit is right.

Blessed.

* * *

Goodness falls asleep next and Lil Bit a short while later. Mrs. M's rumbling snores come and go. Lewis's deep and steady breath calms me. Annalisa is still sedated, her chest the only part of her that moves.

I lie awake and listen to the night sounds around me, and I think about my grandparents' big white house. It's beautiful, but who'd want to live there if you had to live with Neville?

I wonder if he's lonely with Mayme in the guest bedroom and all that space around him. Or is he happy to drift off to sleep knowing his security guards are patrolling the yard? He wouldn't understand six people crammed into one room for the night and how good it feels. That is the last thing I think of before I fall asleep.

24

A hand taps my shoulder, and I crawl from sleep to find Lewis crouched close beside me in the cold dawn light. If my father made my mother feel the way I do right now, all sugary and sweet, then I totally understand why she wants him back so badly.

"I have to help my brothers with deliveries," he whispers. "I'll drop by and see you this afternoon. Your mother seems to be doing fine. I heard her mumble in her sleep a minute ago."

"Oh . . . thanks . . ." I can't make more words than that because my mouth is wide and smiling. Heat stings my cheeks and warms up the cold air around me. This stupid happiness is a feeling I want every day of my life. "Come by anytime."

He nods, and I slip from under the weight of Goodness's arm, which is draped across my collarbone. I am too polite and too much my mother's daughter to not walk him to the door. *Good manners*, Annalisa says, *cost nothing*.

I pad to the front door, turn the locks, and pull it open. "Thank you for staying over. Your Auntie Mags was right. All of us being together made a difference."

"Happy to do it again." Lewis steps out of the house and straight into Maggie Mabula, who holds Primrose, her one-eared dog, in the crook of her arm. Her mouth drops open to see Lewis leaving through the front door in broad daylight.

"Oh . . ." Her gaze drifts to my stomach as if she expects it to go from flat to pregnant in an instant. "Sorry to disturb."

"Lewis was just leaving." Annalisa has taught me well. I do not squirm or blush. I look Maggie Mabula straight in the eyes and smile, knowing that the gossip about Lewis Dumisa and *that colored girl* will spread through Sugar Town faster than a winter flu. This does not bother me. Like Lil Bit, I have lived through worse.

"Again tonight?" Lewis takes my hand and laces his fingers through mine—giving Maggie a piece of gossip she will be unable to stop herself from repeating—all over town. It's hard to keep a straight face. It's ridiculous: Maggie thinking that Lewis and I took advantage of my mother being stabbed to get busy and sweaty in a room full of people.

"Come earlier." I join the game and squeeze Lewis's hand. "That way we'll have all night together."

"I can't wait to see you again. Hold you again." Lewis winks and saunters toward Sisulu Street. He has a sense of humor, and Lord knows, he will need it. Goodness told her mother where she and Lewis were spending the night, but when Mrs. Dumisa catches word of what Lewis said and the way he said it, she will not be pleased.

"What can I do for you, Miss Mabula?" I wait till Lewis has turned the corner and disappeared. Primrose, the dog, pants.

"An old white man with spring-up hair is asking for directions to your house. City men have no business in Sugar Town, but the woman sitting next to him? She has your looks. Same nose. Same freckles. Your granny, I'm guessing?"

Maggie is fishing for a second piece of information to share over the back fence. A one-night stand—maybe even a teen pregnancy, with a *Dumisa* no less, and a white grandma that turned up out of nowhere . . . she'll be hectic for days repeating this story.

"I'll go see who it is." I will not confirm nor deny that the white stranger is my grandmother. It's time for Maggie to find her scandals somewhere else.

"No, you stay." She moves fast out of the gate. "Get the house tidy. I'll bring them to you, my own self. It's safer that way."

Please! It's daylight. There's no danger lurking in the lane, but Maggie smells the chance to make some money, and if Maggie loves anything more than Primrose, it's the crinkly sound of banknotes being pushed inside her bra for safekeeping. Her courier business is strictly cash on delivery. But if cash is tight, she'll take fresh eggs, canned food, and baked goods instead. If she expects a special payment for hand-delivering Mayme and Father Gibson to our home, she'll be sadly disappointed. I plan to hang on to the money that we have.

"Thank you, Maggie. Bring them over."

"My pleasure." She runs in the direction of Sisulu Street with Primrose tucked under her arm like a fluffy handbag.

I turn and crack the front door open to peek inside. The room is tidy but crowded. Mrs. M snores in the cot across from a pale and still Annalisa. In sleep, her face is smooth and relaxed. She looks younger, less worn down by unpaved roads and unpaid bills. Lil Bit and Goodness curl together on the floor in a tangle of limbs and thin blankets. They seem to belong together somehow. They balance each other out, a sports-mad soccer star and a book-mad bandit.

I tiptoe into the kitchen area, grab two cans of beef in gravy from the cupboard, and slink out of the room. The sun breaks from behind a cloud. Father Gibson and Mayme here in Sugar Town. Family history and all its rules are changing fast.

"Amandla." Maggie sweeps her free hand in a grand gesture. Primrose barks, adding to the drama of the moment. "See what I found."

Father Gibson and Mayme stand outside the garden gate with dazed expressions. Father Gibson's nighttime visit did not prepare him fully for the daytime visuals of township life. Hard light bounces off the flat tin roofs and strands of barbed wire curl around window frames like poison ivy. A stranger with no shoes picks through a pile of garbage a few houses down.

Mayme's face is drawn tight. She's aged ten years overnight. The lines at the corners of her mouth and eyes are deeper than I remember. Hearing about the attack on Annalisa and seeing how we really live has shocked her. She has no way of knowing that the lane between Sisulu and Tugela is not the bottom of the bottom. Plenty of people are far worse off than us.

"For you, Miss Mabula."

Maggie raises an eyebrow at the dented cans, and under normal circumstances, I'd be ashamed of how little we have.

These are not normal times, though. I am not my usual self. I choose to be honest. "That's all I have to give you."

She throws Mayme a glance. The glance is a question: *What about the white lady?* I give a shrug that says, *Take it or leave it, sister. I won't beg for money from my grandmother.* Maggie grabs the cans and shuffles off.

"Come. Don't be scared." I walk out to Mayme and pull her gently through the gate and into our dead yard. There must be a way to change the soil and introduce a living patch of green. Mrs. M will know how. Plans for later.

Father Gibson follows us, glancing at the houses without windows. On the map, we are less than thirty kilometers from the big white house where I met him, but it might as well be another country.

The door opens before we reach it, and Lil Bit's head pokes out. "Amandla," she calls. "Come quick. Mrs. M needs your help."

* * *

Annalisa thrashes in bed. Her hair is wild, and her eyes are wilder. The front of her T-shirt is soaked with blood. Mrs. M tries to gently hold her down, but Annalisa fights. She twists and turns and says in a ragged voice:

"Just a little farther. Hold on, baby girl. We have to keep moving. We have to get out of here . . ."

Mrs. M says, "Talk to her, Amandla. Tell her that you are here. That you are safe."

I try to speak, but nothing comes out. My lungs feel like they're being crushed. There's blood everywhere. It's on Mrs. M's hands, on the sheets, and on Annalisa's nightgown, which will have to be burned in the fire barrel that Lewis rolled into the front yard last night.

"Shhh . . ." Mayme pushes past me and kneels on the grass mat beside Annalisa's bed. She takes her hands, gentle. "I'm here. Mummy is here with you."

The sound of Mayme's voice calms Annalisa. She stops thrashing and leans back against the wall like a puppet with broken strings. "You're home. You're safe."

"Amandla?" Mrs. Mashanini's voice breaks through the haze in my head. "Come and help me with your mother. Slow and gentle now . . ."

I blink and edge past Mayme kneeling on the grass mat. A red bloom spreads across the right side of Annalisa's chest, and I try to ready myself to be covered in my own mother's blood. Mrs. M tears the neckline of Annalisa's gown open and grabs a wet cloth from a bowl of water beside the cot. How can she stay so calm?

"Keep talking." Mrs. M wipes blood from Annalisa's neck and collarbone. "Tell her an old story. Give her something nice to remember. Amandla, come closer and help me take off your mother's gown. We need to wash and rebandage the wound."

"Does she need to go to the emergency ward, like Dr. Dlamini said?"

Say no. Please say no.

"Not yet," Mrs. M says. "After the dressing is changed, I will give her a sedative. She needs to sleep and rest."

Thank heaven. My medical knowledge is limited, but I'd prefer that Annalisa stays at home. At least here she has Mrs. M to look after her, one on one. And she has me. Mayme pushes up her sleeves and says, "What can I do to help, Mrs. Mashanini?"

Father Gibson leans across the foot of the cot, worried. "Take it easy, Amanda. Try not to put a strain on your heart."

She waves him away. *I have to do this, Tony.*

After years of staying away, Mayme has finally chosen to be here with Annalisa and me, against Neville's wishes, I'm sure. The white house is spectacular, but there is no place on Earth that she'd rather be than right here beside her daughter's bed.

"If you need me, I'll be outside having a cigarette." Father Gibson bows out and backs away. Despite his flyaway hair and rumpled appearance, he understands the need for this meeting of Harden women. He brought Mayme here, after all.

"Go home, girls," Mrs. M tells Lil Bit and Goodness. "Your mothers are waiting to see you, and Miss Harden needs her privacy."

Goodness doesn't want to leave, but this morning, she does what she's told. Even she gets that the business between Mayme and Annalisa is old and painful and private.

"Catch you soon, Amandla." Lil Bit grabs Goodness's hand and leads her out of the house and into the yard. The door closes behind her with a metal click. Mrs. M instructs Mayme and me to remove Annalisa's stained gown and help wipe the blood from her chest and shoulders. Mrs. M changes her bandages, and once we have wrestled Annalisa into a clean nightgown, we lay her back against the pillows. She sighs and closes her eyes, tired from everything that's happened in the last twenty-four hours. Everything that's happened in the last fifteen years.

"Wipe her forehead with this." Mrs. M hands me the damp cloth. "I'll be back in twenty minutes to give her another dose of painkillers. For now, the sound of your voices is all she needs."

Mrs. M scoops the bloodied blankets from the floor and bundles them under her arm. Blind Auntie will have them washed and hung out to dry on the metal clothesline in the backyard before the sun is overhead. Blind Auntie's hands are never idle.

Mrs. M leaves, and it's just us. Three generations of one family, women with the weight of a silent, unresolved history resting on our shoulders. Mayme plucks at Annalisa's clean sheets.

"Talk to her," I say.

"Words aren't enough to fix what I did," she says. "Words won't change anything."

That is not true. Words have power. String enough words together and you get a story. That is what Annalisa needs right now. Her own story, told to her in her mother's voice.

"Here." I unzip my backpack and pull out the private investigator's report, still unopened. "Read this and tell Annalisa what happened fifteen years ago. Tell her everything. Do it for yourself. Do it for her."

Annalisa's soft breath breaks the silence that fills the room. The report hangs in midair as I wait for Mayme to make a move. Minutes pass. My arm grows heavy, and my patience begins to evaporate. Right now, she needs to put Annalisa's suffering ahead of her own fear.

"It's hard to face what's in there," she whispers. "I can't do it."

Oh, cry me a river, rich white lady. Life is hard. And life in Sugar Town is even harder. I don't have the time to protect you from all the bad and the sad things that we deal with every day.

"Look around and tell me how hard your life is." My voice vibrates with anger. "This is all we have. Two cots. A table. Four chairs. A sink and a stove and a toilet in the backyard. Annalisa gets up every day and cleans the house from top to bottom. She has made this tin room our home, and she has done it by herself. Your money helps, but it's not enough to make Annalisa's life easy. Or mine. Our life is hard, but guess what? We are grateful. I know that 'into each life some rain must fall,' but if you believe that reading a report is harder than being stabbed in an alley to stop your daughter from being killed by a maniac, then you are not my grandmother."

I fling the report into Mayme's lap, tired of carrying the weight for the women in my family. Once, just once, I need someone else to do the heavy lifting. I've had enough. "Take the report. Father Gibson will drive you home. Mrs. Mashanini and I will look after Annalisa."

Still, she doesn't move.

"Please go. Leave us alone the way that you've done for fifteen years. We'll be fine. We're used to you not being here." The fury drains from me, but I don't regret anything that I've said. Every word is true.

"You look like me, but you take after her." Mayme's voice is low and soft. "When she was younger, Annalisa was fierce; you *had* to listen to her. Her boldness made me uncomfortable sometimes, and other times, I was proud of her strength. Much stronger than me. I have wasted so much time on meaningless things . . ."

Anger I was prepared for, not honesty. An ache grows inside my chest. Mayme has thought about where her life went wrong, many times.

"You're right to criticize me," she continues. "I never got my hands dirty. Think of all the years that you lived so close. A forty-minute drive away, but I never set foot here till this morning. I didn't visit you because I was scared. Scared to stand up and claim you and Annalisa in public. I did not stand up and claim you because I was ashamed of who Annalisa was: poor and broken and with an illegitimate child from a black man . . . I did offer Annalisa more money, but she refused. For some reason, she didn't want Neville to know where she lived. She couldn't tell me why. I should have confronted Neville and fought for you both, but I let things slide. By staying away and making up stories about Annalisa, I could keep being a queen bee . . . Mrs. Bollard . . . whatever that means . . . It's the worst exchange I ever made."

She rips open the envelope with shaking hands and takes a deep breath. "Now I'm dying, and you deserve the truth. Annalisa deserves the truth. Please forgive me, if you can."

Mayme is about to give this family what it needs. Love. Honesty. Courage. Closeness. She's an old lady who has found the bravery to take a step that will likely damage her heart. I knew it was in her somewhere. Her fingers slide along the back of the envelope . . .

"Wait." I hold my hand out to stop her. There is danger inside the report; is it enough to kill a sick old lady made weaker by her own guilt? "*I'll* read it. But not here. I have to go somewhere by myself. You stay here with Annalisa. I'll be back in an hour."

"No, we go together." She runs her thumbs over the smooth skin of Annalisa's fingers, perhaps remembering a time when Mother's tiny hand fit perfectly inside hers. "When I die, I want to go knowing that, for once in my life, I was brave."

"I know the perfect place for us to go and read the report." I grab the envelope and my backpack on the way out of the house. Father Gibson leans against the gate and lights up a smoke. Not his first. There's a stack of cigarette butts piled neatly by his feet.

"Keep Annalisa company while we're gone," Mayme tells the priest. "And tell Mrs. Mashanini that we'll be back soon."

"Is it wise to—"

"Shush, Tony. Amandla is with me. I'll be fine."

We leave through the gate and walk slowly to the water tower with Nelson Mandela's face beaming his warmth and wisdom onto all of South Africa. We sit side by side on upturned milk crates and read the neatly typed pages. We cry our eyes out. Our hearts are broken. Nelson says nothing, but he knows.

25

When we return to the house, empty of tears and filled with rage, Lil Bit and Goodness are waiting for us in the front yard. They look worried, frightened, even. It's eleven thirty in the morning, but from their expressions, you'd think we'd been out walking at three in the morning. I hurry through the gate, with my pulse racing. What happened in the hour that we were gone?

"Is Annalisa all right?"

"She's fine, you idiot. The priest is with her and Mrs. M has gone home to water her seedlings. It was you who had us worried." Goodness punches my arm hard enough to sting. "What's in your head, sister? Auntie Mags said we were supposed to stay together. Lil Bit thought that—"

"Thought what?"

"That Jacob's gang found you." She talks so soft that I have to lean in to hear.

The twins with the prison tattoos. In the flood of stuff that's happened in the last twenty-four hours, I'd forgotten about them. Lil Bit is right, I should have been more careful; I should have remembered *Pain Is Love* inked across Twin Number One's cheek. The same twin who said he could break Lil Bit in two and she might like it. No wonder she's worried.

"I don't think they were Jacob's friends . . . not really. They might have smoked meth together, but they probably don't live in Sugar Town. We would remember seeing them and those tatts, for sure," I say. "I doubt we'll bump into them again. Now that Jacob's gone."

"You can't assume that," Lil Bit says, stubborn.

"That's true but the odds are . . ." The rest of the sentence dies away. Lil Bit is right. The twins might be fifty miles away or they might be right around the corner.

"Chill out." Goodness throw her arm across Lil Bit's shoulder, lets the weight rest. "If it makes you feel better, I'll get my father to tell the cops about those gangster boys. If they show up in the township again, the cops'll be on them in a second."

Lil Bit says, "I can't ask you to—"

"It's no problem. My father loves it when I run to him for help. It gives him a chance to be the big man." Goodness lifts her chin in my direction. "In the meantime, we're supposed to wash the blood off us, like Auntie Mags said. We haven't done that yet, which means that we're easy meat for the bad spirits. Next time, tell us where you're going."

"I'm sorry, girls. We're fine, really," Mayme says. "Amandla took me to the water tower to finish up some old business."

Lil Bit raises an eyebrow. *And what business was that?*

"We had to read this." I hold up the manila envelope marked *Private and Confidential.* "Now we're back."

"You look awful," Lil Bit says. "Worse than I felt when we couldn't find you."

"What is that?" Goodness points at the envelope.

"It says what happened to Annalisa. It says why we're here."

Lil Bit reads my face, heavy with sadness, and frowns.

"That bad?" she says.

I nod yes.

"Goodness and me will help you through. Tell us what to do."

A lump blocks my throat, and the angry spirit inside me stills. This lane, thick with shacks and rising dust, is my home. Mrs. M hums over rows of green seedlings across the way, and on the porch, Blind Auntie knits scarves for the orphans. I will leave here someday. I know I will. But for now, everything and every*one* I need is right here.

"We're going into town tomorrow morning," Mayme says. "To visit the Bollard Company headquarters."

"You guys want to come with us?" I ask. "I'll need my crew."

"We're in!" Goodness grins, and rubs her hands together. "Just like we planned. It's time to mess with the old man. We fu—" She stops, embarrassed at the swear word that almost escaped her lips in front of an older woman. A white one.

"We fuck him up," Mayme says.

* * *

The argument in my head as I walk to Lewis's office on Monday morning goes something like this: *What you're asking him to do is wrong, Amandla. Turn around and go home. You leave for the city in an hour. There isn't even enough time.*

My feet keep moving toward the Build 'Em Up. It's as if they know better than I do what I need.

You have your words. You have the truth, and the truth is a powerful weapon. You don't need anything else.

No. Words won't be enough. Neville will deny everything. I can't take that chance.

What would Nelson Mandela do in the same situation?

I ask the question, but I can't answer it. My feet seem to be answering for me, though.

I come to a stop outside the gates to the busy timber yard. I ask myself again: *What* would *Nelson do?* The answer is complicated. Nelson on the water tower is a saint, forever radiating goodwill onto Sugar Town. The real Nelson Mandela believed in armed struggle. He was a freedom fighter before he became the leader of a nation.

Once you do this, you can't go back.

It's too late. I've made my decision. Today, I decide to follow the freedom fighter's footsteps.

I grab the strap of my backpack and run into the yard. No hesitation. No doubts. I take the metal stairs to the upper level. The office door is open. I peek inside and motion for Lewis to come out. We need to talk. He comes right out and closes the door behind him to give us privacy.

"Tell me," he says, reading my flustered expression at a glance.

I rise up on tiptoes to whisper my request in his ear.

* * *

The reception area at Neville's office is massive. The furniture is plush, with Persian carpets and floor-to-ceiling windows that look across the sapphire blue of the Indian Ocean. The air-conditioning hums. There's a glass case with a model of a building in it. Tiny cars and people give it scale. It's huge.

The luxury on display in the waiting area is intimidating. Self-doubt creeps over me. An old woman with heart problems, a priest, and three teenaged girls from the township are here for justice. Who are we kidding? We do not have the power to fuck up Neville. We don't even have the power to put a dent in his armor. He has all the cards. He always wins. Mayme senses my rising panic and reaches out to take my hand.

Her voice is tight with anger. "The furniture is window dressing, Amandla. A show. We know who Neville is. We know what he's done. We know."

She's right. We've seen behind the mask, and that knowledge makes us stronger than the steel beams that hold up the twenty-story glass-and-steel tower that is home to the Bollard Company. Lil Bit sits next to Father Gibson on a wide velvet couch, calmly waiting, while Goodness paces back and forth.

"Sit," Mayme tells her. "Neville's secretary, the Mamba, will be out in a minute. I call her that because . . . well, you'll see . . ."

Mambas are one of the most venomous snakes in Africa. They are lightning fast and they kill. The nickname doesn't calm me down.

"Not long now." Father Gibson picks at a jam stain on his shirt and spreads the mess even further. He is here to witness

Mayme's words. A white priest and a family friend. No one will doubt his honesty. Lil Bit, Goodness, and I are the Sugar Town backup.

The door to Neville's office opens, and a white woman wearing a peach pantsuit comes out with pursed lips and a frown: part stern headmistress, part prison guard. Her gaze flickers over us one by one and stops on Mayme.

"Mrs Bollard," she says in an icy voice. "This is a surprise."

"Yes, it has been a while since my last visit, Beatrice, but as you can see, I'm alive and well. Thank you for asking." Mayme's voice has a sting—Beatrice knows that Mayme's been sick and didn't mention it at all. Beatrice's mouth pinches tightly to seal in the words she wishes she could say.

"We're here to see Neville." Father Gibson smiles at the Mamba. "We don't have an appointment, but I really think he should make the time."

"Mr. Bollard is on an important call. Perhaps you could come back when it's convenient?" Beatrice plants herself in the doorway, a human roadblock. The power to keep us on the wrong side of the door makes her face shine with pleasure. She's enjoying herself. The cow. Beside me, Mayme's breath grows loud and uneven. She hates conflict, has avoided it all her life. A fact that the Mamba has, no doubt, figured out over the years. I bet this isn't the first time she's barred my grandmother from seeing her own husband.

Well, not today, lady. I did not come here to seek your permission.

I stand and walk straight to the imposing doors that dominate the waiting area. Goodness and Lil Bit fall in behind me.

Beatrice holds her ground, eyes hard. This close up, I can see her hair is sprayed into a helmet.

"Tell my grandfather that his wife and his granddaughter are here to see him."

Beatrice hesitates a moment, shocked. A mixed-race granddaughter in the clan is a surprise. She gathers herself quickly and says, "Mr. Bollard is on an important phone call. You will have to wait till he is finished."

Goodness sucks her teeth, impatient. "We heard you the first time, now you hear this: Move out of the way or we will move you. Take a good look at me and my sisters. We are Sugar Town Queens, and Sugar Town Queens *never* back down from a fight."

"Never," Lil Bit says. "Don't even know how to."

"The priest is only here to make sure we don't hurt you. We're from the township. We've got nothing to lose."

Goodness has elevated our status. We are queens now, sprinkled in sugar and dust, sweet and dangerous.

Beatrice's lips thin out into a red slash. "I will not be threatened at work by anyone. Least of all by you people."

The phrase *you people* makes Lil Bit's and Goodness's eyes go wide.

"Woman!" Lil Bit says. "I'm gonna kick . . ."

"How long have you worked for the Bollard Company, Beatrice?" Mayme, shockingly, has stepped up. Her soft tone is velvet-covered steel. "It must be fifteen or sixteen years by now. Certainly long enough for you to remember who I am."

"Certainly, Mrs. Bollard."

"That's wonderful. You had me worried for a moment. Imagine how embarrassing it would be for all of us if security removed you from the building for blocking me from my husband's office." She puts an arm around my waist, her palm pressed warm against my hip bone. "This is my granddaughter, Amandla. She's a member of the family. All the privileges that apply to me, apply to her. Are we clear?"

Beatrice looks ready to explode, but she also wants to keep her paycheck.

"Of course." She grabs the giant handle and opens the door. "Mr. Bollard? Father Gibson; Mrs. Bollard; your granddaughter, Amandla; and her friends are here to see you."

* * *

Together, we walk into a wide room filled with light. Mayme keeps her arm looped around my waist to give me strength, or maybe so she can use mine, it's hard to know. Neville sits behind a sleek desk made of blond wood. On the desk is a silver computer, a notepad, and a row of sterling-silver pens. Two matching blond wood chairs for visitors. Real minimalist stuff. Another floor-to-ceiling window on the right side of the office lets in views of the sky, soaring birds, and the distant blue of the ocean. All the beauty that money can buy.

"Amanda. You should be at home, resting." Neville stands up but stays behind his desk, a man in control. "What are you doing here? And why did you bring her?"

"Her name is Amandla Zenzile Harden. Annalisa's daughter. Our granddaughter." Mayme is calm and polite. "And we have something for you."

I take the private investigator's report from my backpack and place it gently on the desk. No township toughness here. Just me, cool and in control, for as long as I can fake it.

I say, "This explains how Annalisa disappeared."

Neville ignores the folder and me. Dressed in a crisp blue shirt and dark trousers, he is every inch a rich businessman, though old-school. His hair is trimmed and neat, and his mouth is curved in a smile that, to my eyes, is 100 percent fake. "Amanda, darling, you need to stop this," he says. "You need to go home and rest."

"Oh no, I don't, Neville," Mayme says.

He turns his BS smile onto me. "Then you have to stop this. You're killing your grandmother. Do the decent thing. Leave Amanda in peace and take your friends with you."

His appeal to my decency is funny. *You've got to give a little to get a little, old man.* In my experience, Neville is anything but decent. "No." I stand firm. "I'll stay for as long as Mayme wants me to."

"Should I call security, Mr. Bollard?" Beatrice, the Mamba, says from the doorway. Her loyalty to my grandfather tests my cool. Lil Bit clicks her tongue.

"If somebody doesn't get that woman out of here, I cannot be responsible for what I do next," she says. I love this township-tough side of her.

"Leave, Beatrice." Mayme is firm. "This is family business."

Neville nods, and Beatrice withdraws with her jaw clenched. *Wake up, lady. Your long years of service do not make you a Bollard, and this is strictly Bollard business.*

"Keep the door open, and get Julien," Mayme says to Beatrice's back. I hide a smile. This new version of grandma is all kinds of good. Like Lil Bit, everything that's happened over the last few days has made her braver than she used to be. It suits them both.

"Come and sit, Amandla." She takes one of the blond wood chairs and pats the other. "Let's make ourselves comfortable while Neville tries to lie his way out of the situation. Tony," she calls out to Father Gibson, "there's whiskey in the cupboard behind that white panel. Girls, help yourselves to soft drinks and any snacks that you find. We'll be here awhile."

Goodness reaches the white panel first and grunts. There's no handle. No way to open the magic cabinet. Lil Bit reaches past her and pushes her fingertip to the edge of the panel, which springs open to reveal three shelves of soda cans and booze bottles in bright colors.

"Whoa! See all this?" Lil Bit calls out across the huge space. "Want anything, Mayme? You, Amandla?"

"Whiskey," Mayme calls back, enjoying the moment. "Two ice cubes, please."

"Amanda. Drinking is bad for your heart," Neville says. "Think of the damage—"

Mayme waves him off with a flick of her finger. "Shut it, Neville. When you talk, all I hear is noise."

Seeing her so calm and in control makes me proud. Reading the report changed her. Reading the report shone a light into the dark corners of her life that she was too scared to look into. Now that she's faced the truth, she has to make things right.

She can't . . . she won't back down. And damn, if Mayme hasn't stepped up and stepped out. We Harden women are no pushovers.

"What are you doing here, Amanda?" Neville asks as Goodness and Lil Bit make a show of chugging cans of Pepsi Mango and ripping open packets of chips. "With them?"

Mayme takes a brimming tumbler of scotch with two ice cubes from Father Gibson and raises it in a silent toast. She sips, in no hurry to answer Neville's question. She is playing a deep game that I don't understand. It's amusing and frustrating. Mayme takes another hit of scotch and thumps the tumbler onto the table. Liquid sloshes over the sides and splashes onto the immaculate blond wood. Neville flinches.

"If you had loved me even a little," she says, "you would never have kicked Annalisa out of the house because she was dating a black man. And if I'd felt loved and secure, I might have tried to stop you. Instead, I let you have your way, as I did with everything."

Neville sits back in his chair with a wounded expression. "Amanda," he says, "I have no idea what you're talking about."

Mayme sighs, tired of the lying game. "Tell the truth, Neville, and maybe you can salvage something good from all the bad that you've done."

He stays silent, and anger knots my stomach. I was right. Neville will never confess; he will never suffer the pain and anguish that he caused Annalisa. His money will protect him. The tall walls around the white house will keep him safe. It's not fair. It's not right. My fingertips dip past the open zipper of my backpack, and my hand slides inside. Neville will pay. I'll make sure of it.

"Last chance to tell the truth," I say. "It's not hard. Just repeat after me, 'I am a bigot and a liar. I threw my own daughter out of home because she was dating a black man. When she stood up for—' "

Uncle Julien chooses that exact moment to walk into the room. He is red-faced and flustered, with the Mamba whispering in his ear. I wonder how long he has been outside the door, listening and doing nothing. On her worst days, Annalisa has more spine than he has on his best.

"You have it wrong," he says to me. "Your mother wasn't kicked out of home. She ran away to Johannesburg. If Father knew where she was, he would have helped her."

None so blind as those who will not see. Annalisa got that right.

Mayme sighs and turns to Julien. "Your sister did not run away." She speaks slowly and clearly, the way she might to an old pet that's lost its hearing. "When Annalisa got pregnant, Neville *did* lavish her with his help. A bed in a mental institution. Electric shock treatment. Imprisonment. And, most kind of all, he arranged for a couple to adopt her baby after it was born. But you know Annalisa. Too stubborn to know what's good for her. Instead of being grateful, she set fire to the institution and burned it down. Then she escaped with Amandla. She walked ten miles on dirt roads with no shoes before she found shelter. Imagine that. My girl is a warrior."

The tips of Uncle Julien's ears glow hot. Annalisa pushed back against Neville in ways he cannot imagine, not even in his dreams. I almost feel sorry for him, but only almost; he had a chance to show us kindness at the police station and he failed. For now, Uncle Julien is on his own.

"Is that true?" he asks Neville. "About Annalisa and the mental institution . . . the shock treatments?"

Neville pulls a worried face. "Your mother's heart condition has made it hard for her to live a full life, so she builds castles in the air and believes they're real. It's not her fault."

Every time Neville speaks, he makes it easier for me to hate him.

"Who do you believe?" Mayme asks Uncle Julien. "Your father or me?"

26

I hold my breath and wait for Uncle Julien's answer. He stands at the crossroads of two different lives. If he sides with Neville, he will spend the rest of his days doing what he has always done—trying to please his father. If he sides with Mayme, the future is new and uncertain.

Your move, brah.

"Where did you find out about the asylum and Annalisa being committed?" he says, still trying to decide on the best path to take.

I admit that Annalisa's story sounds far-fetched, but luckily, we have proof that every twist and turn is real. I take the report from the envelope and hand it to Uncle. "It's all here. With times, dates, and pictures. Mayme had this done years ago but couldn't bring herself to open it. So we did it together."

Julien flicks through the report, scanning the contents. His face goes crimson and then white as he reads the true story of Annalisa's disappearance. "My God, Dad . . ." he whispers. "How could you do this to your own child?"

"Don't tell me you believe the rubbish in that report," Neville snaps, and for the first time since entering the office, I see the unease growing inside him. He expected Uncle Julien to take his side no matter what. "None of it is true."

Lil Bit walks over to the table and throws me a can of guava juice. I catch it on the fly and rip it open to drink a mouthful of the sweet pink liquid. She turns to Neville and smiles. What is she up to?

"*Some* words in the report *are* true. Your name. Annalisa's name. The address of the white house. The name of the head psychiatrist at Bright Way House, the mental health clinic at the foot of the Drakensberg mountains where Annalisa was committed. Dr. Leonard Milton," she says with perfect recall. "I looked him up. They called him Doc Shock for his fondness for electroshock therapy. The higher the voltage, the better. He fried Annalisa's brain, and you let him. That's why her memory is broken. Call fake news all you want, but the facts are all in the report."

"I don't know anyone named Leonard Milton." Neville's stunning lack of shame remains intact. "How could I instruct a stranger to do everything that you claim?"

Father Gibson wanders over with a tumbler of scotch in his right hand, no ice. He drinks and thinks. "I'm getting on in age, but I do remember Leonard. Tall, dark hair, eyes set too close together. You introduced us at your engagement party to Amanda and again at the wedding reception . . . or am I a liar, too?"

Silence falls over the room, broken only by the distant crash of waves on North Beach. I say nothing. Neville taps his fingertips on the desktop. Is he trying to find the right words to ask for forgiveness or is he searching for a way to deflect blame for his actions?

"But why?" Julien mutters. "She was your favorite. You promised her the company."

Neville's hands make fists. "And she threw it all away for a black man who worked in a bar. Nobody in their right mind exchanges a seat in the boardroom for a barstool. I sent her to Bright Way to clear her mind. Everything I did was for her own good."

Mayme goes still, and her shoulders slump. I reach out, afraid of the strain that this conversation is taking on her heart. "You punished Annalisa for turning her back on your plans," she says. "You broke our beautiful girl. Things will never be the same between us."

"Please go home, Amanda." Neville amps up the concerned tone. "You need to rest and take care of your heart. We'll talk tonight. I promise."

Mayme snorts in disbelief. "You bring up my heart whenever you want me to shut up and go away. I've lost count of the times you barked and I backed down. I'm not backing down today. Tell the truth or there's nothing left for us to talk about."

Preach it, sister.

Neville's arctic-blue gaze drifts from Mayme to Julien and then to Father Gibson, whose cheeks glow from the scotch. We Sugar Town girls are beneath his notice. If we shouted his sins from the rooftops, nobody would believe us. Neville knows that. He knows that all the prejudiced perceptions of nonwhite women still hold sway. *Black girls lie. Dark girls will, given the chance, maliciously attempt to blackmail a powerful white man for money. It's in our blood: this need to deceive and steal and use our bodies for gain.* Social media will eat us alive.

"There are a million things for us to talk about, Amanda," Neville says. "But not here. Not surrounded by people who don't have your best interests at heart."

Lil Bit, Goodness, and me are the "people." He means black people. All nonwhites. Lazy. Scheming. Violent. His racism poisons the room. The city. The whole world.

"You'll feel better at home, surrounded by your pots and plants. And when I get home tonight, we'll go over everything in that report. We'll find a way out of this. Together."

I shoot Mayme a sideways glance. Is she buying Neville's bullshit? He's softened his eyes and mellowed his voice. He's an amazing liar with years of practice. I worry that Mayme will fall for his act and that we'll leave with nothing. Not good enough. I need to hear Neville confess to what he's done. I need him to beg forgiveness for wrecking Annalisa's life. And after he's confessed, he needs to fix what he shattered. I don't know how, but he has to try. It's still inside the room. Then:

"It's too late to sell your lies as the truth," Mayme says. "Words won't change what you did to Annalisa and Amandla. To me and to you, too, Julien. You need to suffer the way that you made us suffer."

The change in Neville is swift and frightening. The veins on his forehead pop out, and his jaw clenches. He might actually be grinding his teeth. His smooth front evaporates. He burns with rage.

"You don't have the power to punish me, Amanda," he sneers. "But go ahead and try. Let's see who wins this fight."

Mayme holds herself still and upright. She doesn't flinch in the face of Neville's dark mood and ugly threats. This is not the first time she's been bullied and belittled. I hate that, even after all his lies and crimes have been exposed, Neville refuses to show remorse for what he's done.

He will never change. Speaking truth to power is so much bullshit. Power only respects power.

* * *

I reach into my backpack and wrap my hand around a smooth polymer handle. The rough grip presses into my palm. A perfect fit. I stand up and pull a black Ruger Security 9 pistol from the interior. My hand shakes but I manage to hold the pistol steady as I aim the muzzle at Neville's heart. Or close to it. I'm no expert. We lock eyes. His are wide with shock, and mine are narrowed in determination.

All around me is noise and confusion. Everyone talks, but all I hear is white noise.

"Amandla . . ." Mayme's voice breaks through the buzz. "Put that down."

"Nah . . ." I say. "I'm cool."

Lil Bit rushes to my side. Father Gibson is right behind her; both of them are shocked. "Don't," Lil Bit says. "He's not worth it. Put the gun down."

"Killing Neville won't change what he did," Father Gibson says. "Violence isn't the answer, Amandla."

Yeah, I know, but seeing Neville scared is so satisfying. I could feed on his fear all day. "Are you sure that violence isn't the answer, Father?" I say, and keep the pistol aimed across the desk at Neville. I have his full attention. "'Cause right now it feels pretty good to me."

Goodness strolls over and stands next to Uncle Julien, who is frozen with fear.

"Shoot him in the shoulder or the arm," she says. "It will hurt like hell, but he'll live. And once a judge has read the report, you'll get off with community service. I mean, after what he did to your ma, he has it coming."

"Put the gun down!" Neville says. "Right now."

"No," I say. "Close your eyes, Neville."

He shakes his head no. I lean forward with my finger touching the trigger. "Now."

His shoulders tense, and his eyes squeeze shut, expecting a bullet. I say, "Imagine that you're running for your life on a dirt road in your bare feet for hours. You run till the skin on your burned feet rips to pieces. Your arms are exhausted from cradling the only thing you have left to love." I keep the gun in a steady, two-handed grip. Part of me wants to put down the weapon before things get out of control, but I want justice. I want tears.

"Amandla. Please . . ." Lil Bit is at my shoulder. She's waiting for the right moment to stop me from committing a crime. She's worried, but she shouldn't be. My heart rate is slow and my hand is steady.

"Take it easy, Lil Bit." I walk around the blond wood table with even steps. "It's all good."

I have taken care of my mother my whole life. I have picked up her pieces by myself with nothing. Who could Annalisa and I have been if Neville had just left her alone? I put the pistol barrel to Neville's arm. He's sweating now.

"The shock therapy wiped out most of Annalisa's memories, but she still has nightmares about smoke and fire, and pain, and running with me in her arms. She wakes up terrified because of you. She hid us inside the township because she was scared. Of you. I was born in a mental hospital because of you." I lift the barrel and press it to his temple. "You like playing God, so use your all-knowing power and tell me: How far will the bullet go? If I shoot you in the head, will it go all the way out the other side of your skull or will it get stuck in your brain?"

"Don't do it, Amandla," Mayme whispers. "I can't lose you. Not when we have so little time left."

Neville blinks and tears roll down his face. They hit the desk with wet splashes, and I smile. He is right where I want him to be. Powerless. In pain and in tears. Afraid. Maybe tonight he will dream about this moment and wake up sweating and terrified and remember what it is to be afraid for his life.

My job here is done. It is time to end the farce. I step back, hit the magazine release, and let it drop into the palm of my hand. Then I show the magazine to the group.

No bullets.

Neville sees the empty magazine and goes from scared to furious in a split second. He grabs the phone, hits three buttons, and opens an internal line. The phone is picked up on the other end. "Security," he snaps. "Three guards to my office. Now!"

Too late. I got the tears that I came for.

Mayme sits back and presses her hand to her mouth. She is shaking and afraid. And I am an idiot. My stunt could have ended with Mayme dead. Who was I kidding? Nelson the freedom fighter would never have used violence to settle a personal score. And he would have had bullets, too. Nothing that I did was for the greater good. I feel shame and triumph at the same time.

"I'm sorry, Mayme. I wasn't sure that I was actually going to use the gun, but I lost my temper and . . . I didn't even think what it would do to you."

"I'll be fine in a moment." She takes a long swallow of her abandoned scotch. "Are you hungry? It's long past lunchtime, and I'm starved."

The sudden switch from guns to food is jarring. Then I get it. Mayme wants to get us back to normal as soon as possible. She needs to erase the fear that gripped her as she waited for me to pull the trigger. I'd like to forget that moment, too.

"Any idea what you'd like to eat?" I ask, joining in.

"Let me think." She takes a minute. "Fried chicken and then chocolate?"

"Perfect." We are so calm, we might as well be talking about the possibility of rain in the afternoon. I slide the magazine back into place, and Father Gibson holds out his hand. I give him the gun, and it disappears. Neville's close call with a non-existent bullet leaves him white with rage and speechless for the moment.

Goodness says, "The Hot Dip on Makeba Street does amazing fried chicken. They have chocolate bars and chocolate malva pudding, too."

"Lead the way," Father Gibson says as two security guards in blue uniforms walk into the room. They wait for orders.

Neville snaps, "I asked for three of you."

The Indian guard looks out the window, uncomfortable. "We're here on Mrs. Bollard's request, sir."

"What!" Neville pales, and something clicks inside his head. He reaches out to take Mayme's hand, and she pulls away from him. "Everything I did was for Annalisa," he says. "To stop her from ruining her life."

I snap, "Stop lying, brah. You didn't like Annalisa being with a black man because you're a racist. Be honest with yourself and maybe, just maybe, you can change your ways." Calling my father *a black man* suddenly feels wrong. He was more than the color of his skin. He loved cold beer and the AmaZulu Football Club. He had a life and he had a name that I will not say aloud in front of Neville. Annalisa will be the first person to hear it from my lips.

"I'm not a racist," Neville says. "Do you know how many black people I employ? Hundreds and—"

"Don't waste your breath and our time." Mayme stares him down. "You committed Annalisa so you could control her. You arranged for Amandla to be adopted out to punish her. There was no love or care in what you did. And speaking of control . . . you do realize that, between us, Julien and I control the majority shares in M-Tech, Sage Property Development, and BVL Investments? Till now I've let you take care of the business, but that's all changed. My lawyer will sort out the details, but in the meantime, security is here to escort you from what is now *my* office. All right with you, Julien?"

"Yes," Julien says. "That's fine with me, Mum."

Now it is my turn to be stunned. I made Neville shed a few tears, but Mayme has taken control of the company and grabbed Neville's lifeblood. She presses her palm to her heart and takes a deep breath. I search her face for pain and see none. She is serene. A fortress. We walk to the office door side by side, our shoulders touching.

"We're going to get lunch," she tells Julien. "Are you coming?"

"I'd love to," he says, and joins us.

Neville springs to his feet. "You can't—"

"I can and I will. We're leaving, Neville," Mayme says from the door. "Security will help you out once we're gone."

27

Mayme and Uncle Julien buy enough fried chicken to feed everyone who lives on the lane. Mrs. M sets up her clean seedling bench in our front yard, and Lil Bit, Goodness, and I bring out chairs from the kitchen for people to sit on. Uncle Julien does his best to act laid-back and cool, but his nervous smile and stiff shoulders give him away. Poverty is something he reads about on the internet or sees on the evening news. He might occasionally drive by a township with his car doors locked and the windows up, but meeting the people who live inside the crooked streets and jumbled houses is different.

I bet he's sorry that he brought Sam and Harry with him. Too late now. I love that my cousins are here in Sugar Town and close to Annalisa and me. And who knows, the sound of her family's voices might reach into her subconscious and pull her back to the present. Mrs. M checks in every hour, but for now, Annalisa is sleeping like a mermaid at the bottom of the ocean.

"Where did you get it?" Lil Bit asks when we finish helping

Mrs. M load the food onto the seedling bench from where she will serve it to everyone. "Tell me, Amandla."

"Get what?" I fall into an empty chair and bite into a crispy chicken wing. I promised not to tell and I won't. Not yet.

"The gun, you fool!" Lil Bit says. "Did you steal it?"

"No." I take a second bite of the wing and roll my eyes. "Mmm. You're right, Goodness. This is the best fried chicken I've ever had. Like . . . the best."

She grabs for the wing, and I duck out of the way, laughing. Both she and Lil Bit have been burning to know all about the black Ruger pistol, which Father Gibson gave back once we reached the township. "Tell me before I make you," Goodness says, and stops to squint through the cloud of dust raised by running children. "What's *he* doing here? The Build 'Em Up is open till six."

Lewis walks through the gate and straight toward me. He squats beside my chair and holds out his hand, not a word spoken. I dip into my backpack and lay the pistol across his palm. "Everything go okay?" he asks.

"Yeah, and thanks. It did the trick."

"Good." He stands and shoves the pistol into the waistband of his jeans. "Remember, if my dad hears that I borrowed one of his guns, I'm dead."

"Understood."

Then he walks through the gate and into the lane. In a minute, he's disappeared into Tugela Way. He does not look back or wave, and I wish that he would. I need to know that asking for the pistol hasn't damaged things between us, that we are still sweet. Goodness punches me hard in the arm. The pain takes my mind off the uncomfortable feeling that the invisible thread that holds Lewis and me together could be broken.

"He gave it to you?" Goodness squeals. "Lewis hates guns. Never touches them. How did you manage to convince him?"

"I asked."

"That's it?"

"Yes."

Goodness's mouth falls open. "Oh my God. There's only one word for what he did for you!"

Stupid? Blind? Irrational?

"Love." Lil Bit laughs. "Am I right?"

Goodness and Lil Bit giggle and throw their arms around each other, cheek to cheek and hip to hip. They are making fun, but somehow, I think that they are telling each other the truth about how they feel without saying it out loud.

"Yeah," I say. "It's love."

Mayme and Uncle Julien come out of our house with Sam and Harry. I hadn't even realized they had gone inside. After this morning, the shape of the family has changed, though I'm not sure what that means for Annalisa and me. For now, though, there's food to eat with our friends and neighbors.

Mrs. Khoza brings her twins to meet Mayme and everyone gathered in our yard. Father Gibson is relaxed. He balances a Khoza baby on each hip and rocks side to side, to the amusement of Mrs. Khoza and Mrs. M. He is, it turns out, fabulous with babies.

"Here." I break a chocolate bar into pieces and share it with Lil Bit and the Bollard boys, who sit on plastic milk crates collected from the surrounding streets. Goodness passes on the chocolate. She's more of a savory girl.

I sigh and lean back. There is beauty in our shabby lane, but it only becomes obvious when you really look. The soft color of the sky and children's laughter. A woman's song caught on the breeze. In this hard place, life is all around. Full and vibrant and humming. I soak it all in. I commit the details to memory. Deep in my heart, I know that my time here is coming to an end. But not today.

* * *

Annalisa has gone deep inside herself to heal. Mrs. M says that she might sleep for an hour or for a week. It's impossible to tell. Mayme suggests we read the report aloud in the hope that the sound of our voices will bring her back to us.

We sit side by side on my cot and take turns reading. Together, we tell Annalisa her story. We give her back her lost memories. When she wakes, I will read it to her again, as many times as she likes. The information might stick in her head or it might drain away, but at least she'll know what happened sixteen years ago and why. Not all knowledge is sweet. Some of it is bitter but worth the pain.

Mayme finishes reading the second-to-last page and puts the report down. My turn. I pick it up and see that my hand is shaking. I know what comes next, and it sits like a stone on my heart. I could bury the report in our murderous front yard, where the soil will kill every word in it. I won't.

I lean close to Annalisa's cot. I tell her the truth in my own way. "On the night you met, Joseph Funani Malaba made the perfect Sazerac cocktail in a chilled old-fashioned glass. 'A perfect cocktail for a perfect girl,' he said. A pickup line for sure, but you noticed him. Tall as a lala palm. Dark as a moonless night. His long, elegant fingers wrapped around the chilled glass, and he had a smile to melt the ice cubes in it. You stayed till the bar closed. Six months later, you picked out an ivory silk dress for yourself and a sharp gray suit with a blue tie, iridescent like peacock feathers, for him. Wedding clothes."

I stop and take a long breath. I need a minute to find the right words to finish the story. Mayme takes over. "That was the plan. To marry in a civil ceremony with a witness pulled off the street. You knew to keep it a secret, but your father found out. He had you committed the day before the wedding. Neville told everyone that you'd run away. I'm your mother. I'm sorry. I should have known that he was lying."

She stops, short of breath and out of words. It's up to me to finish.

"Joseph stood on the steps of City Hall in his suit and tie from nine o'clock in the morning till nine o'clock at night, waiting for you. When you didn't show up, he went to your apartment. The apartment was empty. He came back every day for three weeks to search for you. When you didn't show, he left Durban and went to live with his parents in the countryside." I reach across the space that divides us and take Annalisa's hand. "Five weeks later, Joseph drowned crossing a river at night. Nobody knows why he went to the river or why at night, but

I imagine his mind was in a daze from losing you. At least that's what the report suggests."

Annalisa sleeps through the revelation. The shock treatments tore a hole in her memories of Joseph. How they met. Where they met. His name. How they came to be separated . . . Gone. All that was left were images of a tall black man with curly hair who loved to dance and to kiss and who would, one day, come back to her. She has no idea that this man, whose name she could not remember, is dead. My own sadness is almost overwhelming. Next time I tell her the story, maybe the hurt in my heart will have softened. "Joseph," I say, "isn't coming home."

Joseph Funani Malaba, my father, is gone. Fact.

Mayme takes Annalisa's other hand. She talks softly, her voice a balm to heal all wounds. "Joseph wanted a life with you, Annie. A home. Children. The future you planned was stolen from you both, but you escaped. You saved yourself and you saved Amandla. His daughter. He'd be proud of you, Annie. I am proud of you."

I blink back tears and wait for the dam inside me to burst and for the water to drown me the way it did my father. Then I wait for the darkness to swallow me the way it swallows my mother. I sit and wait, but the darkness doesn't come. My heart beats slowly and steadily.

I am Amandla Zenzile Harden, daughter of Annalisa Honey-Blossom Harden and Joseph Funani Malaba. My father's faraway voice whispers from the other side. It tells me to turn and face the sun.

28

On the fourth morning of Annalisa's deep sleep, Mayme and I sit and play cards at the kitchen table with our ears strained for any change in Mother's breathing. Cot springs creak, and we turn to find Annalisa awake and blinking at the ceiling. She is small and pale under the blankets, and I'm afraid that, if I make a sound, she'll close her eyes and disappear again.

"I met your father last night," she says. "He was sitting on a rock, waiting for me."

"Oh?" My heart beats out of my chest.

She turns to face me and Mayme with a dreamy half smile. "I had to cross a river to find him. The water was deep and cold, and he pulled me onto the opposite bank. We sat on a rock in the sun, holding hands. It was beautiful. The days went by so quickly. I wanted to stay with Joseph, but he said the time was wrong, that I had to cross the river again and go home. To take care of our daughter."

I blink back tears. It is the first time I have heard my father's name spoken aloud by Annalisa.

"He said that when I'm ready to cross over a second time, he'll be there, waiting. He has all the time in the world, he said. I begged him to come home, but the river wouldn't allow it. He can't make the crossing. He lives on the other side now. Do you know what means, Amandla?"

"Yes," I whisper. "I understand."

"I would have stayed with him if it weren't for you," she says. "But you need me more, and he promised to wait. I'll know where to find him when the time is right."

"Not yet," I say. "Not for a long time."

"Not for many years." She smiles at Mayme. "I heard your voice. I thought it was a dream, but it's true. You are here."

Mayme sits on the edge of Annalisa's cot. "We don't have to worry about your father anymore. Amandla and I talked to him. We told him to keep his hands out of our business, and he listened. I can go wherever I want, and I want to be here with you."

They sit together in silence, enjoying the closeness. I fill the teakettle and unpack the mixed box of coconut and gingersnap biscuits that Mayme brought. She always brings too many, and Mrs. M's grandchildren and Blind Auntie are happy to finish whatever is left over. I dump tea leaves into the teapot, and the warm, woody smell of rooibos fills the room. Annalisa whispers a question, and Mayme leans in close to answer. They need time together alone.

"Tea is brewing in the pot," I say. "Me, Goodness, and Lil Bit are going to check out the Christ Our Lord Is Risen! yard sale. I'll be back in an hour or so."

Annalisa sits up with Mayme's help and says, "Goodness, Lil Bit, and I."

I laugh at the correction. Five minutes awake and she's already schooling me in the "proper" way to speak. In time, we will find a way back to our own kind of normal. I stop in the doorway and turn to Annalisa and Mayme: two Harden women with no more lies between them. "It's good to have the both of you here and together. Don't you go anywhere without telling me, Ma!"

Annalisa laughs, and Mayme smiles to hear it. I do, too.

* * *

Families pack the yard of the gospel hall. Stalls selling cakes, counterfeit-brand clothes, and ingredients for muti—traditional medicine—take up a small amount of ground. Children run wild. I pick through a pile of dried leaves at the muti stand, just browsing, while Lil Bit and Goodness test out the beauty products that Miss Shembe cooks up in her kitchen.

Lewis walks through a crowd of little girls chasing soap bubbles. I am surprised to see him at a church yard sale in the middle of a workday. He stands next to me in sneakers and jeans, his T-shirt stained with wood sap. Even when he's messy, he's a gorgeous hunk of boy.

"Hi," I say. *Classic opening line*, I think. "It's a workday. What are you doing here?"

He blushes. I kick myself. Good work, Amandla. Push him out of the yard, why don't you?

"It's lunchtime." Lewis grabs a bunch of twigs and flips them over in his hands. "I thought I'd come over and check out what's cooking. No reason. Just filling time."

He clears his throat, aware of how bad *just filling time* sounds. We like each other. That's obvious, but who takes the next step? Me or him or the both of us at the same time? Mrs. Gabaza, wrinkled and missing an eye, comes over to us. She points to the bundle in Lewis's hand and grins.

"Boil two of the sticks for two hours. Drink the liquid and you will go all night and all day. Satisfaction *guaranteed.*"

Wait. Is she talking about . . . ? Mrs. Gabaza winks her good eye at me, and yes, she is talking about exactly what I think she is. Lewis drops the twigs like they have teeth, and I laugh. He is mortified. I love how his skin darkens in a blush.

"Let's walk," I say. "Goodness and Lil Bit will be ages."

We start a slow circuit of the yard. The stalls are set well apart, with plenty of space between them for awkward silences to build.

"How's your ma?" he asks.

"Better. She woke up this morning and talked to me and Mayme." I stand in the thin shade of a jacaranda tree. "Mrs. M thinks that the trauma from the attack will fade in time, but the scar is there to stay."

"Show me yours," he says, and takes my hand.

"What?" My face goes hot.

"Your scar." He turns my hand over and lifts it to the light. A long red wound cuts across the width of my palm. It marks out a new lifeline that will lead me to who knows where. "Does it hurt?"

"Sometimes. When I close my hand."

Lewis moves around to the other side of the jacaranda tree and takes me with him. I go willingly. Nervous and thrilled. This is the first move. Lewis lifts my hand and kisses the scar, a soft press of his lips to ease my pain. *Be careful*, Annalisa said. *But not too careful.* I am happy to be not too careful.

He says, "I was wondering if you had a chance to add more names to your list of potential boyfriends? It's been nearly a week since your ma got hurt, and a lot has changed since then."

My hand tingles, and the scar throbs with the opposite of pain. The list is the last thing on my mind. It's hard to keep my thoughts straight.

"There's still only one name on my list," I say. "And nothing has changed."

He smiles. "As soon as your mother is well enough, your grandma will pull the two of you out of Sugar Town. It's only a matter of time. A few weeks and it's goodbye."

Maybe. Maybe not. The future is unfolding one day at a time, and I only know about right now. This very minute under the Jacaranda tree with Lewis, my hand tingles from his kiss. Now is perfect. Now is all I want. He's nervous, though.

"What about you?" I ask. "Is there still only one name on your list?"

"Yes, but the girl will break my heart when she leaves me, and she will leave."

He's so certain I will walk away without a backward glance. That was my plan: to leave and never come back. Now I'm not sure. So much has happened. Lewis has happened. "The girl grew up in Sugar Town, but she doesn't know where she'll end up," I say. "The world is a big place."

Lewis runs his fingertip across my palm, slow and smooth. "There's a new housing development going up just before the turnoff to town. It's close to the city and close to Sugar Town . . . a good place for the girl to get used to living on paved streets and eating in nice restaurants. Once she's moved, she doesn't have to see anyone from Sugar Town again."

Though our move from the township now seems inevitable, Lewis is pushing me out before I'm ready to go. He wants to protect his heart, but ending things between us is a lose-lose situation. I'm not ready to walk away.

"So what do you want?" I ask. "A marriage certificate and five kids to prove that the girl is still interested?"

"No," he says. "Just a kiss to test the waters. But only if she wants."

I tilt my head and examine the dips and curves of Lewis's lips, and the word that comes to mind is *mouthwatering*. Better than *juicy*, but not by much. I will leave Sugar Town one day, but for now, I want that kiss. I want Lewis right now, in the fenced yard of the Christ Our Lord Is Risen! Gospel Hall.

"The girl on your list would like a kiss," I say. "But besides a few dry pecks and wet slobbers in primary school, she doesn't know much about kissing, while the boy on her list probably has experience."

Lewis keeps a straight face. He gives the matter thought. "All right. How about she kisses him? All she has to do is follow her instincts."

I take his advice. I follow my instincts and trace the shape of his mouth with my fingertips. I reach up and press my lips to his and slowly, slowly move my mouth across his. The contact creates a delicious friction that sends a shiver through me. I nip and press and lick. He does the same, and then we are kissing, and it feels exquisite, amazing, and new.

I could do this all day.

A soccer ball hits the fence close to us: a stray kick or warning from an old granny to respect the house of the Lord or go home.

Lewis steps back and says, "Worth doing again?"

"Yes," I say, breathless. "Absolutely yes."

So we do it again. And again, careful to keep the trunk of the jacaranda between us and the yard. Pastor Mbuli preaches on the coming days of heaven—how the gates to paradise will open only if we are good and serve the Lord. He's wrong, I think. Kissing a beautiful boy in the dusty churchyard is heaven. Right here. Right now.

* * *

Lil Bit walks me home after the yard sale. *Correction*. She walks. I float. Lil Bit loves to eat, but I think kissing is better than the best food in the world. Kissing is a feast. I slant Lil Bit a curious sideways look. I wonder . . .

"Have you kissed Goodness yet?"

"What?" Lil Bit snaps back. "Why would I do that?"

"Because," I say. "I've seen how you act around her . . . A light goes on inside you when Goodness is close. You like her. You like her the same way that I like Lewis."

She shakes her head. *No. No way.* "If I liked her that way, that would mean that my father and I are both, you know . . . Imagine the gossip. The things the church ladies would say."

I can imagine very well, but Lil Bit didn't deny her feelings for Goodness. Instead, she focused on all the negative ways that a relationship with another girl will mess up her life. She's afraid of the gossip. Of being labeled *unnatural*.

"Look on the bright side, Lil Bit. If you stick with Goodness, the church ladies will stop asking you to babysit their children. You'll be free of them."

Lil Bit smiles. "True, but what about my mother? She barely leaves the house after what Father did. Another scandal will kill her."

It won't, but the feeling that she is responsible for her mother is strong. I understand. It's hard to think of your own needs when your parent needs so much care and attention. You live your life in service to them.

"Your ma won't change no matter what you do. She has to fix herself. You can help, but that's all you can do. It's all anyone can do." I throw my arm around her shoulder. "Meanwhile, you are missing out on kissing those juicy Dumisa lips."

"You pervert!" Lil Bit snorts. "Juicy?"

"Yes," I say. "You have to try it."

"Maybe . . ." Lil Bit says. "Maybe I will. But if you tell anyone about this conversation, I will be forced to kill you."

We walk down the street with our arms around each other, sisters and secret members of the newly formed Dumisa Appreciation Society.

29

A fist bangs against our tin door, and the walls creak. Annalisa sleeps through the noise with the help of painkillers, but I am up and across the small kitchen space in three seconds flat. It's seven fifteen in the morning, too early for Mayme's daily visit and too late for the police raids that occasionally sweep through the township.

"Amandla," a voice calls. "It's me."

"Sam?!" I open the door and find him standing in the dirt yard, his cheeks flushed and a gaping hole in his T-shirt. "What happened?"

He says, "I jumped out my bedroom window and went over the garden wall. I threw a blanket over the wires, but I got caught on the way across."

The razor wire that's coiled on the top of the tall walls in nice parts of town has slashed his T-shirt. *Shhh.* I put my finger to my lips and pull him inside.

"Sit. Lemme see." He sits at the table, and I yank up his T-shirt to check the damage. A tiny scratch crusted with dried blood. He is already healing. Sam is all right. He is in Sugar Town and in my house.

"Why did you scale the wall when you could have walked out the front door?"

"No choice," he says. "Dad won't let me come visit you by myself, and he's too busy kicking Grandpa out of the company to find the time to bring me out. 'When things have settled,' he says, but I couldn't wait."

"All right, but you still could have used the door."

He laughs. "True, but no lie, I've always wanted to go over the wall just to see what it's like. And I left a note saying where I was."

"Good work." I take his hand and lead him across the small space to the bedroom area. We stand at the foot of Annalisa's cot and watch the peaceful rise and fall of her chest in the early morning light.

"Will your mother be all right?"

"Yeah, the knife wound healed up nicely. She's walking and talking and getting stronger every day." How sweet it is to say those words out loud. "But in the meantime, do you want a tea or coffee?"

"Coffee, please," he says, and follows me into the kitchen. He's not completely at home inside our tin walls, but the worn floors and rusted roof don't freak him out, either. Where is his mother, I wonder, and how did he get to be so at home in his own skin?

"Mayme will be here in a few hours. How long can you stick around?"

"All day." He takes two cups from the cupboard like he has lived here forever. "Or until my dad sends someone to find me. Though I'd rather not be here when that happens."

"I can arrange that. How are your lungs?"

He frowns. "Fine as far as I know. Why?"

"I'm taking you some place where screaming is encouraged."

* * *

The wooden grandstand sways and groans as the crowd jumps to their feet to shout encouragement at a player taking a run at goal. Shouts of "He scores! He scores!" thunder from all sides when the Sugar Town Shakers put one in the net. A little boy on the edge of the field breaks into a victory dance and sends dirt flying into the air.

I check Annalisa out the corner of my eye, concerned that the noise and the relentless energy of the soccer match might be too much for her. She's calm. Her visit to the land of the dead changed her. She still has sad moments and blanks, but knowing that Joseph is waiting on the other side of the river has, somehow, anchored her in the here and now. Things will never be perfect, though. The damage done by the shock treatments can't be repaired. Finding out the truth about what Neville did has changed my reaction to Annalisa's mind drifts. Now when she forgets and asks me when Father will be back, I tell her soon; I tell her that he misses her and thinks about her every day. I lean my shoulder against hers. We are both perfectly imperfect, and knowing that makes our relationship easier.

Mayme sits between Sam and Lil Bit and smiles at the little boy dancing in the dust. This is her first township soccer match, a "winter warmer" before the opening of the official season, and despite Mrs. M's warnings about the noise, she refused to stay on the lane. *My heart can take it*, she said.

She is determined to live every last minute of the time that's left to her.

"Goodness has talent," Annalisa tells me when the noise dies down. "If she wants to play on the women's national team, she has to step up a league and get herself noticed."

I am no longer Annalisa's sole focus. She has plans for Lil Bit (a scholarship to a *decent* university) and Goodness (*international* soccer stardom) and Lewis (his *own* construction business). She aims high on all our accounts.

On the field, Goodness swats a ball away from the net to keep the Sugar Town Shakers in the lead. The crowd roars. "She saves! She saves!" Goodness is the only female on the team. The men accept her because she is a superstar; her talent is too big to be contained inside the township. When she kicks the ball, it makes a sound like a rifle shot and flies down the field to land at the feet of a Sugar Town striker who flies toward the opposition goalie. He aims the ball at a right angle and curves it into the back of the net.

Annalisa stands up and claps, and I stand with her. Laughter and chants of "He scores!" surround us. The man next to Mayme lifts his arms and throws her a prodding look that says, *Come on, sister. Give it power!*

Mayme stands and lifts her hands above her head. Sam and Lil Bit lock their arms around her waist to keep her steady. The atmosphere is electric. And infectious. I grab Annalisa's hand

and call out at the top of my voice, "He scores! He scores!" She laughs and joins in the chanting till we are both hoarse and breathless. It feels good to make noise. To raise our voices in a chorus of celebration.

I turn to check on Mayme. Dust motes float around her head like a halo. Her face shines with joy. Life is all around her, full and overflowing. She is beautiful, and my heart hurts to see her so radiant and present.

* * *

We slowly walk home, glowing from the Sugar Town Shakers' 3–2 victory over the Durban Diamonds. Goodness blocked a shot at goal in the dying minutes of the match. A close call. My throat is raw from screaming useless instructions from the stands. "Watch out. Stop that ball!" Goodness managed to save the match without my help.

We turn into Tugela Way. Sam, Goodness, and Lil Bit run ahead, kicking a ball from one to the other. Where Goodness gets the energy to keep going, I don't know. When the action and excitement have died down, she'll need a quiet place to just breathe. Lil Bit could be that quiet resting place for her. I hope they will soon figure out how perfectly they balance each other out.

Mayme squeezes my hand. It hurts a little, but the feeling of our bones pressed together is heaven. I think maybe she's imprinting the memory of herself on my skin, on me. Our time together is running out. Do we have days or weeks left? That's not enough. I want years, not months.

I can't help myself. The words spill out.

"Lil Bit looked up the stats. Open-heart surgery is nasty and the recovery is painful, but . . . if you survive the operation, you could live for years longer. Will you please think about it? Annalisa wants more time with you. I want more time with you."

We walk on in silence. A noisy voice fills the quiet space inside my head. *Mayme knows all about heart operations. She doesn't need you to tell her how it is or what she should do with her own life. You pushed her into a corner. You asked her to do something that she has already told you she doesn't want to do. Smooth move, Amandla.*

Minutes go by. Mayme doesn't say a word, and that makes me anxious.

"I'm sorry . . . I shouldn't have—"

"No. You did right." Mayme stops at the mouth of the lane. "I've lived with a broken heart my whole life. And now, for the first time, I have a chance to fix it. Not just the weak muscle inside my chest, but the contents. I have plenty of sadness and fear stored away. From now on, I want to fill my heart with happiness and good memories."

Does that mean Mayme has changed her mind about the operation? I turn to ask and see tears in her eyes. Annalisa sees them, too, and dips into her bag for tissues. She pulls out a linen handkerchief with the initials *BBZ* monogrammed on the corner and gives it to Mayme. A second later, she pulls out a beaded necklace with a wide, flat pendant designed to sit at the base of the neck. The colors are gorgeous. Copper, brown, and pearl beads woven into intricate diamond shapes.

"A Zulu love letter," Goodness whispers, mindful of Mayme's tears. "The diamond shapes represent a married woman, but the colors have a secret meaning that only the woman who made it and the man she sent it to understand."

"Oh." Annalisa holds the necklace out to Mayme. "You're the only married woman here. This is for you."

The necklace is a mystery, both vintage and modern at the same time. Was it made by a lovesick woman decades ago or hand-sewn by a design student in a city studio last week? It doesn't matter. Seeing the necklace makes Mayme forget her tears. It makes her smile.

"Lean forward." Annalisa slips the necklace around Mayme's neck and closes the clasp. The beaded panel sits snug against the breastbone. It could have been made for her. Maybe Annalisa's bag is magic after all.

"I love it," Mayme says, and runs her fingers over the beads to feel the rough texture. "And yes, Amandla. I'll talk to my surgeon in the morning and schedule the operation. I've decided to live fast and die old."

Thank you, Father, and all the saints in heaven. Mayme will be at my high school graduation and my eighteenth-birthday party, which I have decided will be big and flashy, with a thumping DJ and close dancing. Annalisa might be right. There really might be angels whose job it is to listen to our dreams and help them catch the light.

30

That night, Annalisa shakes me from sleep, and I roll onto my back, disoriented. A single candle throws light onto the rusted walls, enough for me to see that she is barefoot and in her flannel nightdress. She leans close to my face.

"Get up, Amandla. Someone is coming."

I get up and get out of bed. I don't argue. Annalisa might be emerging from the tail end of a nightmare that woke her or she might be having one of her episodes. It's impossible to know, so I surrender to whatever is happening. She opens the wardrobe, pulls out a pale yellow dressing gown with a moth-eaten silk collar, and gives it to me. I've never seen it before. "Wait outside the door. Not too far into the yard," she says in an urgent voice. "I don't want to hear what they have to say."

She's scared, and now so am I.

"Go, Amandla."

I wrap myself in the too-big dressing gown and flick on the electricity on my way out of the house. It's still dark outside, and the light spilling from the open door will help me see what's coming. I go halfway to the gate and search the lane in both directions. A three-quarter moon hangs over the rooftops, and a dog barks in Tugela Way. The lane is asleep. Annalisa's visions have been wrong more times than they've been right. This is one of those times. I turn back to the house, relieved, and then I hear footsteps on the road. I turn and see two human shapes in the moonlight.

It's hard to make out who they are, but my heart knows. It's Father Gibson and Sam. They have come with news that I don't want to hear. I hold up my hand to stop them from getting any closer.

"Go away," I call out. "I don't want to talk to you."

Father Gibson rests his hand on the gate. He is a wreck in wrinkled clothes, his face drawn tight with sadness. Sam hangs back in the darkness, and the sound of him crying is loud in the stillness.

"Amandla . . ." Father Gibson opens the gate and walks toward me. "I'm so sorry—"

"No!" I cut him off. "It's too soon. She still has time to get the operation."

He shakes his head and holds out his hands to take mine. I step back. Does he not understand what I said? *It is too soon.*

"No," I say again. "Just. No."

Sam comes into the yard, with puffy eyes and cheeks wet with tears. "You're right," he says. "Mayme left too soon, but I think she died happy."

"Happy to leave me and Annalisa after one week together?" *Wrong answer!* "You had fifteen years with her. I had days. Days! It's not fair."

My knees give way, and Father Gibson catches me before I hit the ground. My heart hurts inside my chest, and I can't breathe. White spots float in front of my eyes, and I suck in a mouthful of air. A wailing sound comes from inside the house. Annalisa is in pain and falling apart. This is where I run and help her. It is my job to save her from the darkness.

"Sam," Father Gibson says, "take care of your cousin while I see to Annalisa."

I slide to the ground the moment Father Gibson's hands leave my shoulders. I sit in the dirt, and Sam sits next to me. Tears stream down his face, and seeing him cry makes me cry. I lay my head on his shoulder and let the tears come.

"I'm sorry your time with Mayme was so short." Sam wipes his nose on his sleeve and clears his throat. "If it helps . . . this last week was the happiest I ever saw her. She got to live her life on her own terms before she died. You helped her do that. *You did that, Amandla.*"

Maybe someday in the future, I will be glad that I helped Mayme reclaim some of her power, find some joy, and find her family again. Right now, though, grief has shattered me into a million pieces.

* * *

Saint Luke's Mission by the Sea is built of stone. It has stained-glass windows and a steeple that pierces the sky. The church towers over wild grass fields and looks down on the distant blue of the Indian Ocean. If I was God, I'd want to live here.

We walk through the parking lot toward the front doors, and my mouth sags open at the collection of luxury cars around us. Shiny cars with working stereos and leather seats. Cars with horned bulls and winged ladies on the hood and not a speck of rust.

I shrink an inch with every step that we take toward the carved wooden doors. The feeling of not belonging comes in a wave. Nobody inside of Saint Luke's has ever haggled over the price of chicken necks. Of this I am sure. My heart beats loud in my ears, and it's difficult for me to move forward.

"We've come too far to turn back, Amandla." Annalisa straightens her spine. "The congregation might judge our clothes and our hair, but Mayme never did. All she sees right now is her daughter and her granddaughter coming to say good-bye. And I know it makes her happy."

Lewis presses his hand to the small of my back and urges me on. Annalisa and I have come all this way, not for the living, but for the dead. We are here for Amanda Iris Harden Bollard, who broke out of her golden cage to spend the last days of her life with us in Sugar Town.

"Keep your head up high and don't walk too fast," Annalisa whispers as we step through the open doors and into the cool interior of the church. The pews on either side of us are filled with people: mostly white faces I've never seen before, and a sprinkling of black, Indian, and mixed-race faces, too. All are dressed in dark suits and black dresses. Even if we'd come early and sat in a corner, our group would stand out. We add a bright pop of color to the somber atmosphere. Mayme would have liked that, too, I think.

Mrs. M is in a hot-pink suit, and Lil Bit and Goodness and me wear shweshwe print dresses covered with blue and red starbursts. Annalisa's black silk pants, white silk shirt, and zebra-print scarf score an 80 percent match for the right colors but only 5 percent for proper funeral clothes. Lewis wears a light blue suit with a white shirt and white high-tops with blue laces. He is a beautiful dream of a boy. I'm scared to look at him for more than a few seconds in case what I'm feeling for him is written all over my face.

Annalisa walks to the very front of the church, a journey that takes us past the hundreds of mourners inside Saint Luke's. People stare. Mouths fall open and eyebrows shoot up. It's as if they've seen a ghost. I hear whispers from both sides of the aisle. "That's definitely her," "Where's she been for all this time?" and "I heard she was *dead*."

Annalisa's presence is a shock. It rattles the congregation to see her alive and with her mixed-race daughter. No doubt they heard and believed the story that she ran away to Jozi and fell in with a bad crowd. Maybe they still believe that. I force my legs to keep moving. It's a challenge. Saint Luke's is a sacred space dressed in acres of white flowers and lit by white candles, and I am dragging my dusty shoes right through the heart of it.

I throw Mum a sideways glance and find her in full untouchable mode. She looks neither left nor right. She sails down the aisle with her focus pinned on the high altar and the red-haired woman playing the church organ behind it. Sam stands at the end of an empty pew two rows from the front and guards the space.

"Thank you." Annalisa kisses his cheek, and he steps aside to let all of us into the reserved seats. Nobody tries to stop us, and there's plenty of room. I sit and try to relax. Members of the family who are strangers to me turn and stare. Fair. I am the first mixed girl to sit in the family pews, and with my black friends, no less. An older man with a red-veined nose turns and glares at us. He is a heavyset version of Neville with thin lips and a thick neck.

Annalisa says, "Amandla, meet my uncle Rupert. Your grandpa's brother."

"Have you no shame?" Uncle Rupert asks in a loud whisper. "Take your brat and get."

Get.

Neville said the same thing to me in the rooftop garden at the institute. Neville, who is now losing the fight to keep his control over the Bollard Company's vast holdings: a diamond mine, a tech company, a real estate empire, and a financial investment firm. *Too bad, so sad.* Neville, who has no family left but this puffed-up old codger with a drinker's nose. His attitude is offensive, but I am not offended. I am calm.

"Get what, exactly?"

"Get out," he says between clenched teeth. "Take your disgrace for a mother and leave."

"No, I don't think we will. We have a right to be here."

"You are an embarrassment." My great-uncle leans close, all the better to intimidate me with his bulky white richness. "You have no place here."

My calm disappears. Mayme bore my mother and my mother bore me in an unbroken chain of female labor and pain. No man can break that hold.

"Catch up. Times have changed. In Nelson's South Africa, we all belong. You better get used to it, because Annalisa and I are here to stay. With, or without, your permission." I shake my head at the red color in Great-Uncle's face. "And turn the heat down before you catch fire and burn the church down."

"Listen here . . ."

The organ music swells, and Father Gibson, dressed in a white robe with a strip of bright purple fabric layered over the top, lifts both his hands in a gesture for us to rise. I hesitate, afraid of making a mistake in front of a church full of posh people who know when to sit and when to stand. Annalisa probably grew up going to this church with these cousins and agitated great-uncles while I am just a stranger from the township. I follow her lead, and Lewis, Lil Bit, and Goodness follow mine. Mrs. M, a regular churchgoer, is relaxed and at ease.

Father Gibson prays, and Annalisa grips my hand so tightly that my fingers go numb. I turn to the entrance and see the reason for her fierce hold. Six pallbearers in black suits walk through the church doors with a coffin balanced on their shoulders. The polished wooden casket is dressed in white flowers, and the gold handles shine in the low light.

"Oh, Mayme," I whisper through tears. My heart hurts inside my chest. This is the final goodbye for a grandmother who passed through my life like a comet, bright and beautiful. I hate that she's gone. Her dying has left a hole inside me that can't ever be repaired, and I wonder if Neville has a hole inside him as well. Maybe, in our grief, we can find the grace to forgive and start again. He is my grandfather, and secretly, I hope for his redemption.

I sway on my feet. Lewis takes my right hand and Annalisa my left. The mourners bend their heads in quiet respect as the pallbearers move slowly down the aisle and rest the casket in front of the altar. Uncle Julien and Neville, both pale and drained, walk to the family pews. I don't know the other pallbearers.

Neville stops dead when he sees Annalisa and me in the space reserved for family. Lewis tenses, ready to fight for my right to mourn in peace. Uncle Julien moves around Grandpa and holds his hand out to his youngest son. Harry joins him, and together, they join us in the rebel pew. Sam greets his father and brother with a smile, and we shuffle closer to make space for them.

Neville stands in front of the first pew, isolated and alone. I am sorry for him, but he has to be the one to ask for forgiveness for what he's done. He must change his ways. Annalisa barely notices him. Her attention is on the coffin and the cascade of white roses that release a sweet perfume into the air. Father Gibson places a framed picture of Mayme on the casket. In the photo, Mayme wears a flowered silk dress and a double strand of pearls. She is every inch the great and good Mrs. Bollard, rich society matron and generous philanthropist. Then Father Gibson reaches into his robes and pulls out the beaded necklace that Annalisa found in the depths of her magic bag. He loops it around the base of the photograph. The earth colors and the vibrant Zulu patterns transform the untouchable Mrs. Bollard into Mayme, loved grandmother, passionate gardener, and late-blooming soccer fan.

I wipe away tears and focus on her. Neville is alive. He has time to fix what he broke. This is Mayme's funeral. This is her time.

"Please, sit." Father Gibson's voice breaks on the words. Conducting this service is going to be hard for him. Neville sits next to Uncle Rupert. He is so close . . . *Please, Jesus. Keep him away from us!* I do not have the strength to deal with another insult from a nasty Bollard man. Rupert leans into his brother and says, "I tried to get them to leave, but that half-caste piece has a mouth on her . . . like so many of them do. She—"

Neville says, "Be quiet, Rupert. Amanda loved the girl."

I stare at Neville, stunned. To his credit, he does not claim to love or even like me. He is being polite for Mayme's sake. And while he didn't exactly defend me, he didn't use the words *kaffir* or *township trash*, either. A low bar to jump, but a small step in the right direction. It might take him a decade to call me granddaughter or Amandla, but I'm not going anywhere. I am part of the Bollard family now.

Neville, I notice, is sick-looking, like he's lost a part of himself—because he has. Mayme's passing has hit him hard. Perhaps harder than he imagined it would. He turns and pulls an envelope out of his jacket pocket. He gives it to me.

"From your mayme," he says.

"When did . . ."

"The night she died. Her time was running out, and it was you that she thought of. You and Annalisa."

I take the envelope, and he turns to face the front. It's strange that Mayme went back to the big white house after the bust-up at the office, but I understand. She raised Annalisa and Julien there. Planted trees and a garden. Lived the life of a perfect society wife behind the gates, before she found her own path. Neville does not deserve her grace, but I think he's trying to earn it back.

Annalisa slumps against my shoulder and presses her face into the crook of my neck. Her tears soak the collar of my dress. I want to be strong for her, but my sadness makes me weak. We hold each other tightly and cry together. Tears are the only way to release the grief inside us.

Lewis sits close and quiet. He is a rock in the storm for me and for Goodness and Lil Bit: Mayme's Sugar Town Queens who stared down "the Mamba" and gave Mayme the courage to stand up for herself. It's a miracle that we are all here with Mrs. M, Uncle Julien, and the boys. Mrs. M pats Sam's hand, and he leans his head against her shoulder for comfort. We are separate individuals joined together by our loss and our compassion for each other.

This, I think, is Ubuntu.

31

I sit in the shade of a Natal mahogany tree planted at the edge of the graveyard while the others go down to the hidden cove below the church grounds. The parking lot is empty now, the mourners are on their way to the wake at the big white house. Neville invited us, but first we have business to take care of.

I lean back against the tree trunk with Mayme's letter in my hand. My name is written on the front of the envelope in dark ink, in Mayme's familiar sloping hand. Her last words. For me. There will never be a perfect time to read what she's written. I tear the envelope open and I begin:

Dearest Amandla,

Your mother says that you are named after me, but that's not right. Your name means power in Zulu and Xhosa, and you already have more power than I ever did. The power to do things. To make change. Don't settle for anything less than what's in your dreams.

There is too much to say and not enough time to say it. Times like this, I like to make a list. Lists help me put my thoughts in order. They give the world shape. Through this letter and the will, I have tried to be brave in the last hour. Now. At last. Too bloody late for us, but not too late for you, Amandla. I'm at my end and you are at your beginning.

My list of hopes/wishes/dreams,
in no particular order:

1. Forgive me.
2. Be the woman that I never was:
   strong, confident, and powerful.
3. Be kind to Neville if you can. Give
   him time. I know that he will come
   to love and appreciate you as I do.
4. Fall in love with whomever you want
   (no matter what color), and may
   that person be kind and generous
   and love you in return.
5. Visit me now and again.
   My favorite flowers are white roses.

I have left you two gifts. The first is half my shares in the family company, which will come to you on your twenty-first birthday. Till then, you and Sam will learn the business from Julien and from the board of directors. I know you will use this gift for good.

The second and more important gift is a name: Poppy Malaba. Poppy is your other grandmother, and she lives north of Richards Bay. If you're reading this, then I'm gone, but you have another family besides the Bollards. They are waiting to hear from you: Joseph's daughter. His living legacy. His blood. Kiss your grandmother for me.

And one last thing. Thank you for taking care of Annalisa. You are the light of her eyes, and even now, with the dark shadow of death hanging over me, you are the light of mine. Forever and for all time.

With love and gratitude,
Mayme Amanda

* * *

The path to the cove below the church winds through tall grass and coastal scrub. Waves pound the shore, and gulls sweep across the water, skimming for fish. Clouds float on the horizon, white castles in the air. Two large boulders sit like giant marbles in the sand. More rocks rise out of the ocean, and the waves turn to foam as they try to get around them. Tears sting my eyes as I stumble onto the beach.

Father Gibson and Sam, who insisted on joining the Zulu cleansing ritual, collect twigs from the underbrush with wet hair and wet towels wrapped around their shoulders. Annalisa waves from the water. I kick off my shoes and shed my clothes down to my underwear. Mrs. M, also in her undies, runs onto shore, shivering.

"In you go, my girl," she says. "Make sure that the water covers your whole body and also your head. That is the only way to wash away the past."

I run across the sand and plunge under the foaming crest of a wave. The cold is a shock, and I surface with a scream. Annalisa swims over to me and rubs warmth into my arms and shoulders. "Come out when you're ready," she says, and swims hard for the shore, where Sam and Father Gibson have built a small fire to heat us up after the dip in the cool ocean.

Lewis surfaces next to me, and I turn to him like a flower turns to the sun. We tangle together with our limbs entwined and our bodies rising and falling with the surge of the ocean. We kiss, all salty and delicious, and he shivers, from the cold or from our closeness, I don't have enough experience to tell which. Feeling bold, I lean forward and lick the groove of his dimples. Mmm. Nice. He shivers again, and this time, I know that my dimple licking is the cause. It's hard to remember that we are here on serious business. I concentrate.

"Where are Lil Bit and Goodness?"

"Having a private moment behind that rock to our right," he says. "I thought it was better to leave them to it."

"About time they figured it out." A wave pushes me against Lewis's cold chest. "Go and get warm. I'll be out soon."

"Are you sure?"

"Very sure," I say, and kiss him again so that he understands that I am fully sure about being here with him on a wild beach below a graveyard. He kisses me back and swims to shore with slow, powerful strokes.

* * *

I breach the surface of a wave and blink the salt water from my eyes. The ocean stretches all the way to the horizon, but the current tugs me back toward the shore, where everyone now crowds around the fire to dry off. Father Gibson swam with us. He does not believe that the waves will magically wash away all the bad muti from the attack in the alley, but he does believe that the ocean is powerful enough to heal wounds.

I dive below the water. I imagine Jacob Caluza's blood and my guilt dissolving off me and drifting out to sea. With the right wind and a high tide, the weight of both these burdens will float out beyond the breakers and into the open ocean. They might reach the island of Madagascar or travel up north as far as Somalia on the horn of Africa. And then, just disappear.

I flip onto my back and float on the surface. The water holds my weight, and the sunshine warms my face. I close my eyes and lie suspended between the ocean and the sky. I try to make a list of all the things I need to do to make sure that my future is a good one.

My mind refuses. There is only water and sand and the motion of the waves.

"Amandla!" Annalisa calls to me from the beach. "Come sit with us by the fire!"

I float for a moment, then I turn and swim toward shore.

To love and adventure.

To family and friends.

Turn the page for an excerpt of
the *Los Angeles Times* Book Prize winner

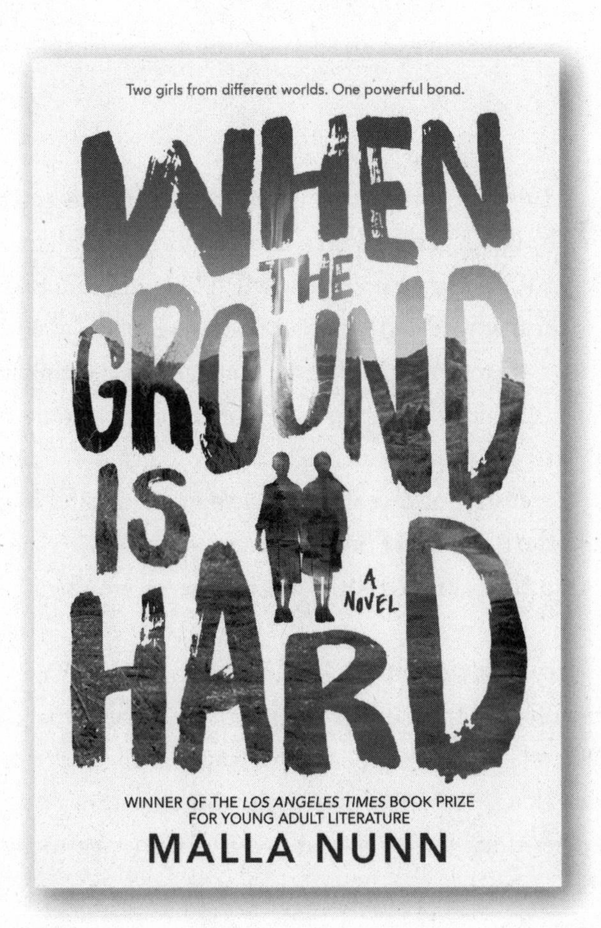

1

Dying Days

It's Thursday night, so we walk down Live Long Street to the public telephone booth at the intersection of three footpaths called Left Path, Right Path, and Center Path. My flashlight beam bounces the length of the dirt road and picks out uneven ground and potholes, of which there are many. Mrs. Button, who lives in the pink house behind the mechanic's workshop, says that all streets should be paved like they are in England, but we're not in England—we are in the British protectorate of Swaziland, fenced in on all sides by Mozambique and the Republic of South Africa—so what does she know?

"Pick up the pace," Mother says in a fierce whisper. "We can't be late."

We hurry past cement-brick houses with cracks of light spilling from under locked front doors. Dogs bark in fenced yards. A curtain twitches, and a face peers at us through a space the width of a hand. The face belongs to Miriam Dube, the church minister's wife, who makes it her duty to spy on our weekly pilgrimage to the public phone box. It's dark, but I imagine that Mrs. Dube's expression is smug disapproval.

Mother holds her head high, like she is balancing the weight of an iron crown or suffering a garland of thorns. The neighbors are jealous, she says. Jealous gossips who frown on her high heels and her dresses straight from Johannesburg that show too much leg. They know we have carpet in the living room, she says. We also have Christmas bicycles with flashing chrome, in the backyard, and new Bata school shoes that still smell of the factory, under our beds.

They have concrete floors, and if they do have rugs, they are sure to be ugly when compared to the tufted field of purple flowers that blossom under our feet when we walk from the settee to the kitchen. That's why they hate us. That's why they don't stop to give us a lift when they see us walking at the side of the road, weighed down with shopping bags. The Manzini market is three miles from our house, Mother says. Three miles across dry fields pocked with snake and scorpion holes. A dangerous walk. A Christian would see our suffering and pick us up. But our neighbors—who call themselves Christians and stuff the church pews every Sunday—they drive by and leave us in their dust.

The phone booth appears in my flashlight beam: a rectangle of silver metal cemented into the red earth. Right Path, Left Path, and Center Path split off and disappear into vacant land covered in weeds. Bored children and drunks have left their initials and their boot prints on the glass walls, but, by some miracle, the interior light still gives off a dim glow, which attracts a circling cloud of white moths.

Mother feeds four silver coins into the change slot and dials a number. Her hands shake, and her breath comes short from walking the uneven road in high heels. As a rule, she never leaves our house in flat sandals or, Lord save us, the loose cotton slippers worn by women who value comfort over fashion sense. The coins drop, and she shapes her mouth into a smile.

"It's me," she says in a throaty voice that she reserves for the telephone.

The voice on the other end says something that makes her laugh, and she flashes me a triumphant glare. *You see?* her look says. *I call every Thursday night to talk about what's happening with you, me, and your brother, Rian, and he answers just like that . . .*

Mother wants me to know that, no matter what names the church ladies call her, her relationship with him is special. She has a good man she can rely on, and how many "loose women" and "tramps" can say the same thing? Zero. *That's* how many. Mother, I think, wants me to be proud of our weekly walk to the phone box.

I pick a twitching moth from my hair and blow it into the air. Its wings leave a fine white powder on my fingertips, and I brush it off onto the front of my skirt while Mother talks low and soft into the receiver.

"Of course. Adele is right here." She snaps her fingers to get my attention. "She's dying to talk to you."

I take the receiver from her and say, "Hello. . . . I'm fine. How are you?"

The voice tells me that he's tired but it's good to hear my voice and Mother's. Did the rest of the Christmas holidays go well? Am I ready for my second-to-last year of high school, and, good heavens, where does the time go? He pays the fees, so I tell him, "Yes, yes, I can't wait to go back to Keziah Christian Academy." It's January 21, three days before the term starts, but my bags are already packed. "It will be good to see my friends again." Phone time is precious. I can't waste a second of it by mentioning the bad food or the sharp edge of Mr. Newman's ruler that raps against my knuckles when I get a wrong answer or look at the mountains through the classroom window for too long. Mother says: *Have some pride, girl. Nobody wants to hear your problems. Nurse your sorrows in private like the rest of us.* She double-snaps her fingers to let me know that my time is up.

"See you soon, I hope." I surrender the receiver and step away to give her privacy. A cloud of moths beats a white circle around the phone box while others lie on the ground with broken wings.

I pull a strand of wild grass from the side of the road and chew the sweet end while Mother whispers promises into the telephone. Her right hip and shoulder press against the glass, and in that moment, surrounded by fields of rustling weeds and the low night sky, she seems small and completely alone. Just her and the moths dancing together in the pale light while darkness swallows everything around them.

Minutes pass. She hangs up and strides across the pockmarked road with her high heels clicking and her hips swinging to a tune that only she can hear. A loose curl bounces against her flushed right cheek, the way it always does after she's talked to him on the telephone. I can't tell if winding a strand of hair around her index finger is a nervous habit or a soothing motion. She throws her arms wide and hugs me tight. Air escapes my lungs with a hard whoosh.

"He's coming," she whispers into my ear.

"When?" I want dates and times. In one way or another, he is always on his way. He tells us he'll be in Mkuze, only five hours' drive from us. Or he has a meeting coming up in Golela, and it's a quick hop across the border from South Africa to us. Next, he's visiting Kruger Park with the other children and he might drop by for a few hours. Maybe he'll show up. Maybe he'll come this weekend . . .

"Saturday." Mother is giddy with joy. "He wants to see you before you leave for boarding school. And he wants to see Rian. You know how he worries about Rian's asthma. Missing school. He cares about us, my girl, but you know how things are."

Yes, I know "how things are." I am an expert in the unwritten rules that govern our family and the boundaries that can't be crossed or even mentioned out loud. I was born knowing. Mother reminds me of "how things are," on a regular basis so I'll remember that certain things in life can't be changed.

"Come." Mother grabs my arm, and we retrace our footsteps back in the direction of home. The vacant land around us rustles with sounds: secretive porcupines digging up roots, the soft pads of a house cat hunting small creatures through the bush, and a nightjar's escalating song. Mother hums "Oh Happy Day" under her breath. She used to sing in the church choir, and she has a lovely voice even now.

Car headlights swing off Center Path, and two bright beams illuminate the craggy length of Live Long Street. We automatically jump off the road and into the tall grass that grows thick along the edge. A truck speeds past, and we tuck our faces into the crooks of our arms to avoid being choked by dust. The white Ford pickup truck with a dented front fender belongs to Fergus Meadows, who lives in the house opposite ours and inherited his father's lumberyard five years ago.

A stone pings my leg, and I see that I'm cut. I wipe the blood away with white powdered fingers and step back onto the street. This is where Mother usually says, *Hooligan! His father would die twice if he knew how spoiled that boy has turned out. He saw us walking in the dark. Don't you think he didn't. Two females. Alone. Yet he doesn't even slow down. Imagine!*

But tonight is different. Instead of criticizing Fergus Meadows's manners, she flicks dust from her skirt and tucks her arm through mine. She hums and smiles at the half-moon in the sky. The neighborhood gossip and the sly glances thrown at her in the aisles of the new hypermarket on Louw Street can't touch her. She is bulletproof. She is armored by a simple fact:

He is coming.

•••

I lie awake to the rasp of my little brother's asthmatic breath in the next room and the hard scrap of steel wool on the kitchen stovetop. Mother is cleaning in preparation for the visit. A maid comes every day except Sunday, but you can't trust them, Mother says. They don't know how to treat nice things. They are careless, and you have to watch they don't break the fine china cups or leave streak marks on the windows.

It's better to do the important things yourself, she says. That way you know they are done right. His arrival is the number one most important thing. The house has to be perfect when he walks through the door on Saturday, so Mother takes care of the details. She cleans the stove, washes the floors, and dusts the porcelain angels on the sideboard next to the settee. Tomorrow, on Friday, she will choose our outfits for his visit: a pretty dress with strappy sandals for me, and a pair of khaki shorts and a collared shirt for Rian. We will be clean and neat, to match the house.

The oven door opens, and the *scratch, scratch, scratch* of the steel-wool pad continues. To my knowledge, he has never once looked inside the oven or opened the cupboards. Maybe this visit he will, so Mother has to make ready.

I roll over and blink at the windup clock on my bedside table. It is twelve minutes to midnight.

Rian coughs and Mother cleans, and I think of the moths suspended above the phone booth, their delicate wings beating the air until dawn.

• • •

Sixteen is four years too old to be sitting on his knee, but when he collapses on the lounge chair, all rumpled and sweaty from driving tar roads and gravel paths and narrow dirt lanes to get to us, I do just that. I take his right knee and Rian takes his left, and we simultaneously plant kisses on opposite cheeks: a ritual that goes back to before my memory begins. Bristles prick my lips, and I think that he is tired, that he is older than when he delivered our Christmas presents five days before Christmas Day. *He wanted to spend the holidays with us*, Mother says, *but you know how things are.*

"Look at you," he says to Rian, who is pale and exhausted from last night's asthma attack. "You'll be bigger than me soon."

That's possible. Rian is thirteen and sprouting fast while our father gets smaller each year, the black strands of his hair now overrun with gray. What he lacks in muscle and youth, he makes up for with brains, Mother says. He is an engineer. He builds the dams that hold the water that feeds the cornfields and fills the bathtubs of the people who live in town who've forgotten how to wash in rivers.

"And you." He pinches my cheek. "You are even more beautiful than the last time I was here. I'll have to buy myself a shotgun to keep the boys away."

The idea of him armed with anything but a pen and a contour map makes me laugh. He loves reading books, drinking scotch, and cutting wood-block puzzles with Rian in the lean-to behind the kitchen. And what good will a gun do when he's not here to take shots at those limber night-boys who might, one day, creep over my windowsill? He lives in faraway Johannesburg with the other children, who I imagine are red-haired and clever, with skin as white as smoke. Family friends stop them on the street corner and marvel at the resemblance. "Goodness," they say. "You certainly take after your father. It's uncanny."

The others naturally take top billing. They are classified "European," and Europeans are the kings and queens of everything. We are not European. Our skin has color. Our hair has curl, but not the steel-wool kink that's hard to get a comb through, and praise Jesus, Mother says, for that small mercy. Our green eyes shine too bright in our brown faces, as if to confirm the combination of white and black blood that flows through our veins.

When he is here, he loves to tell us the story of how they met. Him on a work trip to the land title office in Mbabane, and her, slotting ancient charts into the right pigeonholes in the map room. Mother in a blue polka-dot dress, making order of the chaos. She smiled at him. *A smile like an arrow to my heart*, he says. *Beautiful and shocking, all at once.* And how he knew in a flash that, no matter what, Mother would be a part of his life. And so she is. Not the whole part, he forgets to add, but a small, bright piece of his life that's hidden away in Swaziland. We are an add-on to Father's regular life. We are the secret well that he drinks from when no one else is looking.

Mother sits cross-legged on the flowered carpet and beams to see us perched on his lap. She'd dip the scene in amber to preserve it if she could. We are together for one day and one night, and that will have to be sufficient until the next time.

"Are you thirsty?" she asks.

"Ja . . . I'm parched. The drive took longer than I thought, and Swazi roads . . ." He shakes his head as if remembering the high mountain passes and dangerous hairpin turns. "The minute you cross the border, it's like going back fifty years. Cows and people everywhere, and more potholes than tar."

"Go get a beer from the icebox, Adele." Mother tucks a strand of freshly ironed hair behind her ear and pulls a tragic face. "Daddy has to wash the Swazi dust from his throat."

Father smiles at her comical expression, the way it distorts her features without touching her natural beauty. Whoever picks combinations of skin color, eye color, and body shape got Mother just right. She is mixed-race, like us, with golden-brown skin, flashing green eyes, and pleasing curves.

I go to the kitchen to get the beer. The maid is in the backyard, hanging up my blue-checkered school uniform and the knee-high white socks that go with it. Keeping white socks white in the blooming dust and the red earth of Keziah Christian Academy is almost impossible. I plunge my hand into the icebox, and the shock of the cold bottle against my palm shifts my thoughts from the dying days of the school break. Bowls of stiff porridge and stale toast will come around soon enough.

I shake off my bad feelings about returning to school. He is here and sulking is forbidden. When he is here, we are happy. When he is here, we are grateful and well-behaved so he'll have a good reason to come back and visit us again. *You catch more flies with honey than vinegar*, Mother says, *and don't believe what people tell you, miss. Misery might love company, but misery has to learn to shut up and take care of itself.*

I pop the cap from the beer with a metal opener, and white foam rims the lip. I step into the lounge room, and I remember to smile.

2

And the First Shall Be Last

We are late. Of all the times and places to be late, the Manzini bus station is the worst. Men drag goats through the maze of buses while women hold live chickens with their feet tied together. The women push through the crowd while the chickens flap and squawk. Children and women sell roasted corn, boiled peanuts, and bags of deep-fried fat cakes to passengers about to board the smoky buses, from pans they carry awkwardly in their arms. Passengers also buy pineapples, mangoes, and bananas from woven baskets carried on sellers' heads. Pickup trucks reverse out of narrow spaces, with their horns blaring, their worn tires flattened by the weight of the passengers packed shoulder to shoulder in their open beds.

Dust is everywhere. The purple heads of the bougainvillea strangle the chain-link fence outside of B&B Farm Supplies: YOU NEED IT. WE GOT IT. Red dirt weighs the flowers down. A million motes suspended in the air catch the early-morning sun.

Animals bleat, children cry, and bus-ticket sellers call out their destinations in singsong voices. "Quick, quick time to Johannesburg. No stopping. Best seat for you, Mama." "Smooth ride to Durban by Hlatikulu, Golela, and Jozini. Brothers, sisters . . . all welcome."

We hurry through the dust and noise to the far end of the bus ranks. My heart lurches against my ribs. We are too late. All the good spots are already taken. If Delia, my best school friend, hasn't saved a place for me, I will be forced to the middle of the bus, where the lower-class students sit dressed in hand-me-down clothing, or, worse still, I'll have to make the long walk to the very back of the bus, where the poor and smelly students group together like livestock. I walk faster, and the corner of my suitcase bumps against my knees.

"There." Rian points to a decrepit bus with a faded blue wave painted on the side.

All the buses have names. There's *Thunder Road*, *True Love*, *Lightning Fast*, and finally, the *Ocean Current*, which drops students off at Keziah Christian Academy at the beginning of the school term and picks them up again on the first day of the holidays. It's a public bus, but today the exclusively mixed-race students of the academy will take up most of the spaces. Black people with common sense wait to catch the next bus heading south to the sleepy part of Swaziland. They know that mixed-race children only stand up for white people.

On paper, we are all citizens of the British protectorate of Swaziland, but really, we are one people divided into three separate groups: white people, mixed-race people, and native Swazis. Each group has their own social clubs and schools, their own traditions and rules. Crossover between the groups happens, but it's rare and endlessly talked about on the street corners and inside Bella's Beauty Salon for All Types.

My sweaty palms grip the handle of my suitcase, and my shoulders ache from hauling its dead weight from the crossroads where Father dropped us off on his way back to Johannesburg.

"See? The bus is still here." Mother's breath comes fast. She is annoyed that I rushed us to get here. "All that fuss over nothing, Adele. We have plenty of time."

I give my suitcase to a skinny black man, who throws it onto the roof of the *Ocean Current*, where another skinny black man, barefoot and shining with sweat, adds my case to a mountain of luggage already piled there. Faces peer out of the dusty windows. I look frantically from the front row to the back. I cannot see a vacant window seat.

"Here." Mother gives me a small cardboard box of impago, food packed especially for long road trips and enough to tide me over on the eighty-eight-mile journey ahead. Inside will be boiled eggs, strips of air-dried beef, thick slices of buttered bread, and maybe an orange. Whatever the cupboard had to give.

I say, "Sorry for the rush."

The real reason I have rushed us to the bus station is my secret. Mother grew up in a shack with dirt floors, and the poor girl that she was still haunts her: the two pairs of underwear made from old flour sacks that chafed her skin, a broken comb with six uneven teeth to do the combing, and the daily walk from a mud hut to Keziah Academy in shoes with more holes than leather. She never caught the *Ocean Current* to school, so she has no idea how the seating on the bus works. If she knew, she'd smack me for playing a part in keeping the rich students and the poor students apart, so I'm not about to tell her.

"Be good." She tucks a strand of hair behind my ear and blinks back tears. "Mind your teachers and keep up your marks."

"I will." I let her hug me in front of the crowded bus. Snickers come from the open windows. Hugging is for babies. I love the feeling of being held close, but I keep my face blank. Showing my emotions will get me teased by the bully boys for weeks.

I pull out of Mother's embrace and go to ruffle Rian's hair. He steps back and offers me his hand instead. Already man of the house. Rian's independence annoys me, because showing him affection in public is actually allowed. Everyone knows that Rian is sick. The last time he had a major asthma attack was smack in the middle of second term last year. May 12. I remember the date. Mr. Vincent, the white American principal of Keziah Academy, drove the dirt road from school to the Norwegian hospital in Mahamba with the high beams on and the accelerator pressed to the floor. Steep mountain passes fell away into darkness, and stones pinged the underside of the car. Death rode with us. We heard it shortening Rian's breath, willing him to surrender. To stop breathing.

Mrs. Vincent sang the *Halls of the Holy* hymn book from the first page to the last while I clutched my brother's hand and prayed—not for show, the way I do in chapel, but for real. *Please, God. Don't take him. Take another boy. Take one of the mean ones. Take Richard B, Gordon Number Three, or Matthew with the lazy eye. Please. They deserve to suffer.*

The doctor at the Norwegian hospital said that Rian had severe asthma—up until then, we'd called what he had "the struggles"—and he needed a mother's care and a clinic nearby. Our house is three miles from Christ the Redeemer Hospital, where the Catholic sisters inject the sick with needles and pull rotten teeth out with pliers.

Now Rian stays home and gets his lessons via the mail. In any case, he's too delicate to survive the bullies who control the boys' dormitory, and I am secretly relieved that he has stopped coming to Keziah. Although I tell him I miss him at school, things are easier now that I don't have to defend him from Richard B, Gordon Number Three, or Matthew with the lazy eye.

"Be a good boy for Mummy," I say. "See that she doesn't get too lonely, and make sure to read all the books that Daddy brought you from Johannesburg."

"Of course!" Rian is offended by my advice, which is, after all, just me repeating words I've heard grown-ups say to children.

The ticket seller leans out of the bus with one hand clinging to the top of the chrome lip above the door. He whistles to get our attention. "*Ocean Current* to Durban, leaving now, now, now!"

I tuck the box of impago under my arm, throw Mother and Rian a last look, and climb aboard. I am sick with nerves, because I know what I will find when I reach the top of the stairs: rows of occupied seats stretching all the way to the poor children at the back of the bus. Unless Delia has saved me a place, I am doomed to four hours in rough company. I buy a ticket with the money that Mother gave me and pocket the change. It's enough for me to buy one item a week from the school store.

I step into the aisle and check the first two rows. Both are taken by black teachers from the Cross of Nazareth, a native school fifteen miles from the academy. Mr. Vincent, our American principal, has told us to be polite to the black teachers and to show them respect. We do as we're told, not because we believe that natives are equal to us—they are not—but because we're afraid of being punished for our rudeness.

From row three on, mixed-race students in every shade, from eggshell white to burned charcoal, stare up at me. They are waiting for something, but I can't tell what. I start walking and see Delia in the fifth row. There's an empty seat beside her. She's saved a place for me. Praise be. I hurry toward her, ready to shimmy past her knees to claim the window seat.

I grab the metal handle on the chair back and blink in disbelief when a cinnamon-brown girl with glossy braids dressed with Vaseline pulls a bag of peppermint chews from the box at her feet and sits up in the seat that's meant for me. I don't know her, but her mint-green dress is brand-new, and the heart-shaped locket around her neck is sparkling silver.

"Oh." Delia pulls a face and makes a soft sound of apology. "Sorry, hey. Sandi got here before you. There's no room left."

Liar. Delia's not sorry at all. She is glad to turn me away in front of a busload of our schoolmates. She is the most popular girl in my year. She is the girl who all the other girls want to be friends with, and till now, she was my friend. Tears well up in my eyes, but I can't speak, because the tears are in my throat too.

"This is Sandi Cardoza." The name is velvet in Delia's mouth. "Sandi's parents met and married in Mozambique. They moved to Swaziland just before Christmas. Sandi's mother is Lolly Andrews, from the Andrews family that owns the Heavenly Rest Funeral Home in Manzini, and her father, Mr. Cardoza, owns the hypermarket on Louw Street. You know it?"

I fake a smile. "I've heard of it," I say.

A vast understatement. The hypermarket is the newest and the nicest place to shop in Swaziland. It has all the latest fashions from South Africa and an actual makeup booth. It is the place to be seen spending money. No wonder Delia is lit up. The daughter of a Portuguese businessman and a mixed-race woman whose family owns a funeral home is a big catch. Together, she and Sandi will be the queens of the school.

I've been dropped for a rich girl with a silver necklace and bag of peppermint chews in her impago box. I blush with shame at being left standing in the aisle, and I turn away to hide my face.

•••

I hurry past the first nine rows of students, whose "sometimes fathers" and "always here fathers" have paid their school fees in advance. They wear neat, freshly ironed clothing. Their suitcases are packed with new school uniforms and new school shoes with fresh laces. They have clean faces and nails. They are top-shelf, and the lump in my throat makes it hard to swallow. It's not fair. I am one of them. My "sometimes father" is a white engineer. My fees are paid in full, and my skin smells of Pond's cold cream and lavender soap.

It doesn't matter. The first-class seats are gone. No one offers to move to the back. Why would they? Giving up their prime position would be the same as admitting they are inferior. I move into second class.

Here, students with "sometimes fathers" and "always here fathers" wear a mix of hand-me-downs and new clothing of varying quality and age. Their school fees are paid in installments or whenever money becomes available. They are the middle shelf, and right now I'd give up the best food in my impago box to take a seat among them.

Claire Naidoo, a half-Indian girl with long black hair that is the envy of every student with kink or hard-to-comb curl, shrugs to say, *Sorry. I feel bad for you, but I'm keeping my place.* Other students stare at their hands, their feet, their knees. Anywhere but at me. They are embarrassed for me. Mortified by my public dumping and free-falling status.

I reach the third-class seats, where the bottom-shelf students sit with jutting elbows and sprawled limbs. Between them, they have a mix of "always here fathers," "sometimes fathers," and "many fathers" who pay the school fees whenever and however they can: a pocketful of spare change, a wagonload of chopped wood for the school cooking fires, jars of homemade jam for the kitchen, and loaves of corn bread steamed in corn leaves for the teachers' morning tea.

Third-class parents have no money. If they have jobs, the jobs don't pay well enough to afford the full school fees. Some have no jobs. Mr. Vincent and his wife raise money from overseas to help pay for the poor students' fees. I count five students wearing old school uniforms, and others with holes in their shirts and patched-up shorts. When we get to the academy, the missionaries will pick items out of the donations box for the poor students to wear on the weekends, when our uniforms are being washed.

There are two vacant seats in third class, both equally bad. One is next to Matthew with the lazy eye, who says dirty things to girls. Definitely not. My thighs will be bruised blue by his filthy fingers, and my ears contaminated by sly suggestions that involve physical acts that I've never heard of and don't understand.

"Psst . . . Adele." Lazy-Eye Matthew winks his good eye. "Come, girl. You and I can be friends."

Never! Never!

The other free seat is next to Lottie Diamond, who is half-Jewish, quarter-Scottish, and the rest pure Zulu. Lottie is light-skinned, with blue eyes and brown wavy hair that is hacked short—no doubt to help pick out the lice that live there. And even though she turned out very nearly white, she lives in a tin shack on the edge of a native reserve outside Siteki and spends her holidays washing laundry in the river and mixing with the native Swazis.

Lottie is exactly the kind of girl that Mother, because of her own impoverished background, wants me to be polite to. On the other hand, Delia is the top-shelf girl that Mother, because of her impoverished background, wants me to be fast friends with. I'm supposed to be an improved version of Mother: kind to the poor students but accepted by the sorts of snotty girls who once spurned her.

"Over here, Adele," Lazy-Eye Matthew whispers in a hoarse voice. "Come by me, Adele. Adele . . ."

The Bartholomew twins, dressed in matching blue pinafores, snort with laughter at Matthew's raspy voice. Lottie Diamond shuffles over an inch, a small gesture that invites me to sit down—or to keep standing in the aisle—while Lazy-Eye Matthew croaks my name like a bullfrog looking for a mate. I slide into the seat next to Lottie. I am humiliated and furious at being dumped in front of forty witnesses. I hate Delia, and yet I want to be back by her side, where I'm supposed to be. My bottom lip trembles, and tears sting my eyes.

No, I can't.

If I cry, the others will call me Waterfall or Sprung-a-Leak, or any other clever thing that comes into their heads, for the rest of the term. I will be an easy target for jokes, and the teasing will never get old. Lottie stares out the dusty window and ignores my red face and wet lashes.

I grab the chance to hunch over and slot my impago box between my feet. I stay hunched and press my eyes against my skirt until the cotton absorbs my tears. My stomach aches. Everything inside me hurts. I replay the last five minutes in my mind, hoping to find that my demotion to third class is the result of a terrible misunderstanding. No. The truth is simple. Delia dumped me.

I should have seen it coming. Delia wants the best of everything: the prettiest dresses, the best gossip, the most popular friends. Sandi's rich Portuguese father loved her mother enough to take her to church and make promises in front of God while my father, well, he only made promises to Mother. Mother says, *Hold your head up high, Adele. I'm as good as any church wife*, but the married women and their baptized children know they are superior. Their names are written in the official marriage registers *and* in the Great Book of Life on God's bedside table. If properly married women are diamonds, then the unmarried "little wives" and their unbaptized children are tin.

Delia has traded me for a diamond.

Now I'm stuck next to a girl from the bush, who spits and swears and fights with boys and girls. Lottie wins all her fights, but still . . . it's not nice.

"Hey." A finger taps my shoulder, and I glare at Lottie from my tucked-over position. She points out of the window and ignores my sharp expression, which says, *We are not friends. We will never be friends. Our being next to each other is a horrible mistake. A catastrophe. It means nothing in the long run.* She taps the window again, insistent.

I sit up and lean across her to squint into the swirling dust of the Manzini bus station. Mother and Rian stand on the dirt footpath, their bodies backlit by the strengthening sun. They seem unreal. Phantoms from the life that I'm about to leave behind for too many months to count. The thought of leaving suddenly terrifies me. I don't want to go back to boarding school, where I'll be alone and have to hunt down new friends. And there's a small chance that no one will even have me now that I've been dumped by the top girls. I want to get off the bus and lug my suitcase across the fields until I'm safe at home again.

"Wait . . ." Mother pulls a book from her bag and runs to the window. She reaches up on tiptoes to give it to me. "Daddy forgot this in his car. It's for you. All the way from Johannesburg."

I grab the book through the open window and glance at the title: *Jane Eyre* by Charlotte Brontë. The book is thick, which is good. Thick books take longer to read. Thick books soak up the time between study hall and dinner and help to make the long Sunday afternoon hours fly by. Books are better than gossip, though Delia doesn't think so.

Mother says, "Be good, Adele."

I force a smile and say, "Of course."

I am always good—polite to teachers, reserved with the other students, and all "hallelujah, praise his name" in chapel. That's why what just happened to me is so unfair. If there was a God, I'd be at the front of the bus, where I belong. Mother is right. God is too busy to notice the hurts of a bunch of mixed-race people in a little landlocked African country. The real gods, she says, are the white men in England who draw lines on maps and write the laws that say go here, but don't go there.

Rian steps closer. He understands everything that just happened to me. He sees it in my face and hears it in Delia's distant giggles and in the way that no one on the bus will look at me.

"Don't worry, Adele," he says. "She's not worth it."

"Thanks," I say quietly.

Mother blows me a kiss as the *Ocean Current* lurches from the stand and joins a line of buses snaking their way to the main road. I crane my neck out of to the window to keep her and Rian in my sight for as long as possible. They grow small in the distance. The *Ocean Current* turns onto the road heading south, and Rian and Mother are swallowed by the surge of disembarking passengers and pickup trucks.

"Bet that feels nice, hey, Lottie?" Lazy-Eye Matthew snickers. "Take a mouthful while she's there."

I realize that I am leaned across Lottie with my breasts pressed close to her face. We're not touching, but you know what it looks like. Lottie stares out of the window at the native women cutting grass in the fields and ignores Matthew. She doesn't even blush at his words. It's like there's a wall around her that cannot be breached by bad words or rough hands.

Acknowledgments

Thank you to the following people who make my work possible. Mark Lazarus, my husband and first reader: you elevate my stories and my life with humor and love. My children, Elijah and Sisana—you are the sun in my sky. Pat and Courtney Nunn (mummy and daddy); my sisters, Jan and Penny; and my brother, Byron, for undying support. Dr. Gerald Lazarus and Dr. Audrey Jakubowski-Lazarus for years of care and guidance.

I also send my gratitude to Catherine Drayton at InkWell Management for using her agent magic to make my work stronger and find it a wonderful home. That home is with Stacey Barney at Putnam, who provided brilliant insights along with a powerful commitment to amplifying the voices of black and brown girls everywhere. Mayebuye Africa!

Lastly, I thank my readers for walking side by side with me into new cultures and exotic lands. You are brave and beautiful.